The Ocean

A Novel

By Mia Castile

Entwined Publishing P.O.Box 34274 Indianapolis Indiana 46234,

Visit our website at www.entwinedpublishing.com

First edition: July 2011

Library of Congress Cataloging-in-Publication

Data Available

ISBN 10-0-9835108-2-2   ISBN-139780983510826

The empty spot beside me was suddenly taken. His leg brushed up against mine as Travis shifted to get more comfortable. Though he was dressed, his leg was still wet: it made me shiver. He handed me his hoodie without even looking at me. I put it on and sat looking straight ahead for a short while. Finally, I turned and looked at him. He was smiling his brilliant smile. He leaned back on his elbows as if he didn't have a care in the world.

Travis had taken over my phone and was now DJ-ing for the two of us. We looked at my pictures, and I told him about my small clique of friends back in Indiana. I felt comfortable with Travis, but I was also unbelievably nervous. I'd never felt this way around anyone before. I wasn't my normal witty self. I held back, and I regretted it immediately. As the night wound down, people began to leave. I took my phone from him to check the time; it was nine forty-five.

"Can I see that again?" he whispered. I handed it over. He played with the menu on it and pulled me close to him. With his hand resting against my hip, he told me to smile and held my phone at his arm's length away from us to take our picture. He played with my phone a little more and handed it back to me. "I'm in your favorites, and I hope you don't mind; I texted myself that picture. You'll be speed dial three in my phone, if you were wondering." He leaned closer to me and grinned, "I'll see you tomorrow." He stood and walked away. I sat there staring after him, dumbly unable to process what had just happened. He was leaving. That meant the night was over.

Acknowledgments

First, I would like to thank those closest to my heart. I'd like to thank God for allowing me the blessings that are in my life. He has given me the privilege of a wonderful family and great friends.

Mano, your patience and encouragement have really inspired me along the way. There were so many nights I spent clicking the keys on my laptop and staring at you blankly as you spoke to me. Even though I was so caught up in my plot, you never got too angry with me. Your support is very important to me. *Te quiero mucho, papí, gracias.*

Sofia and Benjamin, you are my inspiration and give me so much material. Thank you for the joy I feel every day. I love you my darlings.

Grandma, thank you for allowing me to sit in my room for hours on end because I was inspired and wanted to write. You never stifled my creativity even though sometimes it broke your heart.

Kristina, how is it that I found you? You are my partner in crime. Our love for fiction fueled each other's creative fire until we had no choice but to burn the forest down! Your generosity is contagious and a blessing.

Chasadee, my sister, my best friend, you are my harshest critic and my safest harbor. I love you.

Brooke, your encouragement and support have been such an inspiration. Thank you.

And Jamie, thank you for being my soundboard, reading my story when you could have easily simply said, "Oh, that's nice." You took the time and invested in me. High school was tough the first time around; I'm just glad that you were there with me and enjoy my excursions back in my imagination.

Sue, Curtis and Kris, thank you, for taking the time out of your busy schedule to go over my manuscript and putting a new set of eyes on it. It truly means a lot to me.

Thank you, you've kept me legit.

I would like to thank Entwined Publishing. You are the platform from which I propelled myself into this wonderful journey. Together we are learning so much along the way.

Sheryl Clark Productions provided the beautiful cover. Your hard work and dedication has truly blessed me.

I would also like to thank you, the reader, for taking the time to get to know my characters. They are very near to my heart. My hope is that they will become close to yours too.

This is For The

Little Girl

Who Overcame Loss.

Chapter 1

As If It Wasn't Enough

Gianna

I hugged Mitchell goodbye. I hoped it wasn't the last time I would ever see him, but a small voice told me it might be. I felt lost. We stood in Chicago's O'Hare Airport, waiting the final moments before I would head off to security.

"You've got your ticket, right?" He nervously checked his pockets as if he were looking for something, pausing only to push his wire-rimmed glasses up his nose. My mother had made a good choice with Mitchell. He was a lawyer, and we lived in a northern suburb of Indianapolis. We had come to Chicago for a final shopping trip before I was exiled to Florida. I was leaving my gated community to return to the first home I had ever lived in. We had struggled over the years, and when it seemed like we were finally happy, boom! Cervical cancer. My mom had passed a month earlier, and though my brother Alex had already been in St. Petersburg for three weeks, I had dragged out the relocation for as long as my biological father, Oliver, would allow. Now, the man I had wished for the past four years to be my father, the man who felt like my real father, was being forced to tell me goodbye.

"Yes, I've got it right here." I held it up to show him.

"Good. One more thing, Gianna." He finally found what he was looking for in his front pocket. He pulled out a small velvet drawstring pouch. I watched him warily because I hated surprises.

"I've been looking for this for a week." He started to chuckle. "Your mom hadn't worn it in years, but I think she would want you to have it." He loosened the top with one hand, cupping my hand with the other as he tipped it over. Out fell a small white gold ring. I knew this ring. It was my mother's wedding gift from her father when she'd married Oliver, my father. In cursive, LOVE was carved on the top of it, the letters connecting and blending into the band. I remembered the story she'd told Alex and me growing up. "My father, a hardworking man, told me that as long as I was loved, I would find my happiness. I was loved by him, and I am loved by you, so no matter where we are, I am happy."

I just stared at it as I said, "I thought she lost this a long time ago; she stopped wearing it when I was still young." I sighed, still admiring it, as I slipped it on the middle finger of my right hand.

"She thought she had too, but I found it in the attic as I was going through some things from before we lived together. It must have slipped off when she was packing the boxes. After I found it, I misplaced it too." I laughed at his absentmindedness. Mitchell was a brilliant litigator, but sometimes he had trouble finding his shoes in the morning when they were in the shoe rack in the mud room where they always went. I didn't know how he'd survive without us.

"There are more things I'm having shipped to Florida, but I wanted to make sure you had this. It's important that you know your mother will always be with you, watching over you and smiling. She was very proud of you and Alex." A single tear threatened to escape my eye. I willed it to stay, at least until I was out of his sight. He had wanted to adopt us when he first married my mom, an act that my father had refused to allow. I couldn't forgive Oliver for that. To be honest, there were a lot of things I couldn't forgive him for. But for that, I wouldn't forgive him. Mitchell promised to visit over our fall break, and I nodded in agreement. I hoped my father wouldn't find a way to prevent that from happening. Mitchell represented stability and integrity, everything that my real father did not. So I hugged him goodbye, trying to remember everything about this moment.

When I found my seat on the plane and buckled myself in, I finally allowed the brimming tear to escape. I sat between a kid who looked as if he were in college and a man in a suit with his laptop open. The business man had huffed annoyance when he realized mine was the middle seat. I didn't like the window seat; I always got dizzy looking out the window. I never liked the aisle seat after a mishap with an airline attendant and drink cart a few years before. The result was three broken fingers on my right hand. It usually wasn't a problem because I sat with Mom and Alex.

Thinking about them together, I allowed another tear to escape my eye. I leaned my head back and looked up at the air vent, waiting for the plane to move, to do anything. Nothing happened. Tear three escaped my eye. The kid on the other side of me looked like he wanted to say something to me, but I ignored his glances. Instead, I closed my eyes and found myself in a happy memory. I closed them tighter, and I could smell the floral arrangements. I saw the four of us standing there on the sandy beach with the wind blowing in our hair, my mother and I wearing flowered halos around loose soft curls, Mitchell and Alex in khaki shorts and button-up Hawaiian shirts, sand between their toes. I saw the Hawaiian justice of the peace smiling at the newly married couple who were so in love. They were married the second day of a three-week family vacation. We'd never been anywhere for a vacation before that. How my mother had found Mitchell was a mystery to me even now.

Another tear slid down my cheek. I opened my eyes to the air vents again and looked down at the ring that said LOVE. I felt a strange sensation, like my mother was wrapping her arms around me in that moment. I closed my eyes again.

The captain came on saying we'd be leaving shortly, and then the flight attendant began speaking about safety procedures. I reached under my seat and grabbed my messenger bag. I found my iPhone and put the ear buds in my ears. Drowning out the flight attendant, I played the loud rock music. I went to my mobile email and sent two messages. First to Alex, it was simple and short.

Alex,

Arriving on time, don't be late!! Phone off now but will turn it on when I land. Luv u

Gia.

The next message I sent was to Mitchell. He wouldn't get it for another three and half hours. Even if it made it to his phone before then, he wouldn't check it while he drove.

Mitchell,

I couldn't say all the things that I've wanted to tell you these past few weeks but thank you, for loving my mom, and for loving us. Even though we couldn't call you dad, you were our dad. Thank you again for the ring; it means the world to me to have a part of Mom with me. I will call when I've settled in.

luv –Gia.

I switched my phone to airplane mode before I glanced at the boy by the window just long enough to see he was still watching me. I leaned my head back as we took off and let the music fill my ears. My eyes unfocused, and I didn't look at anyone or anything. It was me and the music for the rest of the flight.

Finally, we landed. I gathered my guitar and luggage. As I exited the sliding doors from the baggage claim, I was assaulted by the heat and bright sun. I turned on my phone. I had a new text message.

Truck won't start. Find a cab.

"Great," I sighed. I walked up to the first cab I saw. There, leaning against the passenger side door, was a short, skinny Asian man in his forties.

"Where to?" he asked in a thick accent.

"St. Pete." I half smiled.

"That far. You pay, and not stiff me for going so far?" He didn't crack a smile. I dug out my wallet, opened it enough so he could see in as I fanned a row of twenties.

"Do you mind if I see your ID?" I asked as I put my phone on picture mode.

"No. I don't mind, looks like we don't trust each other." I took his ID and took a picture of it. I texted the picture to Alex with the message:

This is my cab driver.

"Hey, you've gotta make a living and I'm a sixteen-year-old girl traveling alone," I smirked as I typed and he helped me load my luggage in the trunk.

"Where, St. Pete?" he asked as we both climbed into the car, him behind the wheel, and me behind the passenger seat.

"Can we go to the St. Pete Pier first?" I was feeling overwhelmed, and I was not looking forward to the reunion with Oliver.

"No problem, your dime, or twenty." Ah, a joke! I smirked again and put my ear buds back in my ears as we drove away from the Tampa Airport. I didn't feel like much more small talk. I watched the scenery change from large city, to beachy forest, to small town. I was here. I was home. We drove up and parked by a meter, the LCD screen on it flashing that it had expired.

"You feed that thing." The driver nodded toward the meter as he reached for a newspaper in the passenger seat.

"I will and feel free to leave the meter running." He looked at me in the rearview mirror with a shocked expression, but he reached and turned it off. I got out and fed the meter. First, I walked to the pier. It was an old gray worn wooden platform with an equally weathered wood railing encompassing it. A few older men sat on a bench with fishing poles, their lines strung out and disappearing in the wavy water. I remembered the last time Alex and I had stood at the end and watched dolphins dance in and out of the water in the distance. He was seven; I was six. This was the only ocean I had ever seen. Alex told me it wasn't the ocean; it was the Gulf of Mexico. To me it was just an ocean.

I stood there for a long time watching the Gulf's choppy water. The breeze chilled my legs beneath my short jean skirt. My black blouse was thin, and my skin goose-bumped under it. I walked the length of the pier to the path that led to the beach. I slipped off my sandals and carried them in one hand. In the distance there were people jogging in pairs, some with dogs. A group of boys were playing football in the distance, and a couple was having a romantic afternoon picnic. About half-way between the couple and the boys I sat down, tucking my skirt under my thighs and pulling my knees up to my chest.

I watched the waves roll in. They rolled out, in, out, as they had always done. There was something comforting in that, knowing how constant this place was even after all these years. This was where I came as a little girl. As soon as I realized I could escape, I came here. Sometimes, I just sat here for hours watching the waves until Alex would come for me. He only came after our father was finished hitting our mother and had either passed out or left to tend the neighborhood bar he owned. Alex never told our parents where I went to escape. It didn't matter where I was in the house or what the time of day, when my mother screamed to us "LEXIE, GIA RUN!" we ran. We each had our hiding place from him. He never came to look for us; he really didn't care. Alex would creep back to check whether it was safe to return. He was always the braver of the two of us; then when he was sure it was OK, he'd return with me. The two of us would put our mother back together, icing her face, bandaging any scrapes, picking up the broken dishes or furniture. I don't remember when it began. I just remember it always happened.

I was lost in thought, so of course, I didn't see the football hurtling toward me. I was entranced by the waves and my memories, but I snapped out of it when I heard, "Hey, look out!" I turned my attention to the direction of the voice. I saw the football sailing toward my head. I leaned a little too much, landing on my side as the football barely missed my head. Sand was everywhere, in my caramel-colored hair, all over my skin, and down my blouse. I was utterly mortified. Running toward me was a tall tan boy, shirtless and wearing long cargo shorts. His messy dark hair that framed his face and white teeth smiling at me captured my attention first. His hazel eyes sparkled, and I gazed at them longer than what I probably should have. I stood, dusting myself off, trying to avoid his gaze and failing miserably. He reached for the ball and as he straightened up, he appraised me from my bare feet up to my eyes, which were scrutinizing him as well. He realized I'd watched him sum me up and looked away briefly, his face darkening slightly with a blush.

"Sorry about that. My buddy," he pointed to another shirtless boy who was waving both hands while yelling "sorry" to me, "has got no aim. Or the best aim in the world, depending on how you look at it. I'm Travis." There was that perfect smile again.

"Gianna, it's OK." I fanned my shirt a little as sand continued to fall out of every crevice of it.

I picked up my sandals as he asked, "Are you new to town or on vacation? I don't remember seeing you around." He shuffled the ball between his hands.

"Just arrived, but now I have to go. Thanks for saving me from the football." I smiled and took a step back from him, captivated by his eyes.

"No problem. Anytime. Really." He stood there and watched me as I inched away. Finally, I turned and walked away. I didn't look back. It was really hard, but I'd seen all the sappy movies where the girl regrets looking back because she usually gets caught by the boy who is still watching her leave. When I made it back to the pier, I turned to walk the final section to the sidewalk, and then I couldn't help myself; I looked over to see if he'd gone back to playing with his friends. He still stood there, shuffling the ball in his hands and staring at me. His focused look suddenly turned into a great big smile that reached his eyes. I chuckled and shook my head, suddenly understanding why it was so much cooler not to look.

I made my way back to the cab. The cabbie looked up from his paper as I climbed in. I told him the address as I leaned back in the seat, but he didn't say anything. It was three streets over and down two blocks. I watched the scenery pass by the window. The neighborhood looked different but still felt the same. He pulled up in front of a house, and I sat there mesmerized by it. I remembered it as blue. Oliver had painted it an olive green color, and the trim was bright white. The porch had a green wooden floor with white pillars along a white railing. A dark cherry wooden door made the home seem welcoming and inviting. My mother's flowers still lined the walkway and flower bed in front of the porch. I was frozen.

"This it, right?" The man turned to me, confused.

"This is it," I sighed. He popped the trunk and opened his door to get out, taking one more look at me. I just kept staring at the house as a flood of memories came back to me.

"Come on girl, or I turn the meter on." I tore my eyes from the house and turned to him. He laughed out loud at my expression and got out of the car. I got out also, leaving some sand on his seats. He helped me take my luggage to the porch where I paid him, giving him a nice tip. He tipped his hat and turned to leave.

As he pulled away, I stood there just looking at the door, willing myself to go inside. Finally, I took my keys out of my messenger bag and found the hot pink key my dad had made and sent to me. Alex's had been army green camo. We talked about switching, just to mess with him, but then thought better of it. I had to give him a D for effort though; he'd gotten the girlie part right. Taking a deep breath, I went in. The living room looked the same, but different. It had the same furniture, but the colorful walls I remembered were freshly painted white. I called out to Alex, then to Oliver, but there was no answer.

"Great," I sighed. I lugged my heavy suitcases upstairs. After three trips I finally stood in my tiny room. The walls had been freshly painted white also but were bare. It looked like the entire house had been painted. I looked at my single bed. It had a new pink comforter with two pink pillows on it. I despised pink.

I began to unpack. My closet was too small. My dresser had no decorations on it and too few drawers. I unpacked half of my bags and decided that I needed more storage. I changed my clothes and texted Alex.

Where are you

My phone sang a pop song almost immediately when Alex called me back. I answered it. "I just got back from the parts store. Oliver is sporting some junker." He didn't even say hello, just jumped into the conversation.

"Um, yeah, my flight was fine. Thanks for asking. Do you think you can take me to the store to get some Rubbermaid storage boxes?" I sat down and surveyed my new smaller living space that looked like a tornado had ripped through it.

"It might make it to the store. How do you like your comforter? I helped pick it out." He was now standing in my door way. He took his phone from his ear and put it in his pocket. He surveyed my room and stifled a laugh. I grimaced in response.

"Tell me you didn't." I glared at him. He seemed to have grown in the three weeks we'd been apart. He was taller than me, with auburn hair, a spray of freckles across his nose, and green eyes that had the girls in Indiana swooning over his every word. The grease stains on his shirt gave him an older look. Eighteen months though, he was only eighteen months older than me. I had to keep telling myself that because sometimes it seemed like I was older than him.

"No, I didn't, and I told him how you hate pink." He plopped down on my bed beside me and looked at his dirty hands, annoyed.

"Where is Daddy Dearest anyway?"

"Working. I know it sucked grabbing a cab, but trust me; it would have been worse to be abandoned by the side of the interstate because Bessie would not have made that trip. Let me change and wash my hands; then we can go. How much money do you have? Enough you think?"

"I'm sure! Mitchell gave me enough allowance to last me the next six months with a raise." Smiling, I raised my eyebrows.

"Give me five minutes." He stood and left the room.

An hour later we were both pushing carts with under-the-bed totes, closet organizing tools, room decorating things, and a duvet cover. We rolled past the mega store's paint section. I looked at Alex forbiddingly.

"You think we should? I've stared at white walls for three weeks. I feel like I need a stark white straight jacket to go with it." He rolled his cart down the aisle full of the rainbow of color swatches. "I call navy," he laughed and stood on the bottom bar of the cart as it continued to roll.

"I obviously call pink." I scrunched my nose in disgust like it smelled bad.

"I'm thinking a silver grey. That color always suited you." He was right. I also picked an accent of sage green. We checked out and went home. Before we unloaded everything from the old beaten down truck, I looked at the back door.

"Do you think he's here?" I asked, suddenly nervous.

"Working until 2 A.M. How a recovering alcoholic can tend bar I'll never figure out," Alex said as he pushed his seat forward to grab the bags and totes from the extended cab section. "Whose room are we gonna paint first?" he asked, unlocking the back door.

"You've been in hell longer, so yours first." I grabbed the rest of the bags.

"It really hasn't been that bad. We stay out of each other's way. He'll probably do the same with you." We walked through the small stark white kitchen to the stairs and up to our rooms. Since Alex's was the most organized, we dumped the stuff in there and sorted our storage units. I took my things to my room and began helping him move furniture across the hall to the guest room. We decided he would sleep in the guest room as his room dried overnight. We took down the blinds, opened the windows, taped off the old wood trim, and began painting. Joking and laughing, we finished in a few hours. It was a total transformation.

"Kinda feels like home," Alex smirked as he picked up the pan and left the room.

"Kinda feels like prison," I whispered under my breath. He didn't hear me.

We then went to my room, and he helped me unpack. We organized and loaded totes. I re-organized my drawers.

"We could paint your room tonight, too." Alex plopped on my bed after everything was organized and put away.

"Where would I sleep? You've already got the guest room," I sighed, really wanting to paint my room and take it away from Oliver, to make it mine.

"You can have the guest room; I'll pull my mattress in the middle of my floor and sleep there," he offered.

"Alexander the Great, so noble." I smiled.

"My lady, I aim to please." He mock bowed from where he sat. Like that, it was decided, so we did it. We did the same process like we were old pros who had been painting rooms for years. Three walls soon were gray, and the wall around the double windows we painted green.

We went downstairs and ate a late dinner of delivery pizza. All felt right with the world, or as right as it could be. We watched the *Reality TV* channel. Alex turned down the volume and gave me his own commentary. We laughed. I had really missed laughing; I had really missed him. Our texting and phone conversations hadn't been enough for me. Finally, after the pizza was gone and the shows became more serious cop programs, we turned off the TV.

I decided to drag my mattress into my room, too, and we went to bed. I didn't hear Oliver come in, but I did hear my bedroom door open and saw a light across my walls; then the door closed again. I heard Alex's door open and shut, and then I heard Oliver's bedroom door slam shut. I wasn't sure if he was angry because I was actually here or because we'd messed up three of his bedrooms. I didn't really care to find out right then. I put my earphones back in and went back to sleep. Eventually.

Chapter 2

Wide Awake, But Wishing

I Was Still Dreaming

Gianna

I woke up at the crack of dawn, literally, because my room faced east and my blinds were in the guest room. I lay there for a long time, staring at my pretty gray walls and soaking in my surroundings. Once I heard someone moving around, I decided to risk it and get up. I quietly descended the stairs as the TV came on. There in the too-bright living room was my messy haired brother eating a big bowl of cereal. He was watching *Cartoon Network*, the constant child in him showing through. The Frosted Flakes and milk sat on the coffee table just waiting for me to partake.

"Is it OK that we eat in here? Shouldn't we eat in the dining room? I looked at the table guiltily.

"Nah, as long as we don't spill and clean up after ourselves, Oliver doesn't care. He's actually pretty laid back. Like I said, we stay out of his way, he stays out of ours." Alex took a big bite of his cereal. I went into the kitchen and got a bowl and spoon. When I returned, he was refilling his bowl.

"Are you ready for school tomorrow?" He asked in between bites.

"Ugh, don't remind me. I'm so not looking forward to that. How about you? Are you still pissed that you don't get to graduate with your friends?" Alex had a few choice words for Oliver for dragging us back here before he left three weeks ago. He simply shrugged.

"I've made friends, so it's not as bad; some of the guys are pretty cool. I like the football team although they need work. I'm just glad they let me join. The coach didn't have to; the roster was picked last year, you know."

"Yeah, but I bet once they saw you play, they didn't have a choice." I laughed. He nodded his head in agreement. He knew he was a good player. He had led our old school to state championships two years in a row.

"Well, at least you'll have Abby; she stopped by last week thinking you were in town," he said. I thought about Abby, my best friend from preschool and kindergarten, and my pen pal from over the years. Our moms had made sure we stayed connected over the years. She was a bright light in a gloomy storm.

"I can't wait to see her," I said. He smiled, at his memories I assumed. She and I got into a lot of mischief together, and he was usually blamed for it. He was a good sport, and I think deep down our mom knew it was Abby and me.

"Did you get your school supplies yet?"

"Yeah, I went last week. Did Mitchell take you before you left?"

"Yeah, and we got you a few new clothes too," I added casually as I watched him out of the corner of my eye. I knew once our money ran out we were fending for ourselves. By the looks of Oliver's truck and the furniture in the house, we wouldn't have much of a clothing allowance.

"Why didn't you tell me last night?" He jumped up, almost knocking over the cereal box.

"Let's clean up this mess and try not to wake up sleeping beauty first." I motioned upstairs. It only took a moment to clean up, and then we went to my room. I took the last suitcase out of my closet, the only one I hadn't unpacked and had made sure to put away before he saw it. I unzipped it on my bed and showed him the new jeans, gym shorts, cargo shorts, tank tops, t-shirts and polo shirts that were completely his style. There was a theme to the new clothes, black and navy. Alex and I had agreed to incorporate black into our wardrobe to mourn our mom. However long it took, we'd have on something that was black. Mitchell and I also bought him a few pair of sneakers and running shoes. He was very pleased. We quietly put our rooms back together, and by the time we finished, it was time to eat lunch. I made us lunch meat sandwiches and found chips to add.

We were sitting at the dining room table when Oliver finally graced us with his presence. As he descended the stairs, I held my breath, waiting for his first words to me in almost ten years.

"Good morning, Lexie; good morning, Gia. I take it you're settling in comfortably." His Italian accent was thicker than I remembered. I stiffened at the nickname that I'd only heard our mother call Alex for years. Alex wasn't as affected by it; I wondered how comfortable he was with Oliver.

Oliver's formerly jet black hair now was speckled with gray. Long lines in his forehead and frown lines along his lips lined his face. His stubble looked like it hadn't been shaved in a few days. I couldn't believe how old he looked. He walked straight to the coffee machine and set it up to brew his coffee

"Yes, I'm settling in fine. I hope you don't mind that we painted our rooms." I felt as though I need to take responsibility for that, especially since Alex hadn't painted until the night I arrived.

"Well, I think it was the splash of color that this old house needed; if you get the urge, feel free kids. This is your home now. Lexie, did you get Bessie running?" Alex raised his eyebrows at me as if to say *I told you so*.

"Yeah, Oliver, she'll run probably another 200 miles before she blows her radiator. It was a quick fix. We should go to the junk yard soon though."

"Good, good. I was worried about how you kids were going to get to school." He didn't even look up as he said it. I looked at Alex, confused. Alex in turn, looked at Oliver with shock.

"What are you talking about?"

"Well, of course you have to fill the tank, I'm not made out of money, unlike *Michael*. But I will help with the repairs on her." He reached into the cabinet and took down a coffee mug.

"His name is Mitchell," I said solemnly. Oliver always seemed to ruin a good moment.

"Yes, that is his name," was all he said as he poured his coffee and went back upstairs. Alex shrugged, but I didn't know how I felt, except for sad. I was very sad that he was undermining our lives, our happy lives that he had ripped apart yet again.

"At least I won't be a senior walking to school, or worse, riding the bus," Alex stated, sounding relieved.

"But you heard him. We have to keep the gas tank filled." I wondered how we would do that once the money Mitchell had given us ran out.

"I'll get a part time job."

"Yeah, along with practice, *and* homework, *and* prepping for college. Just add that to the list of things to keep you busy."

"And out of this house," he added cheerfully.

"Maybe I'll get a job, too." I giggled envious of his genius.

"Hey, you can't steal my gig." He cleared his plate in the trash and put it in the sink.

"We can share the wealth of ideas. Don't forget that; feel free to share." He took my plate and dumped it.

"Hey   , I wasn't done with that!" I mock-pouted.

"It's our final day of freedom and Bessie has a good two hundred miles to go before she needs another repair. Wanna go to Treasure Island? Or we can go over to Clearwater. Let's do something." Alex quickly washed up our plates and cups.

"I need a shower first, but let's go to Treasure Island. I went to the pier yesterday, but I'd like to feel the gulf. It's been a long time since I've felt the ocean water."

"Get a move on because I need one, too, and might have to beat you there; we only have one bathroom you know." That was all it took, and we were racing up the stairs tripping each other. I was in my room first. I tore under my bed for my tote that had jean shorts in it; then I found a black tank top in the other one. I grabbed undies from my dresser, and I was running for the bath at the end of the hall. I knew this was tricky because it was closer to his bedroom. But I heard him still rummaging through his drawers. I made it to the door and promptly banged my head against it. It was locked. Alex came and stood in the doorway with his arm above his head leaning on the door jam.

"Um, yeah. Did I forget to mention? Oliver's in there now and I call dibs." Damn it! Dibs. He had me now! I glared at him. He must have known before he went into his room.

"Dibs doesn't matter if I'm here when he comes out," I laughed in my evilest laugh, though it was pretty pathetic.

"You're such a brat." He gave me a cheesy grin and went back into his room.

"And you love me anyway!" I called after him. Just then the door opened as Oliver stepped out. I startled him.

"I've got to get used to a full house again, I guess," he mumbled under his breath. I stepped back out of his way to let him pass and took my turn in the bathroom. I came back to my room and took out my make-up case. I put on eye shadow, mascara, lip gloss, and blush. I surveyed my face. It was my mother's face. As a little girl I'd looked at pictures of her when she was my age. I had her almond eyes, so dark brown that they looked black; olive skin that was sun kissed now, from a summer in Indiana; and an oval face. It was my face, but it was hers also. I even had her hourglass figure shape. I felt guilty for looking so much like her. There was a knock at my door and Alex entered.

"You ready?" He was wearing a plain navy t-shirt and khaki cargo shorts with boat shoes.

"Yeah, I'm ready." I slipped on my sandals, and we were heading down the stairs. Alex watched my confused expression; I expected Oliver to be sitting on the couch but he wasn't.

"He said he had some errands to run. He took Bessie, so wherever we go we need to walk."

"So much for Treasure Island," I huffed.

"Let's go toward the Pier instead."

After an afternoon of walking down the beach collecting broken shells and looking for dolphins, we watched the sun inch closer to the horizon. Once it sank out of sight, we began our trek back home. As we rounded the path to the pier, we came upon a large group of kids. I walked close behind Alex. We walked past them, and I kept my eyes on the ground, but I felt their curious eyes on me.

"Alex, dude, where are you going?" A big beefy blond guy was addressing him. "And who's your chick? She's hot!" My face burned. Alex paused, and I hid behind him looking away.

"Chiz, this is my *sister*; show some respect! We're just heading home. What are you guys getting into?" The tension of his first statement gone from his voice, Alex was always so cool and collected.

"Sister, huh?" I felt his eyes boring a hole through me. "We're just heading up this way for some late evening surfing and a bonfire. You should join us."

"I'm not sure. Gia?"

Before I could even answer, I heard, "Yeah, Gianna, you should come." I looked to find the other voice. Travis stepped forward next to Chiz. Alex shrugged at me like it was my decision. I shrugged back. So it was decided; we were lemmings. We turned and followed the group.

Some girls laid a few blankets out, and I sat by Alex. Other girls sat on the other side of him, and he entertained his subjects. I interjected occasionally just to remind him that I was listening to the crap he was spitting to the girls. I had one of my ear buds in with the music to keep me company. What I was really trying to do was keep from watching Travis surf in the distance. I was failing miserably.

"Yeah, state champs two years in a row. I don't know how they're going to do it this year." I laughed at his modesty. I'd lost track of Travis.

"You're gonna take us to the state championship this year." Chiz and the other boys that had been surfing came and joined us at the blankets. Alex nodded his head "yes" and they did a knuckle bump secret handshake.

The empty spot beside me was suddenly taken. His leg brushed up against mine as Travis shifted to get more comfortable. Though he was dressed, his leg was still wet: it made me shiver. He handed me his hoodie without even looking at me. I put it on and sat looking straight ahead for a short while. Finally, I turned and looked at him. He was smiling his brilliant smile. He leaned back on his elbows as if he didn't have a care in the world. I turned back to the conversation that was still going on. They were now talking about plays and how to defeat their opponents. Boring.

"Our last night on parole," Travis leaned in and whispered in my ear. He was so close to me it sent chills down my spine.

"We might as well be strategizing how we're going to work the prison yard tomorrow." I chuckled so quietly that only he heard it. He continued, "Though it wouldn't be so bad, as long as they give us plastic spoons so we can make shivs."

"OK, that comment just got your shoelaces taken away." I giggled softly again.

"Aw, shoelaces are overrated. So what's your story?" His question took me by surprise.

"You didn't get our story from Alex already?" I asked, not really knowing what he was asking.

"Yeah, yeah. From Indiana, he plays sports, doesn't have a girl. So what's *your* story?" He winked at me.

"I'm from Indiana, I hang out, and I don't have a girl either." I winked back at him.

"You're gonna make me ask aren't you?" He looked at his hand that was digging in the sand and then letting it fall slowly between his fingers.

"So what's your story?" I asked, taking the focus off me.

"Lived here my whole life with my mom and my little sister, sports, and hanging out, I don't have a girl either. I guess we have stuff in common." He took the other ear bud and put it in his ear. He started moving his head with the music. "A lot of stuff in common." He approved.

At some point the other kids managed to start the bonfire, and Alex gravitated away from us, so I no longer was sitting by him. Travis had taken over my phone and was now DJ-ing for the two of us. He would make a comment about my old school rap versus my punk rock and pop music. I would give him informative facts about the bands. We looked at my pictures, and I told him about my small clique of friends back in Indiana. I was never as popular as Alex was. I was popular by association. I felt comfortable with Travis, but I was also unbelievably nervous. I'd never felt this way around anyone before. I wasn't my normal witty self. I held back, and I regretted it immediately. As the night wound down, people began to leave. I took my phone from him to check the time; it was nine forty-five.

"Can I see that again?" he whispered. I handed it over. He played with the menu on it and pulled me close to him. With his hand resting against my hip, he told me to smile and held my phone at his arm's length away from us to take our picture. He played with my phone a little more and handed it back to me. "I'm in your favorites, and I hope you don't mind; I texted myself that picture. You'll be speed dial three in my phone, if you were wondering." He leaned closer to me and grinned, "I'll see you tomorrow." He stood and walked away. I sat there staring after him, dumbly unable to process what had just happened. He was leaving. That meant the night was over.

Chiz gave us a ride home in his monster SUV with great big tires and a license plate that said "DA CHIZ." He made me uncomfortable as he kept watching me in the rearview mirror. Alex didn't seem to notice, which annoyed me; he was my protector.

Bessie wasn't in the drive, so we went in and got ready for bed. It looked like we weren't the only ones trying to avoid something, or someone.

Chapter 3

Of All The Places in The World

Travis

I tossed and turned. I couldn't believe my luck! She hadn't been a tourist. She was Alex's sister. I ran my mind over all our conversations, trying to get a handle on Gianna. Gia was what Alex called her. His mom had died. I filed that under things not to bring up. His sister was a junior; she was funny. What else had he said? I racked my brain. Before I met her, Alex had seemed insignificant almost. He was a typical jock who came in at the last hour with promises to save the team this season from the embarrassment of the last eight years. Chiz liked him right away, so that had warned me to keep my distance. Chiz didn't like anyone who didn't benefit him. Why was I thinking about Chiz? I wanted to think about Gia. What else did I remember? He hated their dad, probably another forbidden topic. This Alex hadn't said; he just called him by his first name, and his voice was thick with contempt when he spoke of him.

Gia. The day I'd seen her on the beach, I felt my heart would explode; it pounded out of my chest. As luck would have it, Mason threw the ball that far out of my reach. I still hadn't found out if he'd thrown it like that on purpose or not. From the time she had stepped onto the pier, I was keenly aware of her. Sitting on the sand, she'd looked so sad. She was entranced by the waves off the Gulf. I'd yelled for her to look out twice before she actually did the third time. Then when she fell over, her legs sprawled; she had legs that went on forever. When she looked up, so fragile, I imagined kissing her and what it would feel like. She caught me sizing her up; she was quick. I liked that too. I willed her to look back at me when she left. Finally she did. Gia.

I couldn't believe it when I saw her leaving the beach with Alex tonight. Until that moment, I hadn't put it together, that she might actually be real and that I might see her again. Chiz and Mason had begged me to go surfing. I'd have preferred staying home and hanging out with Mom on her only day off for two weeks. But she told me to enjoy my last day before school. I now was forever grateful. I couldn't focus on surfing though. I rode a few waves, and I snuck off to my car to change. I was nervous about the way Chiz was looking at her. Alex would probably approve of his friend going for her.

I hadn't been able to think of anything to talk about. Stupid prison jokes. But she played along. She showed me her pictures. She didn't have many friends, but I didn't see any boys groping her in her pictures. That was what I was really looking for. Yeah, there were guys but none that had hands all over her, none that looked at her the way I wanted to look at her. Her style seemed simple. The only piece of jewelry she wore was a ring that said LOVE. I put in my ear buds and remembered some of the songs we had that were the same. I'd make a play list tomorrow, but for now I picked those songs and played them as I stared at my ceiling.

School. It would be here before I knew it, so long as I could go to sleep. The plan. What was the plan? I didn't have a plan. I would wing it. I was really good at winging it. I finally fell asleep after replaying the evening over and over in my head and looking at the picture on my phone a dozen times.

There was a soft buzzing sound. At first in the distance, a low *buzz, buzz, buzz*. Then, as I realized it wasn't supposed to be in my dream, the buzz became louder and louder as I woke up. I heard my mom talking. What did she say? Late? My eyes flashed open.

"I knew that would get your attention; you need to leave in five minutes." I jumped up, ran to my bathroom, brushed my teeth, splashed water through my hair and on my face. I rummaged through the clothes on my floor for a pair of unwrinkled jeans and grabbed a shirt from my drawers. Socks and shoes went on as I stumbled down the stairs. My mom sat eating breakfast with my sister. She tossed me a banana, and I was out the door. I'd put my book bag in my car two days before because I knew I'd forget it if I didn't. It was a good thing, too, because I was at school before I even thought of it.

I found my locker, put my stuff up, and grabbed a notebook for my first class. I slammed my door shut, and there she was a few lockers away from me in a camo army green short pleated skirt and a black cotton top. Was I really this lucky? I stepped sideways toward her.

"Hey," I smiled hopefully. She glanced over, concentrating first and then instantly smiling when she recognized me.

"Hi." She put up her messenger bag; it was army green with buttons, patches, and marker drawings on it. It looked vintage.

"What's your first class?" I was hoping for chemistry.

"English. Then Algebra 3, and then Spanish." She didn't even look at her schedule.

"Then lunch?" I asked, hopeful again.

"Yeah, I think so." She was closing her locker now with a spiral notebook and a worn composition notebook in her hands.

"Alright, I'll see you then." I turned as the five-minute warning bell sounded. I had to be across the building on the third floor by the time the next bell rang. I made myself walk casually. I looked back at her as she disappeared into the herd of students. Once I knew she was gone, I ran. I took two steps at a time up the stairs and made it to an empty seat in the middle of the classroom, the only one left, just as the bell rang. In my rush not to be late to my first class of the first day of school, I didn't bother looking around to see if any of my friends were in my class.

"You were M.I.A. this weekend. Why didn't you return my calls?" I knew that voice. Jillian. Gorgeous, sexy, hot Jill; and before last spring I honestly thought she was the girl I'd probably marry after high school. She had been my girlfriend since the seventh grade. But I had finally realized she took what she wanted and didn't care who she hurt. In her last scheme (or the last scheme that I knew about) a girl had broken her leg, and a teacher had been fired, but Jillian had landed on top of the cheerleaders' pyramid with the title of head cheerleader. When I realized what she had done, I broke up with her. Only recently, after she'd seemed to have made some amends, was I speaking to her casually. I didn't really want to tell her how much she disgusted me. Just because she was mean, didn't mean I had to be. I shrugged and looked toward the teacher who was reading off names. He rambled something about lab partners; I looked at Jill and groaned, realizing he'd just paired us together. Pleased, she smiled.

"Well, the least you can do is walk me to my next class, English. You at least owe me that. I'm going to carry you for this A." She was opening her book to the page the teacher had just instructed us.

"I think you can find it on your own, and for the record," I turned, leaned across the table looking her in the eye so she knew I was serious, "I don't owe you ANYTHING. I can take care of my own grade."

"Travis, please read out loud the first paragraph there." I held her eye contact until she looked away. Mr. Jackson was looking down at me over his glasses.

"What page again?" I turned back and acted innocent.

"Fourteen." He returned to the book on his podium. I found the page and read out loud about exploring the wonders of chemistry.

As if chemistry weren't bad enough, then there was Spanish class, and U.S. History. What kept me sane was the knowledge that lunch was coming. I would have thirty minutes of uninterrupted face time with Gia. I put my history book back in my locker. I began organizing things impatiently, waiting for her to show up. I looked up and down both directions of the hall; she had to be coming soon. Then I saw her head bobbing. I thought she saw me. "Stay calm, be cool," I said under my breath while I concentrated on the bottom of my locker as if I were looking for something.

"GIA! GIA!" We both turned our heads in the direction of the voice. Gia reached her locker, not seeing me but looking at the curly red head bouncing down the hall. *Abby,* I thought. You couldn't miss those curls, now streaked with bleached blond strands making sporadic parts of her hair white. That was new. It would have given her an edge if she weren't an A+ student and on every geek squad this side of the Atlantic. I chuckled to myself. She was a cool girl though, called it like she saw it. She had advised me to "open my eyes," when things started to seem wrong with Jillian. I'd always be grateful to her for that.

"I've been looking for you everywhere," Abby gushed. "Did Alex give you my new number? I stopped by you know. *Ohmigawd*, look at you; you're all grown up! I'm totally digging your skirt. Do you have lunch next?" Laughing at Abby, Gia closed her locker.

"Well. . .," she slowly said, pausing for effect, "I didn't even know where to begin looking for you; this school is so confusing." She held up her phone. "Alex gave me *A* number for you; he wrote it down wrong. *And* look at you! You're so gorgeous! I. Love. Your hair. Where'd you get it done? Finally, yes, I have lunch next." She turned toward me. I was still pretending to be searching my locker, but I got the feeling that she had seen me when she was walking up. "Travis was going to eat with me." I looked up when I heard my name, acting as though it was the only part I'd heard.

"You wanna join us Abbs?" I had earned the right to call her that. She'd been a good friend who'd actually kept her distance during school hours and not tried to be my instant best friend, or worse, had a hidden agenda to get me to go out with her, so because of that I'd been able to skip the games of *don't speak to me in the hall, but you can tutor me after school*. She actually did tutor me last year in geometry. I always talked to her in the few classes we had together, sometimes inviting her to the clique outings we went on. She always declined, I think feeling that she didn't fit right in that circle of friends.

"Sure, Travis. How do you two know each other?" She winked at me, instantly approving my interest in her friend. Was I that obvious?

"We met this weekend at the pier. When Mason almost clocked her with a football," I chuckled. Gia's face darkened a little, though I wasn't sure why.

"And then a bonfire last night. I had fun." She smiled at me and then looked to her friend; we were now walking toward the cafeteria.

"I miss all the action!" Abby sighed dramatically.

"Well, I would have invited you if I'd have had the right number for you. Next time you write it down, or at least proofread his note." Gia shook her head, giggling.

We got into line as I surveyed the room. It was set up like the solar system, jocks in the middle next to the cheerleaders, like they were the center of the universe. Then the groups fanned out depending on the popularity of the clique. Band sat somewhere close to the jocks because for some reason a lot of kids were in the marching band. Of course, drummers were cooler than the tuba players, so they were closer to the most popular tables. However, orchestra sat further out, and Chess Club was on the outskirts. I suddenly didn't know where I fit into the picture. I could have easily sat with the popular kids, but then thinking of Gia, I wanted to be alone with her. *Table for two –err three.* As we moved through the line, Gia and Abby chatted about their days so far.

"What do you have next?" Abby asked as we inched along.

"Speech with Franklin, free period, and then Art Composition, finally U.S. History with Martin," she sighed.

"I have speech next." I was relieved to find out I shared an easy class with her.

"I have Art Comp seventh too," Abby added, equally happy.

"Good, because aside from Alex, you guys are my only friends," she laughed, and Abby and I smiled.

"It must be nerve-racking coming to this school, being a new student junior year after you've been at the same school for so long." Abby was voicing my thoughts.

"Well, we moved around a lot before we settled in Fishers five years ago. It would have been nice to graduate with my friends, but I feel worse for Alex; he's a senior." She swiped her prepaid lunch card. Abby followed, then me. "I mean we both went to the same junior high and then high school; it would have been nice, but what can we do? Oliver lives here. He wasn't going to sell his house and the bar to move to Indy for us." There was a deep sadness in her voice, almost like that was what she wished her father had done, to allow them to graduate with their friends.

"Well, I'm glad you're here." Abby hugged her sideways.

"Me, too," I echoed a little softer.

"Where are we going to sit?" Abby abruptly changed the subject, lightening the mood as we surveyed the cafeteria.

"Over there, an empty table." I pointed. Abby led the way. We weren't sitting there very long before Alex and Mason joined us.

"Alex, I can't believe you gave Gia the wrong number!" Abby started in on him.

"I read it back to you!" Alex defended.

"You weren't paying attention. Weren't you watching Cartoon Network?" Abby was relentless.

"Hey, there are some quality shows on that channel. Very educational," Alex still defended.

"Don't worry, Abby, I already ripped him a new one when I called and got the China Castle. 'Best all you can eat crab legs east of the Orient,'" Gia said between bites.

"That sounds really good," Mason piped in, scowling at his meatloaf. "Now I want seafood." We all laughed. Chiz, who had been eating in the center of the room, sauntered over and sat beside Alex, discussing—what else—football plays. Abby and Gia began talking quietly and looking at their phones. Mason turned to me.

"Good call on that air ball Saturday, huh? She seems into you." He winked at me as he drank his Gatorade.

"Dude, I thought you did that on purpose." I nudged him with my elbow. "Definitely, a good call."

"I saw the way you were looking at her when she stood on the pier and you couldn't even see her that well. She's hot," Mason stated matter-of-factly, "but keep your eyes on *that* guy." He motioned toward Chiz. Ah, Mason, wise beyond his years. We were always wary of Chiz.

"You know why they call me Chiz, right?" Chiz had somehow managed to drag Gia into their conversation.

"Because you eat a lot of Cheese Whiz?" she asked innocently. I decided that I might just love this girl.

"Dude! NO! But I do like Cheese Whiz on crackers." He distracted easily; just throw something shiny in front of him.

"Anyway, the ladies gave me that name because I'm so *chiseled*. I mean look at me; I'm a rock." He lifted his shirt and flashed his abs. Mason and I shook our heads and laughed. Chiz had given himself the name and insisted we call him that. Gia looked at Mason and me with her eyebrows raised.

"Well, you know what they say about steroids, right? It makes your wee-wee, well, wee-wee." She held her pointer finger and her thumb an inch apart, but she kept her gaze innocent and smiled politely. Both she and Abby stood with their trays and turned to walk away.

"Baby, this isn't steroids! This is hard work! It took a whole summer to get this ripped! I was puny," he called after her.

"Not helping your point, dude," Mason said. He patted Alex on the back saying, "Good luck," and we stood to take our trays to the return also. Alex had a panicked *don't leave me alone with him* expression on his face. Maybe he was cooler than I'd originally given him credit for, so I saved him.

"Alex, I have those protein bars I was telling you about in my locker. Do you want one for before practice today?"

"Yeah, I'm coming." He didn't even tell Chiz "later" as he ran and caught up with us.

"Thanks, man," he said under his breath.

"No problem."

And to think I almost took choir instead of speech. How glad was I that I hadn't listened to Mrs. Kensington when she said I had a lovely voice. Gia and I arrived in our class and found two seats beside each other. Mr. Franklin was the drama instructor. He was dressed in very bright colors and waved his hands very flamboyantly. If there were a Gay Pride Parade, you would picture him front and center. Maybe he was in a closet of some sort, but he was married to a smoking hot Cuban woman ten years younger than him. They had three rambunctious boys that were involved heavily in the sports program and the community drama program. It was a little awkward to see them out as a family. He was very doting, and she looked at him like she would eat him up. I heard him speak of her once to another faculty member. I remember him saying, "There is something glorious about finding your soul mate. Pita gets me in a way that is amazing. And when we make love, mountains move." I shuddered at the image; I took the memory of a TMI conversation too far. Gia looked over at me quizzically. I half-smiled at her, relieved when Mr. Franklin began speaking.

"We are going to have an amazingly fun year this year. I am going to push you to your dramatic limits, but don't worry; I'll bring you back. That said, this is a safe place where we can share dialogue, and where we can create. We will get to know each other intimately." I looked over at Gia. Her complexion darkened again. He continued, "Through our words we will break down walls. Itineraries." He scanned his podium as he held up a stack of papers, the itineraries. Then he scanned the faces, pausing on Gia's.

He began again as he passed out the papers. "For our first exercise, we will get to know each other. Each of you will have a minute and an half to talk about anything you want. I'd like you all to stand in the back of the room. As I call your name, come forward, introduce yourself, and show me what you've got." We did as instructed. "Jackson Adams." Jackson went forward and spoke of his missionary trip to Haiti. "Mr. Adams, please take this first seat here." Jackson moved his stuff to the new seat.

"Ugh," I groaned, realizing there would be a seating chart.

"Ella Akers?" Ella spoke of how cheering was her life and every student should have school spirit. And so it continued. He was getting increasingly close to my name and still hadn't called Gia's either. "Gianna Moretti?" Gia looked up at me with a shrug. She went to the front and smiled nervously at everyone.

"Hi, I'm Gia. I'm new here." She turned anxiously to Mr. Franklin, and he nodded for her to go on. "I'm from Fishers, Indiana. Well, originally I'm from here, but my mom, brother, and I have lived in Atlanta, New Orleans, Texarkana..." Looking, down under her breath, she said, "For two months." She looked back up determined. "Louisville, Evansville, and finally

Fishers, just outside of Indianapolis. I just moved back Saturday, and I'm excited for the coming year." She paused and glanced out the window. She couldn't meet our eyes as she began to speak fast, nervously. "It's funny how one moment can change and define your life—send you down a path that you didn't even see—like you were in the woods and suddenly you see a path, but it's over grown and you're scared and nervous—because there could be bears, scary snakes, or mountain lions, but you have no choice, because the path you are on is now a circle." She took a deep breath as if she'd been holding it in. "You have no choice but to take that path, the scary one." She looked at me. "Because it might lead you someplace safe; if you can make it to that safe place, the world can be a safe place. But it's scary to take that first step because in one moment your life can change." She looked at the clock nervously, counting the seconds I was sure.

"Very nice, Miss Moretti." She sighed, relieved. "Please take the seat behind Miss Langley. Travis Nichols." I was still moved by Gia's speech as I walked to the front of the room and scanned the faces.

"Hey, I'm Travis. Most of you know that I guess. Um. Well. I love to surf. There is something about being in the ocean and seeing that perfect wave coming toward you." I looked at Gia. "And yeah, it terrifies you because it's big, and it's a lot of water. But you paddle out to it because it calls to you, and you jump up on your board. You feel the sheer strength of the creature, of the wave. And it's frightening. It could turn on you any second, but right now, as you tame it, all you feel is the salty, misty breeze over your head. All you hear is the low rumble of the surf, and in that moment, all is right with the world. And you ride the wave until it becomes a small swell. And you no longer have to stand on your board; you can sit and either wait for the next big wave to come to you, or you can paddle out to it. There's just something amazing about it, and that's why I like to surf." I didn't take my eyes off her, and I felt every eye in the room on me.

   "Well put, Mr. Nichols, please take your seat behind Miss Moretti." I got my things and sat behind her. I ripped out a page in my spiral notebook, scribbled a note, and handed it to her. I sat back in my seat and listened to the rest of the speeches.

Chapter 4

A Wave That Doesn't Kill You,

Only Makes You Stronger

Gianna

The note said,

Go out with me on Friday night after the game.

I didn't know what Oliver's thoughts were about his daughter dating. Mom had always said that when I turned sixteen, I could date, but when she got sick, I didn't think about boys anymore. I knew Oliver would be working, so did it really matter? I decided I needed to talk to Alex first.

I was acutely aware of how close Travis was to me. I preferred sitting beside him, but I currently sat in front of him. I could feel him alternately slouch back and lean forward in his chair. He kept nervously kicking my seat, and I could have sworn I felt his breath on the back of my neck through my hair, but I couldn't turn around to see. Class didn't end soon enough.

When the bell finally rang, I gathered up my stuff. As I stood, I heard Travis ask, "Can I walk you to your free period?"

"Only if it's on your way to your next class."

"Well, it's not, but can I walk you anyway?" We were slowly making our way into the herd of students.

"I thought I answered this question already."

"Did you read the note? Will you go out with me on Friday?" He had seen me read the note. He knew I read the note.

"Yes," I answered hesitantly.

"Yes, you read the note, or yes, you'll go out with me? Or yes to both?" He was almost fidgety; was he nervous?

"Yes, I read the note, but I don't know if I'm allowed to date yet." I was too honest; why couldn't I just say I wanted to think about it? That was mysterious and didn't show all my cards because really I wanted to go out with him *tonight*.

"Um, OK." He didn't seem to believe me.

"Hey, handsome." A blond-haired bombshell stepped in between us and looped her arm in his, smiling at him as if he were the only thing in the hall.

"Jillian, this is Gia." He awkwardly pulled away from her, backstepped, and then sidestepped to me again. "She's new here. We're going out on Friday." Jillian stopped abruptly. Travis and I stopped to keep from knocking her over. Some other kids around us stopped, watching what might happen next. I had a fear that it would be big, whatever it was.

"I thought WE had plans! You said you'd help me get the float ready for homecoming. We are meeting to plan on Friday." She had a pouty face that I assumed had worked on him before.

"That was last year before everything happened. It's not my responsibility; it's yours." He was polite but firm. He put his hand on the small of my back, encouraging me to move forward. I did, but I looked back at her, too. If looks could kill, her head would have exploded, taking out everything in that wing of the school—us included.

"You have to watch out for Jillian," Abby said under her breath, obviously a witness to the conversation between Travis and Jillian. The art instructor was passing out boxes of colored pencils to each table. Abby and I sat in the back corner.

"What's the story?" I kept my eye on the teacher.

"Oh, you know; she's a typical mean girl. She went with Travis from seventh grade until last year. He was clueless as to how she operated. She had the wool pulled over his eyes, and his close friends' eyes too. It kind of exploded in her face last year, and he broke up with her. He hasn't given her the time of day since. Froze her out. That's killing her worse than anything. She wants what she can't have. He doesn't even know about all the *teammates* she slept with while they were dating. He'd have *freaked*!" She raised her eyebrows, emphasizing freaked.

"Wow. Do I want to get involved with all of that," I paused, searching for the right word, "drama?"

"Travis is definitely worth it. He's genuine, and a good guy always does the right thing you know." She winked at me encouragingly.

"I guess we're going out on Friday," I stated, as I copied the notes from the board while the teacher began to lecture about technique. Abby did too.

"You deserve it. You know," she paused and looked at me. "To be happy."

"It just doesn't feel right; it feels like it's too soon." I leaned on my elbow and looked at her out of the corner of my eye.

"I think your mom would want you to move on with your life. You can still mourn Anna, but be happy, too. They are different kinds of love, the two."

"Whoa! Who said love?" I sat up suddenly, and half of the class turned and glared at me. Wow, they took their art seriously.

"No one. You know what I mean, and you could fall in love, you know. It would still be OK." Abby was barely whispering now; we were on the instructor's radar. She kept glancing our way. The conversation ended as my confusion began. Abby throwing the word love into the mix made me wonder what it meant now to get involved with Travis. I'd been able to stay off the mean girl radars at my other school. I blended, became camouflage. Now I felt like a linebacker, headed straight for a line of receivers, or maybe all the linebackers were headed at me holding the ball, and with no pads. I couldn't focus on the lecture anymore, so I began doodling flowers in my margins. Friday loomed in the far-too-distant future. I felt like I couldn't breathe suddenly, like when we'd first left Oliver and my mother couldn't drive away fast enough. I had hyperventilated until we were out of Florida. We went to Atlanta first. She had an aunt there. We stayed with her for six months while my mother worked two jobs. She had to get a better car that could take us further away. When she had some money saved, we went to New Orleans. There was a promise of a new job from a friend of a friend. It fell through, and we were there only long enough to save enough money for the next move. Alex and I didn't even try to make friends once we saw the job had been a hoax. In Texarkana, we had hooked up with some day labor field workers. My mom was desperate and worked long hours for nickels and dimes. We were robbed there; whoever it was took our last thousand dollars. She piled us into her hatchback and went to the grocery store. There she picked up five hundred dollars from Western Union, and we left Texarkana in the dust.

In Louisville, she found a job in a diner during the day shift. She began taking classes in the evening. After a year she was accepted at the University of Evansville. We moved again. By this time Alex and I were used to being latchkey kids. We had our household chores and helped in any way we could. In the early days, dinner for us sometimes was PB and J sandwiches and carrots while our mom ate only a baked potato. She finished her schooling, moved us to Fishers, and took a job with a hospital as an executive administrator in Indianapolis. She had a nursing degree and a minor in business. That was when things began to show a difference for us. The bell rang, ending art and taking me out of my memories.

Mr. Martin was all business in U.S. History. It helped me stay on task, out of my memories and away from wondering what would happen next with Travis. When class was over, I made my way back to my locker. The plan was I'd drive the truck, and Alex would call when he was going into the locker room for me to come get him. I opened my locker and another note fell out. I picked it up and put it in my pocket. Then I grabbed my bag and filled it with the books I needed for homework. I didn't see anyone around I knew, so I made my way to the student parking.

As I pulled into the drive, I caught my breath again at the thought of going back into that house. I stood by the tailgate of the truck for what seemed like hours. Finally, I made my way up the walk to the back door. I opened the door and called out, "Hello?" There was no answer. Relief washed over me. I sat my things down on the kitchen table and perused the refrigerator and freezer for something to put out for dinner. After I found some hamburger, I sat it in the sink. Then I went to the cupboard and looked for something to add to it. Hamburger Helper. Perfect! I brought my bag into the dining room and sat down at the table, a rickety old thing, and spread my books across it. I had reading and questions to answer in literature, a vocabulary assignment, Spanish flash cards to make, and math homework, too. I'd done the U.S. History assignment at the end of class, so I was glad for that. I tried to begin my homework. Instead, I wondered what Travis was doing then. Should I be thinking about him? Maybe this was moving too fast. Maybe I wasn't ready for something like this. His intentions were clear. He'd broken up with Jillian last school year, so I wasn't a rebound. He was interested in me. And not an *I'll show her* kind of intention! He didn't seem to be able to stand Jillian. I felt the note in my pocket again. I pulled it out and unfolded it.

Gia,

I'm sitting here in English, pretending to take notes. Mrs. Bennett might be on to me though. I don't know you yet, but I want to. That's kind of scary to me, but a good scary. I'm sorry about Jillian. I would have liked to have told you about her before you met her. She can be a real Bitch. I'm sure Abby filled you in on our history, but I think you deserve an explanation from me. So here goes. We dated for a long time. She's not a nice person. I didn't find out until it was too late. These days I stay as far away from her as I can. She still sometimes finds me though and puts on a show. I'm going to talk to her about that again; I want to make sure she realizes that I've moved on. I really have. And I'm hoping it can be with you. I don't really know why I'm telling you this, or even how I have the balls to tell you this, but I am. I hope you will give me a chance and go out with me on Friday night. But if you're not ready, I will wait until you are.

Travis.

I sat back and analyzed the note. I read and reread it. I was surprised by how presumptuous he was. I had the feeling he didn't hear the word "no" that often. It didn't matter because I didn't want to tell him no either for some strange reason. His intentions were clear. I wrote him a note back. I decided I'd put it in his locker in the morning. I stuck it in one of the pouches in my bag, and then I tackled my homework. It was close to six in the evening when I finished. I couldn't believe that Alex hadn't called yet; I looked at my phone one more time before I began dinner. When it was ready, I checked my phone again. He still hadn't called or texted. I made a plate for myself and sat down to eat. I heard the front door open and froze, worried it was Oliver. I heard things hitting the floor and voices.

"That was hilarious man! Chiz didn't even know what hit him with Brandon coming at him from nowhere." Alex was talking to someone.

"DUDE! I know! Sometimes Mason has the best arm. Threw it right in there." I stood and walked to the doorway as Travis and Alex gushed.

"I made dinner, Alex. It's still hot. Travis, do you want to stay?" I leaned in the arched doorway between the dining room and living room, trying to look casual but feeling nervous.

"I should probably go, actually; I just wanted to make sure he made it home safe." Travis shuffled his feet.

"What did you make?" Alex called as he ran up the stairs to put his bag up.

"Hamburger Helper," I said, not moving or taking my eyes off Travis.

"Dude, you have to stay for dinner; Gia makes the BEST Hamburger Helper." I knew that wasn't true; I wondered what Alex's motive was. He wasn't being his usual sarcastic self.

"Let me call my mom and see." Travis backed out the front door to the porch to make his call. Alex walked past me through the dining room to the kitchen. I followed him and watched him warily as he scooped out his plate, leaving only enough for Travis.

"What about Oliver?" I asked.

"What about him? He eats at the bar. I wasted so much food cooking for him, and he never eats here." Alex sat down at the table where he could see the front door. It opened, and Travis came back inside.

"What's the word?" he asked.

"She said I could stay. I still have so much homework to do, so I can't stay long." He came into the dining room. I went to the kitchen and made his plate and grabbed some sodas out of the fridge for all of us. I balanced three cans in one hand and a plate in another.

"You'd make a good waitress," Travis said with a smile.

"Not really; she tried it and spilled eight drinks on a table once, drenching her customers." Alex laughed with his mouth full.

"Yeah, with closed containers, I'm good." I smiled while blushing with embarrassment.

"Then let me help." He took the drinks, and I sat down his plate. We ate in silence. *Two meals in one day. I could get used to this.* As soon as I had the thought, I looked at my food wide-eyed. I liked this boy. I liked him a lot, and I didn't know him at all. I was terrified.

Chapter 5

Love at First Sight?

Love at Any Sight!

Travis

Gia was quiet throughout the rest of the dinner. Alex jabbered about the day he'd had. He was also talking about Kiarah, a girl from our school. I knew who she was, but much to Alex's disappointment, I didn't know much about her; she kept to herself. I did know she was artsy, so I told him everything I knew about her.

I tried to stay off the topic of football. I loved the game but hated the hype. I could tell after two weeks of boot camp training and now school, Alex was beginning to feel the same way. I'd offered to bring him home when he mentioned needing to call Gia to pick him up. Getting to share dinner with Gia was a bonus. I could have stayed in the car when he invited me in for a few, but I knew I'd have regretted it. I couldn't help noticing that she seemed so sad again. I didn't feel comfortable asking what was wrong though.

We finished eating. Alex and I washed up the dishes while Gia wiped down the dining room table. It was time for me to say goodbye. Alex told me "later" and was gone, disappearing up the stairs. She walked me to the door. It had to be close to eight o'clock, and I knew I had tons of homework to do. I couldn't avoid it anymore—as much as I wanted to.

"Thanks for bringing him home. It's been a long day, and I hate driving the monster truck back there." She jerked her thumb toward where I assumed she'd parked their truck.

"Yeah, it's no problem." I shuffled my feet nervously, adding, "I can probably bring him home most days. You guys are pretty close to my house. I can let you know if I have to rush home for my mom or something."

"That would be really nice, but you don't have to." She didn't look at me; she just looked out the storm door toward my car.

"It wouldn't be a problem. I'll see you tomorrow at school and lunch right?" I asked as nonchalantly as possible.

"Yes." She smiled. "Oh wait." She turned and went to her bag that was still in the dining room. She came back. "Here, I was going to give this to you tomorrow, but since you're here, I'll give it to you now." Her hand trembled as she handed it to me. *Nerves*, I thought. I began to open it.

"No, wait, 'til later, after your homework or something. Promise me? I know you still have a lot to do." She put her hand on mine to stop me from opening it.

"OK." I smiled. "Tomorrow?" She nodded yes. "Um. Bye then."

"Bye," she almost whispered, it was so soft. I opened the storm door, and she closed the front door behind me. I went to my car and got in with the note, feeling like it was burning a hole in my pocket. I turned up the radio to soothe the heat from it and went home.

I came in to see my mom and my sister sitting on the couch together watching *Nickelodeon*. They giggled at the comedy show for teenagers.

"So how was your first day?" Mom asked. Hailey didn't even look up.

"It was good. Practice was good, but now I need to do homework," I said, beginning to climb the stairs.

"So tell me about Alex. You ate dinner with his family? Are they new in town?"

"No. Well, Alex is. He's on the team. I ate dinner with his sister Gia and him. His dad owns a bar in town; I guess he's been here for a long time. They used to live with their mom, but she died not too long ago." *Might as well get it over with.* My mom's eyebrows rose when she heard *sister.* I knew what she was thinking.

"Is she cute?" she asked bluntly.

"Yes, she's very cute and in my grade. And I really like her. Are you happy now?" I sighed, with my foot on the next stair, ready to make my escape at any moment.

"Sweetie, I'm only happy if you are happy, so please be happy. I don't want you moping around the house anymore. Jill really hurt you, and I just want you to find another nice girl like her." I'd never had the heart to tell Mom who Jill really was. All she knew was that I no longer liked or wanted to be with her.

"I know, Mom, but homework now." I patted my bag.

"Go on; I'll see you in the morning. Set your clock for earlier please; you almost made us late, too." She chuckled and went back to their show where someone had just gotten spaghetti dumped on his head. Turning, I shook my head and climbed the stairs to my room. *That never happened in real life.*

I sat my stuff at the side of my desk. As I slumped in my chair, I pulled out my homework. I did it as fast as I could and as focused as my brain would allow. I still saw her standing by her locker looking cool, and calm—and the smile on her face when she saw me.

I finally finished my homework close to ten. The note in my pocket felt as if it must have burned through to my bone. It hurt me. I was dying to read it. I went to my laptop and quickly made a play list adding *Digital Underground* to the list from the iStore. She'd had that album, too. I synced my iPod and dug out the note. I put my iPod on the keyboard while I waited and stared at it, flipping the note between my fingers. It stared at me, too, taking its time while the circle chased its tail, telling me that I couldn't unplug it yet. Finally, when it was synced, I went to my bed across the room and lay across it sideways. I put my iPod in my clock radio and hit play on the play list that said "GIA." Tu-Pac's "Changes" played. I finally allowed myself to read the note.

Travis,

Thank you for the note; I appreciate your thoughtfulness. You are very sweet. Thank you also for the invitation for Friday night. I will be at the game for Alex, and I'd like to go do something with you too. My mom always told me that I could date when I was sixteen, but Oliver hasn't said what the rules are. I'm not sure if he even knows what they are. We all kind of avoid each other. I'm still mourning my mother and trying to adjust to this new place. I don't know how fair it is to be happy here. It holds a lot of bad memories for Alex and me. When I think of you, I am scared too. I think it's the good kind; it's the scared that makes my heart race and my palms sweaty. I can't really say much more, but I can say that I like your smile and your eyes. And now you'll probably get into trouble for reading this note in class, so I'll close. See you soon.

-Gia

I read the note again immediately after I finished it. She liked my smile and my eyes. I could go on about the things I liked about her, but I wouldn't do that. I grabbed my spiral notebook and began to write her another note. I'd put it in her locker in the morning, but a couple lines in, I paused. She was sad. Her mom obviously meant a lot to her. I rolled on my back once more and read the note. I could move slowly. Was that what she was telling me? That she wanted to take things slow? I thought I could do that. I continued to write.

Gia,

I'm sorry that you had something so terrible happen to your family. I know a little bit about loss. My father left my mom weeks before my sister was born. I was only eight at the time, but I clearly remember that one day he was there and the next day he was gone. My mom cried a lot at first, but she just kept saying it was better this way. I had a hard time believing her though.

I hope you don't feel helpless. Just so you know, I'm a really good listener. I don't really know why I'm telling you all of this, maybe because I want you to know me. I don't know.

For the record though, there are so many things that I like about you. I like your hair, it reminds me of the sun, as it sets in the sky with the brilliant colors of red, purple and gray. Not that I think you're purple although that would be a pretty color on you; but you remind me of the most beautiful part of the day. And I like your eyes. They are so expressive. They draw me into them. Though I'm in a hurry to get to know you, I'm not in a hurry to push you into a relationship. I can be patient. I will be patient if that's what you want. Talk to you soon.

-Travis

I changed to some pajama pants, preparing to go to bed. I lay down but was almost immediately up again, too wired to sleep. I paced my floor tossing a football in my hands. I wanted to hear her, to see her, to touch her. These thoughts were *not* taking it slow. I settled for sending her a text.

U still up?

My phone beeped seconds later.

Yes what's up?

Just read ur note. Thanx.

U started it. I liked urs 2.

It's wrong to say but miss u.

There was a pause of four minutes before the next message came. I went too far I suddenly feared.

Me 2. go 2 bed.

I almost heard her giggling.

In bed. U go 2 bed.

Was asleep u woke me up.

Oops, now I felt bad. But immediately another text came across from her.

Did I make u feel bad I'm j/k lol.

Tease.

I smiled.

Nah. Not a game player.

Good! Had enough of that.

See you in the am?

Definitely.

I set the phone down next to my bed and slowly drifted off to sleep. The next thing I knew was my alarm going off, thirty minutes earlier than the day before. I hit the snooze but rolled over on my back and stared at the ceiling. She liked my smile, she liked my eyes, and she missed me when I wasn't there. I went to the bathroom to get ready for school. I picked out a pair of new jeans that my mom said made my butt look good. It was embarrassing enough coming from my mom, and I also felt like a girl for picking them to wear today because of that reason. I got a t-shirt and put my sneakers on. I fixed my hair twice in the mirror. I was ready. I was more nervous than the day before. I went to the kitchen, had a decent breakfast of Cap'n Crunch, and was out the door on time.

I looked for the big green truck from the early nineties and parked close to it. I assumed they were already inside. I had ten minutes before the warning bell. I approached the front door and there she was, sitting on the stoop reviewing note cards. Her hair fell in loose curls around her face and over her shoulders. She wore some old-looking flare jeans that had holes in the knees, grey sneakers, and a snug black V-neck t-shirt. It came down pretty low. My eyes lingered there long enough to make me think about touching her skin. She looked up mouthing "te quiero" as she saw me. I suddenly couldn't take my eyes off her lips. I froze in place as someone knocked into my shoulder. I didn't see or care who it was. She smiled, laughing at me. I smiled back embarrassed. I walked over to her; she stood and put the cards in her bag.

"Good morning." She smiled still as she threw her bag over her shoulder, and we went inside together.

"Good morning. Did you sleep well?"

"I did. Did you?"

"I did. Before I forget, here." I slid my note into her back pocket. It was just an excuse to touch her. Then I leaned in and whispered in her ear. "Don't get caught with that; it's top secret." She shook her head OK, playing along with a serious face. We were at our lockers now. She went to hers and began unloading her stuff. I did the same. I knew I had only a few minutes, and I didn't want to have to run again.

"See you at lunch?" I smiled and waved.

"Definitely." She smiled. I thought of our textversation from the night before. She must have, too. I turned and went up to my chemistry class, very pleased with the start of my day.

"You never wrote *me* notes." I was trying to ignore Jillian who hadn't shut up since I got to class.

"Every relationship is different," I said under my breath as I tried to keep up with the scribble Mr. Jackson was writing on the board.

"You are not in a relationship with her; you don't even know her. You just met her yesterday. Besides she looks like a Gothic wannabe. Her hair isn't even black, but that's all the freak wears." She almost spit the words at me.

"I will be with whoever I want to be with. You will leave me alone or I'll..." I had turned to face her now.

"You'll what?" She smiled evilly.

"Just leave us alone."

"You'll see. You and me." She pointed her finger from her to me and back. "We're meant to be." She went back to her notes and left me alone the rest of the class. I thought about going to Mr. Jackson after class and asking if I could switch partners, keeping her far away from me, but then I felt pansyish. I'd made my position clear; hopefully, that was enough.

I didn't see Gia again until we met at our lockers for lunch. Abby was right behind us. We walked to the cafeteria together as the girls chattered. I kept brushing her hand with mine. It was all I was thinking about. I didn't want to push her, but I wanted to hold her hand. She looked up at me quizzically as our hands brushed again. I was about to take a chance and reach for her hand when I felt a slap sting my back. I winced.

"Dude, are you gonna pay attention at practice today? No more fumbles," chastised Chiz, our ever-motivating team captain.

"I didn't drop the ball," I insisted, trying to wiggle out of his hand now on my shoulder holding me in what looked like a friendly hold, but was anything but.

"Whatever, man." But he kept his hand there. We got into line, got our food, and paid for it. Then we went toward the same table as yesterday, off to the side. Chiz looked torn, like he wanted to sit with us, but that it might hurt his rep. He finally chose the table at the center of the room. Alex and Mason were already sitting at our table. Kiarah joined us too, sitting by Alex across from Gia and me.

"Wicked ring." Kiarah pointed to Gia's ring.

"Thanks; it was my mother's." She shared a glance with Alex and moved her hand down to her lap. Kiarah continued the conversation she had been having with Alex.

"That is why I feel so strongly about it. I just can't eat something with a face. It'd be like eating you. I couldn't do that to you." She batted her eyes at him, and he melted. Girls didn't realize the power they had over us.

Gia passed me a note under the table. On the fold it said, "After speech." She didn't want me to read it in front of her. As hard as it would be, I would do as she asked. I nodded and put it into my back pocket.

Maybe I couldn't hold her hand, but I could put my arm around her chair. She was leaning forward, suddenly engrossed in the conversation. Abby was stating that though she wasn't a vegetarian, she could definitely see the benefits and was listing them. I leaned back and put my arm around her chair. Mason looked at me with a raised eyebrow.

"I had a friend in Fishers, Alex. Remember Gracie? All she ate was meat. She refused to eat vegetables of any kind for a year," Gia giggled.

"Yeah, and as I recall, she gained ten pounds that year before she finally went off her meat-a-tarian diet," Alex chuckled.

"Yeah, wasn't her best idea." We all laughed.

"Heads up!" Mason said, as he did the opposite and looked down at his food.

"Dude, Brandon just said his parents are going away for the weekend. We're gonna party at his house after the game. Let everyone know!" Chiz stood over our table and paused at the last statement as he surveyed Abby and Kiarah.

"I'll go ahead and respectfully decline," Abby stated, holding Chiz's uncomfortable eye contact.

"Yeah, I have an art showing." Kiarah turned to Alex. "I was hoping you could make it even if it's after the game." He was putty in her hands and nodded his agreement.

"We'll see," Mason added.

"Our first date," I chimed in, as I pointed to Gia and myself, which earned me a glare from him.

"No wonder you guys are sitting over here." Chiz turned and stomped off, much like Jillian sometimes did. I smiled to myself.

"Respectfully decline, huh? What's so important that you don't want to party it up with *The Chiz*?" Mason was leaned into Abby across the table. I would say her level of hotness had dramatically gone up over the summer. Getting rid of the glasses and getting her braces off had definitely improved her looks. Then there were the streaks in her hair, and she'd finally come into her own gypsy style.

"I'm washing my hair," she replied, not even paying attention to him. More cool points.

"Well, that is very important because that hair is a masterpiece." I cringed for him. She rolled her eyes. I looked over at Gia and wondered if I sounded that cheesy to her. She caught my glance and smiled at me. We heard the first bell telling us lunch was over. I walked Gia back to our lockers and then to speech. We took our assigned seats, and she sat sideways as we waited for class to start.

"Did you get snow in Indiana?" Britney Langley asked her, also sitting sideways.

"Yeah, we'd get a few inches every year. It got really cold. The ice is worse than the snow." She smiled politely.

"Did you ever go to a Colts game?" a boy across the room asked. I thought his name was Bryan. He was the editor of the school paper.

"Yeah, my step-dad's law firm had a suite, so we went to a few games. I have a picture with Peyton Manning on my phone if you want to see."

"Yeah!" A few kids crowded her as she flipped through the pictures and then showed it proudly to them. It was her in a Colts jersey and jeans, her hair pulled up in blue and white ribbons in a ponytail with wispy curls around her face. Her brother was in a jersey and jeans also, along with a woman slightly taller than her, but a ghost of her. It could have been Gia in twenty years. They were smiling with Peyton Manning's arms around them.

"That's really cool," Bryan said.

"Yeah, it was a fun night."

"OK, guys, today we're going to talk about basic techniques when giving speeches and how to address the audience," Mr. Franklin began, as he entered the room with a stack of books. I assumed they were for dramatic effect. Everyone took their seats, and Gia smiled nervously at me before she turned around. I wondered what that was about.

I leaned forward to take notes, but couldn't resist staring at the back of her head. She leaned forward and sat back nervously about halfway through the class. Finally, she passed me a note, and I realized she'd been trying to get my attention with her movement.

I don't like sitting in front of you.

Why not? I passed the note back to her.

Because I can't see what you're doing. You're making me nervous.

Don't worry I'm just staring at the back of your head.

Exactly. Stop!

62

I chuckled and heard her snicker when she heard me laugh.

Can't help it. What do you do to your hair to make it such a "masterpiece"?

Lame.

I try.

Well you should try harder.

OK, redo: don't worry, I'm just waiting for this class to be over so I can read your note about five times and write you a response that will blow your mind.

I heard a slight gasp escape when she read it.

Better.

Can I read your note now?

NO.

Please?

NO.

You're so demanding.

You might understand when you read it.

Fine, and honestly, Thanks.

For what?

For writing me a note and distracting me from the back of your head.

Har, har, har. You're welcome.

"Bryan, would you like to demonstrate this technique?" I looked up suddenly. I'd missed the lecture. Bryan went forward. Mr. Franklin handed him a paper. He stepped to the podium and read the statement.

"Very good. Now what could he have done to improve the speech? I will only accept positive constructive criticism. If you are hurtful, or negative, then you will go next, and only negative criticism will be given from the class." He raised his eyebrows to the class. The class cheerfully encouraged him to speak up, and to use his hands more. The bell rang.

"Tomorrow I want to start talking about our first real speech assignment and—" We were out of the class. I was walking so close to her. Again, I just had to reach over a little bit and touch her hand. I could just hold a finger. Our pinkies could touch.

"Gia?" *Not again*, I thought. We'd have to find another way to her next class. Gia turned to see Jillian waving at us.

"Please, no," she said under her breath.

"Hi, I'm Jillian, head cheerleader." Flip of the hair. "I didn't get a chance to welcome you to our wonderful school yesterday. Did you even attend yesterday?" She smiled a syrupy sweet smile.

"I was here yesterday; Travis introduced us, remember?" Her voice was equally syrupy sweet.

"I don't remember. I'm sorry." Tilt of the head, fake confusion.

"Well, it was nice talking to you, but we're going to be late." She turned and took my hand. I pulled her away from the daggers shooting from Jill's eyes. I was holding her hand! I'd wanted to hold her hand all day, and now I was holding her hand.

"Is this OK?" She raised our hands.

"Completely."

I said goodbye to her at the doorway to her free period classroom and turned to go to my class. I made it to my class and found my seat. I didn't listen to the teacher's lecture; I just read her note over and over.

Travis,

Thank you for sharing with me. It does make me feel a little better to know that I'm not going through this alone. I'm sure there are a lot of other kids who have lost their parents, other kids who might even be in worse situations than what I am now. Sometimes life isn't fair. Before my mom died, I enjoyed being the center of attention. I became a little spoiled. After she got sick, though, I felt guilty. Because I became so comfortable in our life and our home, I took it for granted. I didn't appreciate my mom all the time. One time a few years ago, we fought in a department store because I wanted her to spend two hundred dollars on a pair of old-looking ripped up jeans. I told her that she was selfish, didn't want me to be happy, and was a horrible mother. I instantly regretted it. I apologized, but something changed. The next day when I got home from my music classes, the jeans were lying on my bed. I'm actually wearing them today. I kept them because I didn't want to forget how I made her feel. I didn't want to ever risk taking someone that I care so deeply about for granted. I don't really know why I'm unloading like this; I think it's special that you and I can share these personal things.

I do want to get to know you. So I have some questions for you, in our quest of acquainting (I know it's a big word). (1) what is your favorite color? (2) what is your favorite kind of music? (2b) who is your favorite band? (2c) what is your favorite song? (3) what is your favorite movie? (4) what is one of your favorite childhood memories? (5) where is your favorite place to be?

It's just five little questions. You can ask me anything too I will tell you the truth even if it's the brutal truth. I promise. But I think that will keep you occupied for your next note. See you soon.

-Gia

Chapter 6

A Simple Letter, the possible window to my Soul

Gianna

I sat in my free period, trying to start an outline for a paper analyzing one of Edgar Allen Poe's poems. I stared at the blank piece of paper. I wondered if I was foolish for telling Travis about the fight I'd had with my mom. I hadn't even told Alex about it. We were school shopping, and the tantrum I threw after she calmly refused to purchase them was awful. I was going to be a freshman, and I wanted to succeed socially as Alex had. She'd told me not even to try them on. I'd insisted. As soon as I blurted those hurtful words I'd clamped my hands over my mouth. It was the only time she'd ever raised her voice to me. She told me to change and that we were leaving. We didn't buy anything. The next day when I got home from my piano lessons, they were lying on my bed. They were the only thing I got for my school clothes that year instead of the two hundred dollars worth of outfits. The lesson was learned. I didn't pursue my popularity any further than that. Today was the first time I'd worn them since trying them on.

I made it to Art Comp and set my books down. Abby came in with a confused look on her face as she sat down on her stool.

"Mason just asked me if he could help me wash my hair Friday." She looked at me.

"Maybe he likes you?" I giggled.

"Well, yeah, look at me! What's not to like?" She shook her head no in disbelief. A few boys turned their heads and looked at her nodding their approval, which made us giggle more.

"Seriously, do you like him?" I asked.

"It's Mason, I mean, come on. It's Mason. He and Travis are high on the crush list for girls and he can have his pick of whoever he wants. He's Mason," she repeated, as if that explained everything. She looked off in the distance as if she were still trying to wrap her mind around it.

"Yes, we've established that it's Mason we're talking about." I went over to retrieve the projects we were working on. I set them down and began shading. Our teacher walked around the class, keeping her eyes on us. *Still on her radar*, I thought.

"It's not unbelievable that he would like you. Do you like him?" I asked again.

"I've never been liked. Well, I mean as a friend I have, but never *liked*." She looked nervous as if this were uncharted territory.

"Well, then, give him your number and see if he calls." I smiled encouragingly.

"He has my number." She began chewing on her fingernail. I looked at her questioningly. "I tutor a lot of the football team." She shrugged.

"Then maybe you should give him the nudge that it's OK to call you even if it's not just for tutoring." I winked at her. She still looked unsure.

I didn't know how I made it through my final class, but I managed. I went to my locker and got the books I needed for homework. A note fell to the floor. I picked it up and put it in my bag. I was off to The Green Monster. That truck really scared me; it was so big. I really hated driving it, but it was better than walking. I made it home and went inside and put my bag down at the table.

"Oliver?" I called out, as I climbed the stairs to get my laptop. There was no answer. I brought it down and turned it on. While I waited for it to load, I grabbed myself some ice water and returned. It was up and connected to the Wi-Fi. Poor Alex had to go the first week with no internet. It had taken Oliver a week to get it installed. I was sure he hadn't thought this whole thing through. There were expenses to raising children and the lifestyle we'd become accustomed to. I didn't feel sorry for him in the slightest. I opened my email. I had three new messages: one from Gracie, another from Melissa, and the third from Mitchell. I opened his first.

Gia,

Thank you for the email. You haven't called yet. I hope to hear from you soon. Are you getting settled in? Alex told me his first game is Friday. I wish

I could be there. Just know that I will be there in spirit and hope to get all the details.

It's hard being in this house without all of you here. I expect to come home and find your mother making her jambalaya. But she isn't here; neither are you and your brother. This house feels so big and empty. That is why I've decided to put it up for sale. It will be on the market by the end of the week. I felt that I should let you know before I did it. I miss you two. Call me.

Love

Mitchell

It made me sad to know that he missed us so much. We missed him, too. I could have written him that a hundred times. But I didn't like the idea of him putting my mother's house up for sale. She was barely gone a month, yet he was so ready to move on. Those were our memories that he was walking away from. I knew Alex wouldn't be happy either.

I read Gracie's anecdotal email about the first day of school. Then I read Melissa's actual account of their first day. I wrote them both back one email. I told them about my new school. I had to tell them about Chiz; I had a feeling Gracie would have thought he was cute. And I told them about Travis a little. I knew there would be more questions. I told them about Abby's hair because they had liked her a lot when she'd visited me in summers past. Then I wrote Mitchell.

Mitchell,

School is going well. I'm sorry I haven't called. We are getting settled in. The first thing we did was paint our bedrooms. We've been driving Oliver's old truck around. They call it Bessie, but I call it The Green Monster. Alex is really excited about the game. I will tell him you'll be rooting for him.

I hope that you will reconsider selling the house if only for just a little bit. We have a lot of memories there. I know I speak for Alex, too, when I say that we were hoping to have it to come home to when we visit. I understand how hard it is though. I miss my mom so much, and being here has dredged up so many memories that I'm having trouble dealing with. We miss you too, and I promise I will call soon.

Love

-Gia

My arrow hovered over the SEND button. I wondered if I should talk to Alex first. I was pretty sure he'd feel the same way that I did. I hit the SEND button anyway. Then I typed up an outline for my paper. I saw the note poking out of my bag. I wanted to read it, but I decided to reward myself with it after homework. Finally, I attacked my math homework. It was a surprise attack and I defeated my enemy. I figured I made some mistakes though; algebra wasn't my strongest subject. I was on my last problem, also contemplating dinner, when my phone rang. It was Alex.

"Do you need me to come get you today?" Of course, I didn't say hello first.

"No, we're going through a drive through. What do you want?"

"You know me, cheeseburger and fries." I smiled because he didn't need to ask and was probably just giving me warning.

"Sounds good. See you in fifteen." I hung up the phone and began to clear my books, put them in my bag, and carry it and my laptop upstairs. I put my laptop on my dresser and surveyed myself. My hair still hung pretty much in place. I had to put a curling mousse in it to get it to stay in loose curls every day. But if I didn't bother it, it pretty much stayed there the whole day and was still soft to the touch. My face was shiny though. I went to the bathroom and washed it with cleanser. I came back and lightly applied eye shadow and mascara. I looked at my jeans again and sighed.

"I'm sorry, Mom," I whispered. Suddenly my heart felt warm, and I felt that she had forgiven me and understood. I heard the front door bang as they came in.

"Gia must be upstairs," Alex said.

"I'll get her," Travis replied.

"I bet you will," Alex called after him, and Travis came stomping up the stairs. I came to the door as he rounded the corner, and we were face to face. He stepped back as I reached for the doorknob.

"Is that your room?" He looked around me as I pulled the door shut.

"Yes, is the food here?" I stepped past him to descend the stairs. He followed.

"Yes." We came down to Alex separating the food among us. I got condiments, and we all sat down to eat. They filled me in on the latest prank that Chiz and Brandon had played on the freshmen. They didn't really laugh about it, but agreed that it was the right of passage to be part of the team.

"I'm just glad that I'm not part of the team. I don't think I'd be very happy," I said. Travis looked confused.

"Gia doesn't do well with surprises. Last year, her best friends back in Indy threw her a surprise birthday party. She pouted all night," Alex told Travis.

"I just don't see the point. I can help plan it and know what's going on."

"She's sort of a control freak about stuff like that," he told him, ignoring me. Travis laughed. "Just warning you about what you're getting yourself into," Alex added. I stiffened.

Alex cleaned up his wrappers and threw them away. He climbed the stairs and told Travis, "Later." Travis finished and cleared his wrappers. He sat back down and waited on me to finish.

"Two nights in a row; I could get used to this." He smiled.

"It's been nice having you here." I took my final bite.

"I'm glad to hear that." I was, too.

"Does Mason like Abby?" I asked.

"I'm not sure. It seemed like it at lunch, didn't it?" He leaned forward on the table.

"I just don't want my friend to get hurt," I sighed as I cleared the wrappers and got the washcloth to wipe down the table. He looked nervously at the clock that hung above the bay window.

"Do you need to go home now?" I asked, hoping that he didn't.

"I do have a little homework to do." He paused.

"I didn't get a chance to read your letter, so I don't have one for you yet." I hoped that I wasn't disappointing him.

"That's OK." He smiled and stood and stretched. "I'll see you tomorrow." He began heading toward the door. I trailed behind him. He opened the door and turned to give me a brilliant smile. My heart skipped. It was almost like he had a secret from me. He opened the storm door, and he was gone. I closed the door as he pulled away. I went upstairs to my bedroom. I found the note in the bottom of my bag. I sat on my bed, put in my ear buds, and turned on my music.

Gia,

I have a confession. I've never written any one person in my life as much as I've written you in the past two days. I really like it though. I feel a special connection with you. I'm sure your mother has forgiven you for the things you said. You were young, and believe it or not, we all say things we regret. Whether we tell someone that we love them when we don't, that an outfit looks OK, or say something because we're mad. I bet your mom knew you regretted it. I have a feeling that you learned your lesson, and it was reinforced when she went ahead and got you the jeans. Am I right?

Answers to your questions:

(1) What is your favorite color? If I say green, you will think I'm smart right? Well, it is one of my favorite colors, but also orange. Don't ask me why. I guess it's because it's a cross between yellow and red and reminds me of the sunrise and being in the ocean surfing.

(2) What is your favorite kind of music? I like classic rock and rock mostly, but I'm getting turned on to classic rap.

(2b) Who is your favorite band? I like The Beastie Boys, Foo Fighters, Nirvana, Lynyrd Skynyrd, Seger, and The Eagles.

(2c) What is your favorite song? I don't really have a favorite song. In the classic rock genre, I'd have to say "Simple Man," and by the way, just because you put an a, b, and c on it doesn't mean that it's one question. It was seven simple questions, Sweetie.

(3) What is your favorite movie? I really like Russell Crowe. Gladiator was a good movie.

(4) What is one of your favorite childhood memories? Despite the challenge of being raised by a single mom, I had a really good childhood. I was involved in all kinds of sports. I also had a lot of freedom, so probably running around the neighborhood with flashlights playing tag with my friends, and playing football in the street. I was able to be a kid. I think it's important for all kids to be able to just be kids. You know?

(5) Where is your favorite place to be? This is a hard question to answer because it changes. If I were being honest, my favorite place to be is anywhere that you are. It's still scary to me to feel this

strongly about you when I met you four days ago. And maybe the only reason I can tell you this is simply because I'm writing it in a letter. I'd never be able to admit this to your face.

So I give you these seven questions back and add (6) Tell me about you in Indiana. What were you like? (6b) Where did you and your friends hang out? (6c) What music did you study?

I can't wait to read your next letter.

Travis

I lay in my bed and read the words over again and again. "If I were being honest, my favorite place to be is anywhere that you are." And, "I'd never be able to admit this to your face." What was happening here? I didn't understand it. I grabbed my phone.

Just read ur letter. I texted.

Really? Did u like it?

Very much.

Then I took out my notebook. I wanted to write him when it was still fresh in my mind.

Travis,

I definitely agree with a few of your points. It's easier to tell you things this way. I can say what I'm feeling right now. I can only imagine what your reactions will be, but it's OK. You seem to confirm the way I feel with every letter you give me. It makes me happy that we are on the same page, so to speak. I have two favorite colors: grey and green. I really like that combination. My mom painted my bedroom those colors when we first bought our house, and since then they've been my favorite colors. You know what my favorite kinds of music are. You went through my phone that night on the beach, remember? I'd have to say my favorite song is "Dangerously in Love with You" by Beyonc. It has such a beautiful melody and the words take my breath away. My favorite movies would be ones about action heroes: Spiderman, Ironman, and Transformers. I went through a comic book stage from the time I was ten 'til I was thirteen. My favorite childhood memory was probably when we moved to Indy. That was when we actually got new furniture for our house. I remember my mom telling Alex and me to go play outside, and we asked if she wanted us to do our chores first. She said "No, go play." And we did. You really touched my heart when you told me your favorite place to be was with me. I find myself anxiously counting the minutes until I can see you again. You wanted to know what I was like in Indiana; well for the most part I was happy. I played the piano and guitar. I haven't played in a long time, but then music was my life. The day my mom told me and Alex that she had cancer, we argued that the doctors were wrong. She assured us that they had been testing for weeks. Her annual visit with the doctor had revealed an abnormal test result. Then she'd had a biopsy. They had tried to remove it, but it seemed to be too late. Watching her go through chemo was really tough. I stopped playing; I just didn't have the heart for it. Instead I escaped into my play lists and tried to understand why this had to happen to us. She was so strong though. She really fought even until the end. I grew up really fast in the last six months. It's not like I didn't have to grow up before, but I think every time I relaxed, boom, catastrophe.

I have two best friends still in Indiana, Gracie and Melissa. I showed you pictures of them. Do you remember? Gracie is crazy and says inappropriate things all the time. Melissa is reserved and smart. I think I'm a combination of the two of them. We usually hung out in our bedrooms and listened to music and read magazines.

I must sound really depressed. I'm not; I'm just trying to deal with the loss of the only person who cared enough about Alex and me to make a difference. I worry about him too. He seems to be adjusting well, but it's only the surface. I just hope that he doesn't lose it and I can't get to him to help him. He refuses to talk about her, even about his memories of good times. Anything at all.

I understand if after this Letter you think that I've got too much baggage for you to deal with. I sometimes don't want to deal with it, but I have to. But if you can hang in there with me, I might be worth a shot.

-Gia

The next morning I performed my usual routine, sneaking into the bathroom so as not to bother Oliver. Picking out three outfits and finally deciding on one. I'd never put this much thought into what I would wear. Today I wore a black short A-line skirt and a lavender scooped neck cotton shirt. I put on my strappy sandals. I did my make-up and put a couple of skinny headbands in my hair and was down the stairs. Alex was tying his shoes and gave me a low whistle as he surveyed me.

"You're really going all out for this guy, huh?" He grabbed his bag as we went out the kitchen.

"I always try to look my best you know that," I said, as I grabbed two Pop Tarts out of the box and followed him.

"The heels are new," he smirked, as he started the truck.

"I'm a junior, growing up." I passed him an open package, rolling my eyes.

"Not too fast. Do I need to have a chat with Travis before your first date *ever* on Friday and tell him to keep his hands to himself?" He kept his eyes on the road.

"You'd better not!" I said, feeling the heat in my face.

"It's OK, Gia. I already had the talk with him. Yesterday. Actually." He paused for dramatic effect before he laughed.

"You'd better not," I repeated.

"We'll see, I guess."

When I got to school, he wasn't at our lockers. I slid the note into his and went to class. I would see him closer to lunch, and that was OK.

Chapter 7

A Fumbling Bumbling Idiot

Travis

I waited as long as I could by my locker. She had already put the note in it, and I figured it would be a long shot to see her again, but I waited still. With minutes to spare, I finally took off toward my first period. I took my seat as the teacher asked for homework. I snatched it out and passed it forward. I took out the letter and read it. Jill eyed me suspiciously. I was thrilled that Gia shared so much with me. I understood that she was sad. I didn't think she was depressed, and if she was giving me an out, I wasn't going to take it. I was going to tell her that when I saw her. Everything about her was goodness. She was hurting, and I'd have to find a way to help her heal her broken heart.

Gia was talking with Abby by our lockers when I came up and put my things in my locker. She radiated as I stepped beside her and took her hand. She smiled shyly at me as we went to lunch. We sat at our now usual table and were in a comfortable groove. I passed her the note I'd written to her under the table. We shared a smile that no one noticed. On the fold I'd written, "To my favorite suitcase." She smirked as she dropped it into her purse. I didn't pay much attention to the conversation. I breathed her coconut scent. I watched her tilt her head to the side. I memorized the sound of her voice. I looked at her long fingers and imagined her playing the piano. My eyes were drawn to the ring that said LOVE. I would get that story out of her, too, soon enough.

We went to speech together, and we took our seats. Ella was bouncing off the walls about the pep rally set for Friday. I groaned. I hated those things. They used to do them only for basketball, but last year they began hauling everyone out to the football field to improve school spirit. Gia smirked at me quizzically.

"You'll see." I rolled my eyes.

"Hey, if we get out of class I'm for it." She giggled. Mr. Franklin came in with a large bouquet of wild flowers.

"Good afternoon, class." We straightened up and turned toward him. "The first speech I want you to prepare for is a three-minute informative speech. I would like it to be on a relevant topic. I want to see your notes and references by Friday. Homework for tomorrow, though, I will take your topic. Then tomorrow during class we will be going to the school library so that you can begin to gather research. So let's get into this. What is an informative speech?" I began to zone out. I tried to take notes, but my mind wasn't choosing a topic for an informative speech.

I survived the class and as we made our way to her free period, we luckily weren't interrupted by a blond head cheerleader. I made it through the rest of my day and into practice.

We ran our drills, talked about plays, practiced the plays, and I dropped the ball. A lot. Mason threw the ball to me. I tried to focus on it because if I couldn't get hold of it during the game, we would lose. I'd be embarrassed in front of the whole school, and worse yet, I'd be embarrassed in front of Gia. I shook my head as the ball went right through my hands. Again. The coach shook his head, threw down his clipboard, and blew his whistle. We all ran over to where he stood. His face was red, and he pointed at several boys but mostly me.

"This is NOT Little League. You guys are playing like toddlers out there. If you don't get it together NICHOLS, you're going to cost us this game. Everyone else is giving a hundred percent, but you, you're a fumbling, bumbling idiot out there." Chiz smirked and nudged Alex. Alex looked annoyed. "Dixon, you get to run an extra round of tosses with Nichols." Mason groaned. "You need to take your head out of your ass and get it in the game Nichols, or you won't be starting on Friday night." He was now in my face screaming. I just nodded. "Hit the showers everyone." He waved everyone off, but was still in my face. "You. Run plays until YOU get it right!" He poked me in the chest. I held his eye contact, and after a few long seconds, he turned away and followed the rest of the team into the locker room. I ran back onto the field where Mason and Alex were already. Mason threw Alex the ball. He caught it perfectly. I was very envious of him. I fell into position. Alex threw the ball back to him. He had a good arm, too. He stayed where he was, but took a blocker position.

"Seventy-seven, thirteen, sixty-nine," Mason chuckled. That wasn't even a play; what a tool! "Hut, hut, hut." Mason leaned back. I ran. I kept looking back at him and watching for Alex, who was charging me. He and the ball were coming at me at the same speed. They would reach me both at the same time. Alex hit me with his shoulder in my stomach just as the ball was on the tip of my fingers. It began to rotate out of my reach, as Alex pushed me back. I fell on my back, and he jumped to his feet.

"Sorry man, run it 'til you get it, right?" Alex stretched out his hand to help me up. I took it and stood.

"Yeah, next time why don't you bring it a little?" I only half-joked. I was angry that I couldn't quite get it. I didn't know what was wrong with me.

"Oh, you want me to bring it next time?" Alex smirked.

"Will you girls stop flirting and let's do this? I'm starving, and my mom is making lasagna tonight." Mason's hands were in the air.

"You're always starving," I snapped, as I hurled the ball toward him.

"One more time, dude," he yelled to me as he went back to his stance. "Ready. Set. Hut, hut, hut!" I had barely gotten back to my starting point as he was tucking back and throwing the ball. I ran and caught that ball right in my hands. Alex had stood off to the side, not even going for me.

"Again," I called, as I jogged back to my position. And we did it, over and over. Finally, we all hit the showers and were on our way home.

"Thanks for hanging out while I worked on my catch. I've been off this week," I sighed, as I pulled out of the parking lot.

"No problem, man. I know you know the techniques. I've seen you catch, but I think you're thinking about it too much. You have to let it come to you. Be there for when it gets there." He shrugged as he looked out the window.

"I know. I've just got a lot on my mind, I guess." I glanced over at him.

"Well, Gia wouldn't want to be a distraction, so you need to get it together, or she'll decide to break things off with you. We haven't talked much about you, but she likes you. She likes you a lot." He paused and looked at me, and added, "If you don't treat her right, you'll have me to deal with." I looked at him, nodding my head.

"I understand."

We arrived at their house. I worried that I was over-staying my welcome. This was the third day that I ate dinner with them. Mom would be giving me a hard time soon I was sure. I didn't care though; I was going to ride this out as long as I could.

Gia was pulling a meatloaf out of the oven as we came into the kitchen door. Alex took his bags upstairs and left me standing there watching her as she cooked.

"Can I help?" I asked, going to the sink and washing my hands.

"Yes, the rolls in the freezer need to go into the oven," she said. I got the package down. She handed me a pan, and I placed three rolls on the pan. She put them in the oven and stirred the green beans as she checked the potatoes.

"Who taught you how to cook like this?" The meatloaf was making my stomach growl; it smelled so good.

"Who else? My mom, well, and the Betty Crocker cookbook," she smirked.

"Why did your mom leave your dad to begin with if you don't mind me asking?" I leaned against the counter watching her add spices. She looked up to the ceiling for a moment, thinking, and then she looked at me as she sighed.

"My dad wasn't very nice back then; he drank a lot, and used my mom as a punching bag. He grabbed Alex by the collar once, and that was all it took for her to realize that she had to do something. We left the next day when he went to work. He's been in rehab and is supposedly better now. He ignores us now; I haven't seen him since Sunday." She went back to stirring.

"I'm sorry." I reached and touched her arm.

"I was six when she loaded us up and drove to Atlanta. I was scared that he would be mad and come after us, but he never did. In fact," she turned to face me, "he never even contacted us. My mom contacted him for the divorce, and then when she remarried and Mitchell wanted to adopt us. That's what makes all this so hard, being here in this town, in this house." I reached up and caught a tear as it slipped from her eye. She looked away and went back to the stove. She asked for the butter and milk from the refrigerator. Then she mixed the potatoes. She called to Alex, and I helped her set the table. We ate, discussing the upcoming game. His phone rang during dinner, and he disappeared upstairs again.

"He and Kiarah are getting close." She smiled.

"Yeah, he really likes her," I added.

"I hope he doesn't break her heart. He was a bit of a player back home; I mean in Indy." She laughed nervously.

"I can see that. The cheerleaders seem to like him." I smiled.

"It's unbearable being his sister sometimes. He charms everyone, and sometimes I had troubled realizing who were real friends and who were just trying to get to him. I'll be right back." She cleared her plate and went to the kitchen. I heard her banging around. I assumed she was putting away the leftovers. She returned and sat back down. "Just so you know, tomorrow night will be meatloaf, too; we have enough I think," she sighed, relieved.

"You're going to make me fat if you keep cooking like this." I patted my belly that was full. "What are you going to do for your speech next week?"

"I have a couple ideas. What are you doing?" she asked mysteriously.

"I have no ideas. I was hoping to steal one of yours." She laughed at my joke.

"Well, I'd be happy to help." She refilled my cup with tea.

"I have so much homework. Is yours done?" I took a drink.

"Almost. Do you want to do it together? Maybe stay for a little while?" she asked shyly.

"I'd love to." I helped her clear the table. She said Alex would do the dishes, and I retrieved my bag from my car. She was waiting for me by the stairs, and we went up to her room. It was a small room. She had a single bed that was up against the wall long-ways. She had pillows against the wall, and it looked almost like a couch. Beside it were small, white, shelved end tables on each side. Her dresser was in the corner with a tall mirror. She had two large windows that almost took up the far wall. She had a street view. Her closet stood in the corner near the windows. She had a black square box that looked like a small suitcase, a blow dryer, and hair products, along with her laptop, sitting on the dresser. All but for a couple posters of musical artists, her room was very impersonal. She didn't have pictures anywhere; she had a clock radio with a music dock for her phone that sat on an end table and books stacked up on the other one. A guitar case leaned in the corner. She hit PLAY on her phone and music softly filled the room.

"So this is your room," I said.

"We pretty much established that yesterday." She smiled as she sat down cross-legged and pulled an algebra book and note pad out of her bag. I dropped my bag to the floor and sat down beside her. It was so strange to be to be sitting here with her. I took out my notebook and my literature book. I turned to the poem by Edgar Allen Poe. I began my rough draft, outlining the meaning behind it and how it related to my life. She paused and watched me write.

"Which poem are you writing about?" She leaned on her hand bracing her elbow on her knee.

" 'Annabel Lee.' Which one did you choose?"

" 'The Raven.' I like your handwriting. It's really plain for a boy." She smiled as she watched me write.

"My mom used to make me practice for hours in elementary school. She said she wasn't raising a doctor, which was weird. You would think she would want me to make a lot of money when I grew up." I laughed, remembering her tracing the letters and then making me do the same.

"Maybe she was just holding out for a lawyer." She giggled and nudged me. She went back to her homework.

"Maybe." I leaned back against her pillows. "I'm blocked."

"What do you mean?" She looked up again from her homework.

"I keep dropping footballs. I'm going to cost us the game on Friday." I couldn't believe I was admitting it to her.

"Why do you keep dropping it?" she asked.

"I don't know, too much pressure, maybe?" I shrugged.

"Have you pictured the other team naked?" Her face was serious.

"No, I don't think I want to picture that." I looked at her and shrugged off the mental picture.

"Have you pictured the coach naked?" She tapped her pencil against her chin.

"Um, that's worse!" I sat up and looked at her. A wicked smile crept across her lips.

"You could picture the people in the stands naked," she continued with her smile broadening.

"I don't want to see ANYONE naked." My face turned bright red. I could feel the heat pushing its way out. I lied. There was one person I'd thought about seeing naked since the beginning of the week. I'd never admit it.

"That's too bad," she smirked. Her whole intention was to embarrass me. It worked. I couldn't even look at her.

"I'm just teasing you; you're so serious." Her eyes burned into me. "You're taking yourself too seriously." I looked at her searchingly. My intentions were to help her, and here she was helping me.

"It's all in your mind. I've never had that much pressure and practicing can only get you so far." She put her hand on my arm. "But if you just relax and enjoy the game, I bet you will catch every ball that comes your way." She patted me and turned back to her algebra.

"Thanks." I just watched her. After a few minutes, she looked up at me again.

"You're making me a little nervous; you should stop." Her laugh was a little higher than usual. It was adorable.

"I'm avoiding," I sighed.

"So what do you want to do?" She stretched out her legs; I put her feet in my lap and began to analyze her toes. She wiggled her toes and tried to pull her feet away, but I held them there.

"What we're doing now." I smiled at her. She still tried to wiggle her feet out. We laughed. I tightened my hold on her ankles and pulled her down toward me. I began to tickle her, and she laughed. Our books fell to the floor, and I somehow ended up lying beside her, almost on top of her. Realizing at the same time how we were, our eyes held each other. We were both out of breath.

"Thanks again." I propped myself up on my elbow, and as I smoothed her hair from her face, loose curls spilled onto the bed between us.

"For what, being a weakling that you can tackle and torture?" she breathed.

"For distracting me and reminding me to enjoy myself." She just nodded. I put my hand on her stomach. We stared at each other—probably a little too long. I wanted to kiss her. I began to lean into her. I watched her lips part slightly. She took a deep breath and slowly closed her eyes and opened them again. Her chest was rising and falling against me. I was going to kiss her. I was going to do it. My lips inched closer to hers; I looked up to her eyes. She looked panicked. It took me by surprise. I leaned up over her. I sat back on my knees. She leaned up on her elbows.

"Did I do something wrong?" she asked, the look in her eyes now embarrassment.

"No. I'm just—I think—I should go," I said. I looked away as I reached for my books and stuffed them into my bag. I stood and left her room. She stood and followed me, but I ran down the stairs. I was through the dining room, zooming through the kitchen past Alex rinsing out the kitchen sink. I flew out the door. I didn't even answer when he asked me, "You're still here dude?" I had to get out of there. What was I thinking? She wasn't the kind of girl that you conned into her room to make out with before you took her out and showed her how a girl should be treated. I was an idiot. AND then I ran away. She thought she did something wrong. But clearly she wasn't ready for our next step. I was pushing her instead of taking things slow. She didn't do something wrong; I did.

Chapter 8

Friday Night Lights

Gianna

In fifth grade I went out with Jesse Busey for three weeks. He kissed me behind the fort on the playground. It was a kiss on the cheek because I turned my face. He broke up with me the next day by telling all the boys that I wouldn't go to first base with him. That was the first and last boyfriend I'd ever had. I'd just done the equivalent to Travis. The only thing was, I didn't turn my cheek. Something about me was off. Maybe I was too rigid; maybe my breath was stinky. I wasn't sure, but something I did suddenly made me undesirable to him. I tried to catch him, but when I came to the kitchen, he was tearing out of the driveway. I wanted to cry. I looked at Alex, who was putting a folded dish towel in the dish drainer. He smiled at me like he was getting ready to ask me something. I locked the kitchen door and shrugged. I went back to my room. I fell on my bed face first. There was something wrong with me. This was proof. Finally, after listening to John Mayer's version of "Free Falling" on loop, I sat up and finished my homework. I went to the bathroom, washed my face, and came to my room to put on my pajamas. I crawled into my bed and fell asleep.

The next day I decided I was going to avoid him. He could come to me. After all, he was the one who ran away from me. I didn't get that chance though. He was leaning against my locker with that cool lean he did so well. Eyes straight ahead, his leg propped up, and hands in his pockets. I slowed as I approached him. I stood looking at him, waiting for him to move; he didn't. He leaned his head against the locker and turned his face toward me. He didn't say anything.

"You're blocking my locker," I sighed.

"I know." But he didn't move.

"You're going to make me late."

"I'm sorry about last night. I shouldn't have left like that." He continued looking away from me.

"No, you shouldn't have." But he still didn't move. I stepped past him and began walking toward my class. I would just have to take my bag with me.

"We weren't ready for that. I shouldn't have put us in that situation." Travis raced to catch up to me.

"What makes you say that?" I tried to sound bored.

"Because I saw your face; I don't want our first kiss to be when you're not ready." He reached for my arm and turned me toward him.

"Oh," was all I said. He held my hand and led me back toward my locker.

"I'm really sorry. I want to do this right." He weaved us in the opposite flow of the student herd.

"You could have told me this last night." I opened my locker and put my books in.

"I know. I was embarrassed. You didn't do anything wrong. I did." He looked at the floor now.

"You didn't do anything wrong either. It's OK. Can we just put it behind us?" I was ready to be over all the embarrassment, his and mine.

"I can. I'll see you at lunch?" He began to back away.

"Yes." I smiled at him and turned to go to my first class.

I went to class and thought about our conversation. I thought about the past six days and how fast things had changed. I had definitely reached a crossroads when I came to Florida. I hoped I was making the right decisions. Abby met me at my locker for lunch. We waited for Travis. He must have been running late. I didn't see him.

"Do you want to just start toward the cafeteria?" She searched for him with me.

"He'll be here," I smiled nervously.

"There he is." She pointed. He was descending the stairs with Mason and a couple of other guys at the end of the hall. Rounding the corner behind him was Jillian. She reached for his hand and wove hers into his. He looked at her with furrowed eyebrows and pulled away. She then looped her arm through his. He was struggling to pull away from her again. I looked at Abby, and she rolled her eyes.

"I don't know how much more of her I can take." I crossed my arms. "He clearly likes me right? I'm not reading too much into this? He asked me out on Friday." I watched as he repeatedly wiggled away from her. Finally, he stopped and forcefully said something to her. She looked annoyed at me and stomped off. Mason shook his head and said something under his breath as they approached us. Travis was shaking his head. He stepped to me and wrapped his arm around my waist.

"Sorry about that drama," he whispered in my ear. I just nodded. I put my arm around him, too. It felt nice. He squeezed me and took my hand. We walked to the cafeteria together. Today some of the guys from the team joined our table. Kiarah was discussing a local ordinance that she was hoping would pass to protect alligators. It was a heated debate between her and one of the boys who had joined our table.

"So am I invited to work on homework with you again tonight?" Travis leaned in and whispered in my ear again. Shivers ran up my spine.

"We can work in the dining room after dinner." I had turned my face toward him. We were cheek to cheek.

"I can be trusted in your room." I felt his breath on my neck.

"I'm not so sure about that," I giggled. We were back to where we should have been. We were on track.

We went to the library for speech class. I checked out books on coping with loss in the family. He checked out books on domestic abuse. When I saw his books, I smiled my approval. We sat at a table together and did our research. Barely speaking to each other, we both got a lot of work done.

In my free period I did as much homework as I could. In art class I put the finishing touches on my drawing. Our drawings were due at the end of class. I was pretty confident it was already done, but I dragged out my shading. Abby was focused on her work.

"Have you ever kissed a guy?" I asked under my breath. I was pretty sure I knew the answer.

"No, does someone want to kiss me?" She didn't even look up.

"Probably. But Travis and I almost kissed last night." She glanced at me out of the corner of her eye.

"What do you mean almost?"

"Well, we were doing homework; then he was tickling me. Then we almost kissed, but he pulled away and then just left. He said my expression said I wasn't ready. I don't know what it was because I wanted him to kiss me." I looked back down at my paper.

"Have you ever kissed a guy?" She was looking at me, not even pretending to work anymore.

"No, Travis is the first guy who has shown interest in me since Jesse." Abby knew the Jesse story. She had lived through hours of my obsessing and blaming him for no social life all through junior high.

"No, Blake liked you, remember, last year," she corrected me.

"That doesn't count. Blake was a friend, and I couldn't have a boyfriend while my mom was sick," I countered.

"He still showed interest. But maybe Travis was right and you weren't ready, last night. Don't try to rush it; it will happen, and when it does, it will be magic." She went back to her drawing.

I went back to my art work and then navigated the rest of the day. When I got out to my truck, there was a note sitting in the driver's side seat. I put it in my bag and went home.

I came in through the kitchen. I called out to Oliver. There was no answer. I went to my room and sat down on my bed, took out the note, and read it.

Gia,

I wonder how OK it is for me to have such strong feelings for you, but I do. I feel very vulnerable sharing them with you, too. I thought about what you said yesterday, about thinking too much about the game. It's the first game of the season. And it seems trivial to care so much when there is so much more going on in the world. I guess this is my big deal. I keep thinking that if I play well enough, I can get a scholarship and get into a good school, and maybe become a lawyer or something that my mom would be proud of. She has sacrificed so much. She's a nurse you know. She puts long hours in at the hospital and is raising my sister and me without any help from my father.

I might be thinking too much about our relationship, too. I don't want to over analyze it. I want to enjoy my time with you. I feel like I would have a huge hole in my life if I lost you. It's like there was something that was always missing, but I didn't even know it until I met you. I hope you understand what I mean and it makes sense to you, because it doesn't make a lot of sense to me. I guess that's all I can say now. It's time to go to practice. I will not be thinking about the game though. I will just enjoy practice. It's because of you. I can't wait to see you.

Travis

I held the letter to my heart as I fell back on my bed and rested in my happiness. I must have dozed off because the next thing I knew, Alex was sitting beside me on my bed.

"We warmed up the leftovers. Are you going to come and eat?" I blinked as my eyes focused on him, momentarily confused as to what he was talking about. "Dinner is ready Gia."

"I'll be down in a minute." I sat up and rubbed my eyes. He stood and left my room. I looked at myself in the mirror. My hair was a mess, and I had raccoon eyes from my mascara. I went to my closet and took out a square tin box and put the letter in it with all the other letters he'd written me. I went to the bathroom and washed my face, pulled my hair into a pony tail, and smoothed my shirt and jeans. I went downstairs and ate dinner with my brother and Travis. Then Travis and I went upstairs to my room, and we did our homework. We actually did it without many distractions. He was in a very good mood. He told me that he'd gotten his rhythm back. He said I was right, and he was grateful for me. After he told me goodbye, close to nine o'clock, I went upstairs and to bed.

On Friday, the last two periods of class were cancelled. We all filed out onto the football field. Abby and I found a seat somewhere in the middle while Kiarah and a few of her friends sat around us. Finally, when all the students were out there, the cheerleaders bombarded onto the field. They did a dance routine before the marching band came out and played a song. The principal introduced the whole team, all the players one by one. Then a few players and the cheerleaders did a few skits. We laughed at them, more because they were really ridiculous than funny. I saw what Travis meant by "you'll see." He sat down by the field. Even from where I sat, I could tell he was uncomfortable. He'd lean forward, sit back, turn and look in our direction, and the poor guy had to be in one of the skits. They had all worn their jerseys to school, and other students wore school t-shirts. When it was over, we were dismissed for the day. We slowly made our way down the bleachers. He climbed the bleachers two at a time to where we stood talking. He took my hand and spoke conspiratorially with me.

"I don't have to be back until five-thirty. Will you come to my house?" I nodded my head yes.

"Good." He turned to lead me away. I waved to Abby and Kiarah. We went to his car and were on our way.

"You should forget law school and go to Hollywood," I said, trying to keep a straight face.

"You should take your comedy special on the road." He did keep a straight face. He reached for my hand and held it as we pulled into the driveway of a house two blocks away from my home. He turned to me.

"If I asked you to do something, would you?" He seemed nervous. I nodded yes, wondering what I was getting myself into. He got out, and I followed. He led me to his front door. We were inside in seconds. There was a yummy smell to his house. It reminded me of wintertime in Indiana and my mom making stews to warm us up. I stood there a moment taking in the homey fragrance. He led me upstairs to his room. It was a charcoal grey color. He had a desk in the corner, a dresser and chest of drawers lining the other walls. Windows on a wall with a side view and a double bed centered between them. Shelves on the walls held little league trophies that were too many to count from soccer, football, baseball, lacrosse, and basketball. He had pictures of his friends, of his family, one of a woman and a man in black and white. I stepped to it and touched it delicately. He watched me as I turned around his room taking everything in; he had a pile of dirty clothes in the corner. He saw me look at them and blushed.

"Sorry for the mess." He went to one of two closed doors and opened it. From the top shelf he reached and took down a plastic bag. He brought it to his bed, removing a kelly green shirt and a white shirt. He unfolded them. They were the exact same V-neck t-shirt replicas of his jersey—just in different colors. On the front they had St. Petersburg High School and the mascot, the Devils logo; Nichols was printed across the top of the back with a large thirty-one centered in the middle. His number, I suddenly realized, but I looked at him confused. Did he stash t-shirts for all his random admirers?

He handed me the green one and asked, "Will you wear this to the game tonight and to the rest of the games this season?" He looked shyly at me.

"Really?"

"Yeah."

"Yeah, I'd be honored to wear these shirts." I smiled as I held one up. He reached in the bag and pulled out a green zip-up hoodie that had the number thirty-one on the upper left-hand side. These were all women's shirts and in a small.

"Try them on." He pointed to the second door. I went in and found a bathroom. I was assaulted by his scent, his soap, his cologne. My mind wandered to the vision of him shirtless. I managed to changed shirts. It actually fit me perfectly. It looked great with my dark denim straight-legged jeans. I came out and did a twirl.

"Is it OK?"

"Great fit." He smiled as he held open the hoodie for me to try on. I slipped my arms into it.

"They fit perfectly. How did you know my size?" I tested the zipper.

"I asked Alex. I ordered them Tuesday, and they arrived yesterday. This way everyone will know you're my girl." He hugged me to him over my shoulders. I hugged him, too, around his waist. Was this official now?

"Alright, let's go get something to eat." He led me out of his room, as he added, "This isn't our date either, in case you were wondering." I smiled as we came down the stairs.

"Travis!" A little girl with long dark brown hair lunged for him, her book bag still on her back.

"Hailey, hey, baby girl." He caught her in his arms and lifted her up to him. A woman in scrubs came in behind her with an arm full of grocery bags.

"Travis, I have more in the trunk." She hadn't noticed me yet, mainly because I was hiding behind him and Hailey.

"Who are you?" Hailey whispered, as she peered over his shoulder at me with big brown eyes.

"I'm Gia," I spoke softly, too, as I smiled.

Travis cleared his throat, and added, "Mom, I'd like you to meet Gianna." He pulled me around him on the stairs.

"It's nice to finally meet you, Gianna. I'm Melanie. Are you going to stay for dinner? It's the least I can do after you've been feeding Travis all week." She smiled warmly at me. Her brown hair was cut in a sleek bob. She had tan skin and wore minimal make up. She had to be in her mid to late thirties. She was very pretty.

"I was going to take her to get a bite to eat." Travis led me down the rest of the stairs with the hand that wasn't holding his sister.

"No, you don't; you can't hide her from me!" His mom teased him. He set down his sister and looked at me wearily.

"I don't mind," I smiled, as I squeezed his hand.

"Fine, Mom, we'll stay." He kept his eyes on mine as he answered her.

We helped her unload the rest of the groceries and set the table for her while she prepared the food. She had a crock-pot of stew going. That was what I smelled when I first came in. She got to know me by playing the twenty questions game.

"So you just moved here, right? Where are you from?"

"Indiana, Fishers, outside of Indianapolis."

"Are you involved in any of the school activities?"

"Not really. I never really got into sports, and I stopped playing music when my mom got sick." Melanie tactfully changed the subject.

"Do you and Travis have any classes together?" she asked.

"Speech, that's it."

"That's nice. Travis loves to surf. Have you ever surfed?" He groaned and adjusted in his seat. She gave him an annoyed look.

"I haven't. We moved away when I was really young. I wouldn't mind trying it sometime though."

"Do you like to play dress up?" Hailey interjected. "I'm too old for princesses, but I like to dress up in my mom's old clothes." She kept her brown eyes intent on me.

"I only get to play dress up on Halloween, but I used to love it, too." I smiled at her.

And so it continued. Around five, Travis told his mom that we needed to go. He went upstairs to get my other shirts and came back down. We went to leave, but his mother held his arm and said something to him while I stood on the front porch. He came out, a look of relief on his face, and took my hand, leading me to his car.

"Well, you pass with flying colors." He smiled as he started the car.

"Was I being tested?" I asked, only half joking.

"Kind of. She only has Jillian to compare, and she's known her family for a really long time, so I think it was a sort of test."

"Wow, being compared to Jillian, that's a high standard. Do I even make it on the same level?" I felt really insecure. Jillian was gorgeous.

"You surpass her on so many levels. I promise that this is the only time you will be compared to her." True to his word, that was the last time he brought her up to me in that manner. He reached for my hand as he pulled up to the curb.

"I'll see you in a little bit?" he asked.

"Yes, you will." He reached over and touched my hair, and I got out of the car and went inside.

I made it to the bleachers just as the boys were lining up to run out onto the field. I surveyed the crowd in the stands. I didn't see anyone that I knew. My heart began to race. Then I felt an arm wrap itself in mine. I turned, and Abby was standing beside me.

"Let's go find our seats. Nice shirt. Is that a new style? I haven't seen it before." She led me to a spot near the band. We sat and watched the game. Alex played excellently, Mason didn't throw any interceptions, and Travis caught every ball that came his way, having a really good game. I was proud of all of my friends. We barely pulled off a win though; it was a close game. As soon as they disappeared into the locker room, I got a text.

I'll pick you up at your house in thirty minutes.

It was already close to nine in the evening. I didn't know of much that we could do after nine, but I sent him a message that said "*OK*," and asked Abby for a ride home. She took me home, and I took a shower and cleaned up. As I was finishing up surveying myself in my mirror, Alex came to my door and knocked. I wore a short jean skirt and an off-the-shoulder dark purple puffy cotton blouse that gathered at my hips. I slipped on my ballet slippers as I told him to come in. He surveyed me and nodded his head in approval.

"Don't stay out too late." He used his fatherly tone.

"I could say the same to you. Is the art show even still going on?" I winked at him

"Yes, it is. I'm going to change and then head over there. I mean it; don't stay out too late." He began to shut the door and then he added, "He's downstairs waiting on you." My heart sputtered, and I followed him out my bedroom door.

Chapter 9

First Dates, Lasting Impressions

Travis

She descended the stairs and there might as well have been a choir singing and lights making her wings glow. She looked angelic. I stood from the couch and met her at the bottom of the stairs.

"You played an amazing game," she said politely.

"It's all your fault," I smirked, remembering her pep talk.

"I'll take the blame for that." I opened the door, and we made our way to my car, which was sitting on the curb sparkling under the street light. I had run it through the car wash and cleaned it out. She raised her eyebrows as we approached it.

"Where are we going?" I opened the door for her and she climbed in.

"It's a surprise." She cringed as I laughed. I went around and climbed in myself. We drove only a few blocks to the pier. She sighed, a contented sigh. We got out, and I popped the trunk. I took out a picnic basket and met her on the sidewalk. She laced her fingers in mine, and I led her to the place she sat the first day I met her almost a week before. I took out a blanket from the basket, and she helped me spread it. She delicately sat down, tucking her legs under her. I sat facing her and took out two cupcakes on a plate that had clear wrap on it.

"Dessert." I handed her one and set the plate aside.

"Thank you." She delicately peeled away the paper and took a bite, moaning her approval. "Sour cream icing and chocolate chips in the cake mix? How did you know?" She took another bite, closing her eyes as she savored it.

"You probably already know. I asked Alex what your favorite dessert is." She nodded appreciatively.

"I adore them." She smiled. Then it happened so fast I didn't even realize what happened. She was on her knees, leaning into me. She softly pressed her lips to mine, and then it was over. "Thank you," she whispered, her hand on my shoulder. I reached up and brushed her hair away from her neck, pausing for a moment to look at her beautiful eyes. I gently pulled her to me and kissed her. I kissed her softly at first, and then her arms were around my neck, and my free hand was pressing her against me. Her soft lips fit in between mine perfectly. She smiled while our lips were still pressed to each other. I let go of her, and she sat back on her heels. I took my cupcake off the plate and took a bite. I was surprised at how good they were. She raised her eyebrows as she watched me eat it.

"You adore them too, don't you?" She grinned.

"I think I do," I smiled. I pulled her in between my legs as I popped the last of the cupcake into my mouth. I wrapped my arms around her, and she leaned back against my chest. Together we watched the waves come in and out.

"I used to come here when Oliver was angry with my mom," she spoke softly. I tightened my arms around her. "Alex would find me after Oliver left. It seems like sometimes it was a daily event, like it was on the calendar. 'Two P.M. take Gia to piano lessons. Three-thirty hit my wife.' And now he wants to be our dad. Like he had a choice in the matter the whole time." She leaned her head back against my shoulder.

"What was Atlanta like?"

"It was hot. We left in the middle of summer. We stayed with my mom's Aunt Francesca because our car broke down just outside of Atlanta. Aunt Francesca believed that garlic went in everything, including cereal," she softly giggled. "My grandfather had passed by then, and we didn't have anywhere to go. She wasn't happy we were there, said we breathed too much, whatever that meant. So as soon as my mom saved up enough to get a newer car, we moved to New Orleans." She stopped there. I sat there holding her, listening to her breathing sync with mine. It was just us and the waves somewhere in the distance. I'm not sure how long we sat there. It felt right though. It felt like the perfect ending to the most perfect week of my life. I kissed the side of her neck. She sighed and reached up and brushed my cheek with the back of her hand, turning it and softly tracing my jaw line. I leaned down and kissed her once more before we packed everything up and went back to the car. I drove the short drive to her house and walked her up to the front stoop.

"I had a really wonderful time tonight." She looked down at her hands as I put them in mine.

"I did, too. Do you have plans tomorrow? Can I call you?" I shouldn't have still been unsure of her, but I was.

"I'd like that." The porch light came on suddenly, and the door opened at almost exactly the same time. A man stood in the doorway. He wore tan Dickies pants and a dingy white t-shirt that said Moretti Pub and Eatery. His salt and pepper hair was disheveled.

"Gianna, it's late. Who is this fella here, and where is Lexie?" His accent was thick. Gia looked nervously at me.

"I know it's late; I was just coming in. This is Travis, and Alex is at an art showing tonight." She took a step closer to the door and away from me.

"Maybe we need to set some guidelines around here. Come inside now, it's late." He didn't move from the door. She took a deep breath and stepped back to me and kissed my cheek, then let go of my hand.

"Good night, Travis." She turned and went inside. The door shut and the light went off simultaneously. Then I heard the voices, low at first, then rising. I stepped closer.

"Oliver, what was that?" She was calm at first.

"I should know where you are."

"You WOULD know where we are, if you cared. But I don't think you do. You can't just turn on the parenting whenever it's convenient for you." Her voice sounded shaky.

"You will show me respect. You haven't even been in this house a week, and you're disrespecting me like this. I am the only family you have.

You will honor me. You will not see that boy until he comes to me first and asks for permission to date you." His voice was rising.

"So you can control me the way you controlled Mom? I don't think so. This is how it will be. We will stay out of each other's way, and as soon as I turn eighteen, I'll leave, and you can go back to your life." She was stomping up the stairs.

"Gianna, come back here. We are not done with this conversation." At that moment I made a decision that I hoped I wouldn't regret. But it was too late; I was already knocking. I stepped back away from the door. He swung the door open, his face beet red. He stepped out onto the porch, and we were almost touching noses.

"What do you want now?" he demanded.

"I was hoping that you would grant me permission to date your daughter. I have nothing but the utmost respect for her." I didn't step back. I waited for him to. He didn't.

"Are you the boy who's been spending every afternoon here after school?" I didn't know how he knew that since he wasn't even around. She had said herself that she hadn't seen him since the previous Sunday.

"Yes, I am. I have eaten dinner with Alex and Gia. She and I also work on homework together." He finally stepped to the side and walked around me to lean on the post by the stairs, his back to me.

"You play on the football team, don't you?" He was looking out on the street. I turned to face him.

"Yes, I do." I put my hands in my pockets.

"You played well tonight. As long as you respect Gia, you may date her. But if I hear of you hurting her or disrespecting her, you will have me to deal with. She's had enough of that to last her two lifetimes." He didn't look at me. He turned and went back inside. He shut the door and locked it. I stood there a few more minutes taking in what had just happened.

"You did what?" Gia spoke softly into the phone. I had just told her about my conversation with Oliver. I was lying in bed.

"I feel like we should follow Oliver's rules," I spoke a little softer.

"I don't want him telling me who I can spend time with or what I do during that time," she sighed.

"Well, I did it, and now we can be together; I don't regret it. I thought I might, but I don't. This will just make it easier for you." I put my hand on my head, hoping she understood. "So when can I see you today?" I asked.

"I have a list of chores and laundry. Then we'll see." She was still upset. I hadn't known her long, but I had seen her as easy-going and generally crowd-pleasing. This tone was neither of those. "Well, try to be done by four. I'd like to spend the afternoon with you."

"I have things to do then. I'll call you when I'm done, OK?" I had a feeling that was the best I was going to get.

"I'll talk to you soon then."

"Bye."

I stayed in bed a few more minutes, but I could smell the pancakes downstairs, and I was definitely hungry. My door opened, and Hailey came bouncing in. She jumped on my bed with me and crawled under the covers. She cuddled up to me and patted my cheek with her tiny hand.

"I think Gianna is pretty."

"I do, too."

"And she is nice. She really talked to me. I liked that," she said.

"Yes, Gia is very special."

"Do you love her?" she searched my eyes questioningly.

"I only met her a week ago, but I really like her. I think I could love her, but that will take some time," I answered her honestly.

"I think you will if you don't already. Mommy made pancakes; it's time to eat."

"I know. I could smell them. They smell good, huh?" I squeezed her to me.

"Hurry up! Let's go." She giggled.

"Let's go." I pulled her up and threw her over my shoulder as I got up from bed. She continued giggling as I carried her down the stairs and put her in her seat.

"Good morning, sleepyhead." Mom was pouring juice.

"Early to bed and early to rise makes it a school day and not the weekend," I chuckled.

"Well, eat up. I have a shift that starts at noon. You've got Hailey duty this afternoon."

"I have plans," I groaned and looked at Hailey adding, "No offense, baby girl." She nodded.

"Well, Mrs. Kensington has the flu and can't keep her."

"Her house smells funny, and I usually smell like it until Tuesday even with baths." Hailey crinkled her nose.

"So now your plans include Hailey," Mom sighed.

"That means tons of junk food and horror flicks." I elbowed Hailey. She giggled again.

"Yes, that means there's thirty dollars in the drawer; order a pizza and go rent a couple movies." She grinned.

Hailey helped me rinse the dishes and load the dishwasher. Then we did some laundry. My mom left with an approving smile on her face. I picked up my room, and dusted it, something that I never did. We ate lunch and played video games. The thing about my sister was she loved video games, and for an eight-year-old girl, she was very competitive. We spent most of the afternoon playing and talking trash to each other.

My phone rang around three. It was Gia, and she said she could do something. I asked her to come over and explained the Hailey factor. She had no problem with that. We went to the video store, and I got an animated movie, an action movie, and a romantic comedy. I hoped they were OK. We met Gia at my house close to five in the evening. I ordered a pizza, and we started playing board games. If I thought Hailey was ruthless with the video games, she had nothing on Gia; her competitive nature made me wonder why she'd never gone out for sports. She was a beast! I just sat back and watched them go at it. It was enough to entertain me for the night. We let Gia pick the movie she wanted to watch. She picked the animated movie, which won her even more brownie points with Hailey. We settled in and watched the movie, Hailey sitting between us. She fell asleep leaning on Gia toward the end, and I carried her upstairs.

I let Gia pick the next movie we watched. She picked the action adventure. I popped it in as she refreshed our drinks. I dimmed the lights and went to the kitchen, returning with two of her favorite cupcakes. She smiled. We sat back down, and there was suddenly a nervous tension in the air. She sat forward as we watched the previews. Finally, I grabbed her around the waist and pulled her into me. She relaxed and leaned against me. Eating our cupcakes, we watched the movie.

"This is nice, right?" I asked, not really paying attention to the movie. "Better than sneaking around."

"Yes, Travis. After we hung up and I thought about it, this is nicer than hiding. I don't want to have to hide anything that I feel about you." I was glad she couldn't see my face. I'm sure she felt my heart begin to race.

"What exactly might you be hiding if I hadn't asked for permission to date you?" I asked anxiously. She didn't answer right away.

"How strongly I enjoy your company, and I like talking to you. I enjoy reading your letters." She turned to look at me. "And you're not bad to look at either," she smirked, but there was a nervousness I felt, behind her smile.

"Oh, not bad to look at?" I chuckled. She nodded yes.

"Well, thank you." I leaned my head back, watching her squirm.

"What about you? How do you feel about me?" She looked down. I put my hand on her chin and leaned in to kiss her. She let me. I finally pulled away from her only so I could tell her how I really felt; I leaned back and said, "I've never seen anyone as beautiful as you the day I saw you standing on the pier. I'd never met a person as good as you before I wrote you that first note." She leaned her head against me, satisfied with the answer.

Chapter 10

Change, It's Inevitable

Gianna

Over the next two weeks, we settled into a rhythm. Travis and I walked to our classes together and ate lunch and dinner together. We did our homework together. If I weren't with him, I was thinking about him. We wrote each other letters every day.

Gradually, posters about homecoming began appearing on the walls all over the halls. After school, I was looking at one outside of girls' restroom as I waited for Abby. That was when Chiz leaned his back against the wall beside it looking up.

"Do you have a date yet?" He looked over at me in what I believed was his attempt to look sexy. Technically, Travis hadn't asked me, but we were going out on a regular basis, and he referred to me as *his girl* when he talked with his friends.

"I'm probably going with Travis." I looked back at the poster.

"Well, probably is not a definite. I'm extending the offer if he doesn't ask you, but it's only good until the end of the week. I'm in high demand, you know." He straightened up and nodded his head to someone. "Hey, Travis, don't be late for practice." He slapped his shoulder and walked off.

"Hey, Beautiful." Travis kissed my head as he squeezed me to him. "What did he want?" He motioned toward Chiz.

"He asked me to the homecoming dance," I said, shaking my head.

"What did you say?" He almost sounded nervous.

"I said we were probably going together even though you haven't asked me."

"Will you go to the dance with me?" he leaned in and whispered, as Abby swung the door open and came out.

"Yes," I breathed; he had no idea the effect he had on me now. He kissed my cheek goodbye and went to practice. Abby and I went on our outing to the mall.

"So you are officially going with Travis? Alex asked Kiarah two weeks ago, and I have no date. Maybe I won't go." Abby was having a bit of a pity party because Mason hadn't asked her yet.

"He's going to ask you. The dance is still two weeks away. They haven't even announced the homecoming court yet. Maybe we should look at dresses." I concentrated as I was trying to do the math on twenty percent off the shirt I was looking at.

"Nineteen-ninety-nine and I have no problem going stag. Besides, I could go with Bryan. He asked me yesterday, but I'm sure that window won't be open for long." She was now chewing on her nails.

"Why don't you ask him?" I pulled her hand down. She looked unsure.

"Do we have enough clothes to go to the dressing rooms?" she sighed uncomfortably, changing the subject.

In the dressing room, I texted Travis and asked if Mason was going to ask Abby to the dance. He replied that he thought so. I told him to hurry or she was going to tell Bryan "yes." He didn't respond. We made our purchases, and I dropped Abby off at home. By the time I made it home, Alex and Travis were in the kitchen fixing dinner. I didn't want to know what they were fixing, so I took my bags upstairs and began looking for a new place to put the additions to my wardrobe.

"What'd ya get me?" Travis threw himself on my bed. I showed him the black tops and darker shorts and skirts. He put his hands behind his head enjoying the display. He uttered approval at his favorites.

"Dark colors honoring your mom, right?" He looked toward the door.

"Yes," was all I said.

Alex yelled for us. We both went down and ate dinner together.

"I need to know what color your dress is for my suit, so I can coordinate," Travis said.

"I don't know yet, but I'll let you know when I find it," I said, dreading that shopping trip suddenly. It was times like this that I really missed my mom. He leaned against the porch pillar prolonging his visit. We had eaten, washed and put away the dishes, and finished our homework. It was getting late. He took one step down.

"So I'll see you tomorrow?" We were eye to eye.

"Yes, bright-tailed and bushy-eyed." I winked. He chuckled. He put his arms around my waist, and I threw my arms around his neck. He leaned in to kiss me. I closed my eyes. Then I heard someone clear his throat. We both looked in the direction just as our lips brushed each other's. Standing on the sidewalk was Oliver. I rolled my eyes and pecked Travis on the lips. "Tomorrow," I whispered. He hugged me tight and turned to leave. Oliver passed him on the sidewalk.

"Travis," Oliver nodded, his steady gaze fixed on me.

"Mr. Moretti," Travis nodded, as he looked straight ahead. I sat down on the porch. He pulled away with a final wave goodbye.

"It's a lovely evening, don't you think?" Oliver sat down beside me.

"It was," I said.

"Is your homework done?"

"Yes." Were we really going to play this game of idle chat?

"Well, you should come inside; it's getting late and—" he trailed off, staring at the early evening stars. "I know you think I'm a horrible person, and that's OK. I used to be. But I'm not that person anymore. I hope one day you and your brother can forgive me. I'll never replace your mother, but I do and will always love you." He stood and walked to the door. He paused and turned toward me. "Don't stay out much longer." I nodded and sat there for another half hour.

As I lay in bed looking at my white ceiling, listening to my loud rock music, I tried to think. I tried to remember a time when Oliver showed me affection as a child. We flew a kite once. He was happy until I crashed it into the ground and broke the stick that held it together. Then he ripped it in two and threw it at my feet. Turning on my mom, he said it was a stupid idea to try to teach someone like me to fly a kite. He once promised to build a swing set for Alex and me. But after two cases of beer, he threw it out with the trash the following week. "Wasted money," he had sneered. *Wasted daddy,* I had thought. I couldn't sleep; I took out my notebook.

The next day at school as I sat in second period during the morning announcements, they named the homecoming court. I didn't know any of the names except for four: Travis Nichols, Jillian Thomas, Mason Dixon, and Alex Moretti. I slouched in my seat. Of course, Jillian, would be there. I'd bet all the cheerleaders were in the homecoming court. And, of course, the most popular boys on the football team. I wondered what going to the dance with Travis now entailed. I wasn't sure.

As I went to my locker before lunch, I was bumped more than I though was necessary by cheerleaders passing me in the hall. At first I thought that I was delusional, but they were really bumping into me. I almost dropped my books once, but I didn't, and I held my head high. As I put my books into my locker, Travis snuck up behind me, wrapping his arms around me and whispering "Hi" breathily in my ear. It sent chills down my spine and tickled my ear. I giggled.

"Hi, yourself." He stepped over to his locker and dropped his books in. "Homecoming court, huh?" I smirked.

"I'm going to concede and let the next runner up take my spot." He was still digging in his locker.

"Why?" I asked, genuinely curious.

"I'm going to the dance with you, and I don't want to do all the stuff that's involved with homecoming—stand on a float, stand on stage, dance with anyone beside you—I've done it all before. It's not that big of a deal." He peeked at me from around his locker.

"Hmm," was all I said, as I took his hand, letting him lead me toward the cafeteria.

"What's that supposed mean?" he asked, a crooked smile spread on his face.

"I was a little bummed you were on the court, but I understand it. You're popular and a good representation of our school. I just don't want you to give this up for *me*. That's not a good enough reason." I didn't look at him.

"Are you sure? It's not that big of a deal to me. This is our first dance together; that's a big deal to me." He had stopped, and I looked up at him. I sighed.

"I'm sure."

"OK."

I stood staring at the mirror in a flesh-colored, soft flowing dress. It didn't feel right, and it was the fifth dress I'd tried on. Abby had already picked her dress, her shoes, and clutch purse, and was now banging on the door for the third time demanding to see my dress. I opened the door and showed her.

"It's not right," I said softly, as I looked down.

"So, what is right then? Because I don't know if they have any more styles of dresses. You look amazing." I looked back at my reflection.

"No, it doesn't feel right," I sighed.

"You're putting too much pressure on yourself." She leaned her head against the swinging door. She analyzed my face. I could feel her searching my eyes and my expression. "We'll come back another day." She closed the door, and I dressed again.

Abby checked out and was chattering about how Mason had asked her. He'd come over to her house on the pretense of getting help with calculus. Halfway through the tutoring session, he said, "I don't need any more help." She looked at him, not believing him. He continued, "I've never needed help. I've always liked you. I guess I just wanted to spend time with you and never knew how." She was shocked; she had tutored Mason since eighth grade. He had confided in her about girls he liked and about girlfriends. He had told her things that friends tell each other, so she never though more of it. She even admitted to me of confiding in him more than she had been comfortable confiding in anyone else. And then he said it.

"Will you go to the dance with me?" She jumped into his arms, hugging him, and he actually kissed her. Her first kiss, there in her dining room, her parents in the great room watching TV. She said it was nerve-racking. She blushed and giggled with me as I laughed, not because he kissed her, but because I envisioned her parents oblivious to their daughter's make-out session in the next room. She admitted that her heart sank a little when she heard his name announced that morning, but she understood. He and Travis had been on the homecoming court for the past two years.

We made it to my house where she dropped me off. Leaning on his car parked behind the old truck in the driveway was Travis, smiling at me as I got out. His expression turned to confusion as I grabbed only my book bag.

"No dress?" His arms went up in the air.

"No dress," I sighed.

"She needs more help than I can give her," Abby called to him. I looked at her in annoyance. She shrugged, waved goodbye, and was on her way. I began to walk up the stoop to the front door. He caught my hand.

"I thought we could try something different today." I looked at him questioningly. "Dinner at my house? My mom made a roast. We can do homework there, too." He wove his fingers in mine and led me away from the stairs. My eye caught a form move from in front of a window with the blinds open in a house across the street. I couldn't see more than just a dark form, but someone was there watching—maybe Oliver's spy and that's how he seemed to know how much time Travis spent here. I directed my attention back to Travis, his face so hopeful.

"Dinner at your house," I conceded easily.

In the car we didn't say much. Throughout dinner we made small talk about the dance, Travis' courtly duties, and Hailey's new obsession with her colored pencil art. We worked diligently on our homework in his room afterward. I sat on his bed, and he sat at his desk. Sometimes my favorite time with him was when we quietly worked on homework. The ability to just be together and not have to fill the void was a luxury I didn't take for granted. I saw him out of the corner of my eye pause and look at me for a few moments without moving. When I looked up, he had such a questioning in his eyes. I sat up straighter and waited for whatever he was about to drop on me. He looked down at his feet and then back at me.

"Do you really think of yourself as an old broken toy, too broken to be worth anything?" He held my eyes, and I couldn't look away.

"Sometimes." I let out the deep breath I had been unconsciously holding. "When you lose someone or something that you love, and you have no control over it, it hurts deeply. And I've teared up, but I haven't wept. Not like Mitchell did, not like Alex did, not like the rest of my aunts and uncles and cousins that came to the funeral. The first time I cried was on the plane, and it was just a few tears." I remembered the boy watching me as I stared into nothingness. "I wonder what it is you see in me sometimes. And then other times I'm so happy that you see anything in me. I feel guilty because I'm happy with you, and I shouldn't be happy. My mom died seven weeks ago. Seven. Weeks. That's it, and it feels like an eternity." I could hear my voice rising, but I couldn't control it. "I don't deserve you. I don't deserve this." I motioned my hands between us from him to me. He moved from his chair and sat beside me, cradling me in his arms. He smoothed my hair down my back and rocked me, my head in my hands. Leaning against his chest, I tried to find a tear, but it was nowhere to be found. "I don't deserve you," I mumbled into my hands. He shushed me, rocking me slowly back and forth.

"Your mom had no choice in leaving you; she loved you. I see the beautiful person you are; you are kind and gentle. You make me laugh, and you deserve this. Your mother would want you to be happy despite the struggles in life. My mom says that she wouldn't be the person she is today if the things that happened to her and the decisions she made were different. I never quite understood that before I met you. Your mother raised you to be strong and straightforward. And I have a feeling you don't take no shit from no one," he said in a comical gangster tone. I smiled and looked up at him. His eyes were soft, and his smile warmed me inside. "My dad left and didn't look back, and I'm a better person because of it. I know when the time comes to have a family; I won't do to them what he did to me. I'll be more than he ever was. He made me who I am today in that regard." He looked past me now to the white board beside his desk. "My mom is responsible for the rest of me, the best of me." He squeezed me, his eyes finding mine again without that distant look.

Chapter 11

There's a First Time

for Everything

Travis

I'd never felt more in my game as I did during that Friday night's game. It was the third in our season, and though we were at one and one, I thought we might win this. Mason was on. Alex couldn't miss the ball or the open holes left by the defense. I had scored two touchdowns, and every time I looked in the stands, there was my girl, my Gia, cheering me on. She wore my number. Out of all the faces, I could always find hers smiling at me. We huddled up with the bright lights from behind the bleachers shining down on us.

"Chiz, I need better blocking; I almost got sacked on that last one," Mason was shooting off.

"But you didn't," Chiz retorted. Mason gave us the play, and we clapped our hands together, breaking up and running to our positions.

"Hut, hut, hut," Mason yelled. I took off running; a linebacker was headed right for me, but so was Chiz to block. I could see the ball coming, and just as it was on the tip of my fingers, the linebacker was plowing into my stomach, rotating it off my finger. I was on the ground flat on my back. The ball was in the other team's hands. Chiz casually jogged up to me. I jumped up, a little sore around my ribs, but I was too angry to pay much attention to it. I got right in his face.

"What the hell was that? Where were you?" I yelled, pushing my helmet against his.

"I got held up." He pushed back.

"Get it together. You cost us the ball." I took off my helmet and threw it. I knew he did that on purpose.

"You're the one who didn't catch it. YOU cost us the ball." He took off his helmet and ran toward the bench. I kicked my helmet, then ran and got it and joined the team on the bench. I was tired of the stupid games, of the comments he made to Gia. I'd bet she didn't fully get his intention for half of them. I was so sick of Jillian still trying to wiggle her way back in with me. I slammed myself down on the bench as Alex handed me a water bottle.

"He should have blocked him," he said under his breath. He nodded toward Chiz and continued, "He was right there and then just stopped mid-stride." I shook my head. I knew it. I looked back up at Gia; her brows were furrowed. She was worried. I gave her a little smile trying to tell her it was OK; she relaxed a little but still looked worried. Chiz sat out the rest of the game. I guess the coach had noticed his stunt, too.

In the locker room Coach began his speech. He seemed pretty riled up considering we won the game.

"I don't know what you fellas think you're pulling out there, but we take care of our own! Any beef you got with anyone on this team is left outside those locker room doors." He pointed with his clipboard. "Here, we are a family, and we watch out for each other. A guy's a jerk? Here, he's your brother. He's dating the girl you like?" His eyes fixed on Chiz. "You protect him and block for him. I don't want any more stunts like that in practice or during the games. Do I make myself clear?" His eyes focused on me. We all nodded, groaning our agreement. "Now hit the showers. I can't be here all night; I got a hot date with the missus." He turned and went to his office. I began undressing.

"He's dating the girl you like?" Chiz mocked Coach's tone while standing around a few guys. "You steal her and then throw it in his face." He looked over at me. They laughed as he continued. "Who cares who is dating who? I only date cheerleaders and girls from other schools—who are cheerleaders." Mason stood up from the bench he was sitting on a few lockers from me. My hands balled into fists. Chiz went on, "I mean the other girls in this school are so inexperienced, nerdy, and downright artsy freaks. Like there's something WRONG with them. Listen to me when I say, guys." He put his hand on Brandon's shoulder as if he were giving him fatherly advice. "You lose street cred and popular points when you date girls like Gia, Abby, and Kiarah." Before I could stop him, Alex had him slammed up against the locker with Chiz yelping in pain. Then Alex's fist came up so fast it met his nose, and we all heard a crunch. The other guys backed up, shocked that anyone would take on Chiz, but Mason and I pulled Alex off him. Chiz grabbed his nose as blood rushed down his mouth and chin. It was dripping onto his bare chest.

"What is your malfunction, bro?" Chiz yelled, as he steadied himself, looking at the blood on his hands. "Homecoming is a week away! And you broke my nose! You're so dead." Someone handed him some paper towels, and he winced as he wiped the blood away. Alex jerked away from us.

"Don't you ever talk about my SISTER or my girlfriend like that. Keep their names out of your mouth and don't come near them." He pushed him again with both of his hands, slamming him into the lockers again. Chiz groaned. Coach came back out, and said, "Moretti, Chiz, in my office. NOW!" He turned and left, and they followed him. Mason and I looked at each other, not knowing what to do next. After a few minutes, we went ahead and took our showers and dressed. Then we went outside to Abby and Gia waiting for all of us so that we could go to the IHOP.

"Where's Alex?" Gia asked, looking around us toward the locker room doors for her brother.

"There was a slight altercation in the locker room," Mason said, as he nervously rubbed the back of his neck.

"What happened?" she asked.

"He got into a fight with Chiz. I think he broke his nose," I said, squeezing her hand.

"Chiz broke Alex's nose?" Her voice rose, and her face began to darken.

"Um, no, Alex punched Chiz," Mason said.

"No, Alex doesn't fight," she said, shaking her head.

"Yeah, I guess if he thinks it's worth it, he does," Mason reasoned. She sat down as suddenly the color left her face.

"Alex doesn't fight; he knows better," she barely whispered.

"GIANNA!" We heard the strong thick Italian accent of Oliver, and she groaned.

"Over here." She stood so he could see her.

"Where is your brother?" he demanded, as he approached us.

"Mr. Morretti, he's in the coach's office; right through there." I pointed the way.

"Go home, Gianna. I have to deal with your brother, and it's late."

"We were going to go get some food," she stated.

"Well, now you're going home." He walked past us and was gone.

"Do you want us to go with you? We can order a pizza," Mason encouraged.

"I have a feeling you guys don't want to witness their discussion when we get home," she sighed.

"I'll take you home and wait with you at least," I said, then turned to Mason and Abby. "You guys go ahead. Don't let us stop you from having a good night." They nodded reluctantly as Abby and Gia hugged goodbye. I took her through the drive-through, and we got milkshakes. We still beat Alex and their dad home. She walked up and sat down on the stairs of her porch.

"What happened?" she asked, looking out at the night sky.

"Chiz was running his mouth, and I guess Alex had enough," I said, not wanting to tell her what he'd said.

"There's got to be more to it than that. Alex has never thrown a punch."

"Well, for never throwing a punch, he really clocked him one. He's going to have black eyes for homecoming." I chuckled a little, avoiding her statement.

"I'd have liked to seen that," she giggled, as she leaned into me. I put my arm around her. We sat there quietly slurping our milkshakes. Then we saw the head lights of the big green truck coming down the street. It pulled into the drive-way. They went silently into the house by way of the kitchen.

"Do you want me to stay longer?" I asked, squeezing her closer to me.

"I do. I don't want to go in yet." She turned her head to look up at me, and I could feel her warm breath on my neck. I moved her hair and traced the outline of her neck. We both took a deep breath and then began to laugh. That was when we heard the voices.

"I don't care if you're getting beat up; you do not fight. You do not throw the first punch especially."

"He was running his mouth, talking about our girlfriends, about YOUR daughter. You of ALL people don't get to lecture me about hitting people!" Alex's voice boomed. I squeezed her closer to me. They continued arguing.

"What did he say about us?" she whispered.

"He's jealous. He obviously likes you and is annoyed that we're together. He just dragged Abby and Kiarah's names into it to set us off. Mason, Alex, and I spend a lot of time together, and he feels like an outsider. I think he had Alex pegged as one of his entourage. When Alex didn't play along, it made him mad, too. The bad thing is, he figured out Alex's button." She pulled away from me.

"Kiarah?"

"No, you. He's very protective of you. Mason and I had to drag him off Chiz." I pulled her back to me. She leaned into me again, taking a deep breath. The front door opened as the light came on. Oliver stood in the doorway.

"Gianna, it's time to come in. It's getting late." He didn't move, and neither did she.

"I'll be in, in a few minutes, OK?"

"Just hurry up." He shut the door but left the light on.

"I guess that is my cue that it's time to go. Are you going to be around tomorrow around lunch time?"

"Yes."

"Good, I'll pick you up for lunch, and we can hang out." I kissed the top of her head, and she looked up at me with a look that I didn't recognize in her eyes. It made my pulse sputter, and I took a jagged breath. She shifted herself so that she was on the step below me nestled in between my legs, and she placed her arms around my neck as she did. She pressed herself to me and kissed me. I found my fingers lightly tracing her sides, my other hand moving her hair. I breathed her soft coconut scent. Our kiss was soft at first but grew deeper and almost desperate as our lips didn't part and her clutch on me grew tighter. Finally, she pulled away, and she looked at me again with the same expression she had a moment before. I did love this girl. I realized at that moment this was what love felt like. She would always be the first girl I loved. I kissed her again.

Chapter 12

Bygones

Gianna

Travis and Alex were sitting on the couch when I came down from my room. They played video games as Travis waited for me to finish getting ready. He said he'd be picking me up for lunch, but I didn't expect it to be at eleven-thirty. I was still finishing my chores; I was on bathroom duty this week. He told me he wanted to check on Alex anyway, so he came on over.

Alex. He'd gotten in trouble with the coach. He and Chiz would have to stay late after practice every night for a week running laps. I guessed that was the coach's equivalent to detention. At home, he had to attend Oliver's group therapy for a month. He also wasn't allowed to go out for a month, with the exception of homecoming. He'd taken his punishment gracefully. Both he and Travis refused to tell me what exactly was said. Alex said his temper had just gotten the better of him, and he was already mad for the stunt Chiz had pulled during the game.

When I was finally ready, I came down in some cut-off jean shorts and layered tank tops. I'd piled on a few beaded necklaces of different lengths and shapes and sizes. I thought it looked pretty cool. We told Alex "bye" and were on our way to the mall. We got some food at the food court, and as we scanned the place for seats, we saw Hailey and their mom waving to us.

"Hey, look at that. They didn't say they'd be here." He smiled innocently as he led me over to where they sat.

"What's going on here?" I asked, not trusting his innocent act.

"Nothing. Let's go eat with them." We joined them.

After the small talk, Mrs. Nichols turned to me and asked, "Since we're here together, would you like to go dress shopping?" Ah, the set up, I realized. He'd thrown me under the bus.

"Well, that would be nice, but I don't think Hailey would enjoy it much." Hailey looked at me inquisitively.

"That's why Hailey and I are going to the Game Emporium; they have laser tag, indoor go carts, and video games." Travis draped his arm around my chair. Hailey began clapping her hands together and bouncing up and down.

"I love the video games there!" she cheered.

"Then I guess we're all set," I smiled weakly.

"What are you looking for in a dress?" Mrs. Nichols sat down and asked me patiently, after the third store and several dresses already.

"I'm not sure—just something that feels right. None of these dresses feel right. They feel like they're too much, almost too fancy for me. I don't know really." She patted the bench beside her, and I sat down in the frilly green dress that I had just been frowning at in the three-way mirror.

"I don't know much about your situation with your mother except that she has passed. I know it's early just to move on. I think that is your conflict," she paused, and I nodded. "But this is one night that you can just be yourself. Not that you'll forget what's going on, but you can let it go a little. You are sixteen, beautiful, and full of life. As a mother myself, I wouldn't want my daughter to miss out on living life just because I wasn't there to watch her enjoy it." She put her hands on mine. "Are you sure that none of these dresses 'feel right'?" I looked back at the dresses hanging on the hooks and taking up an entire wall of the dressing room.

"I think I'll try the yellow one again." She smiled and patted my hand.

We met up with Travis and Hailey. I had my shoes and clutch purse, plus the costume jewelry his mom graciously bought me. She had giggled like a teenager, saying, "I can't wait until I get to do this with Hailey; it's so much fun." I lost myself in laughter with her. She even hugged me while we checked out, whispering, "Travis won't know what to think when he sees how gorgeous you'll be." She had insisted I call her Melanie and claimed me as one of her new shopping buddies. It was nice. I thought I might enjoy shopping with her from time to time.

When we finally got back to my house, I showed Travis my dress. He smiled his approval and he then joined Alex and they played video games. I loved watching them have fun and enjoying themselves. Around six, I began milling around the kitchen to figure something out for dinner.

"I'm ordering pizza; don't fix anything and get back in here," Travis called. I came back and sat sideways beside him with my feet in the couch. He was on the phone. I wiggled my feet into his lap, and he put one hand on them. It was a nice ending to a good day.

On Monday, I saw Chiz coming down the hall as I was exchanging books at my locker. Both of his eyes were blackened. He had a bandage across the bridge of his nose. When he realized I was watching him, he averted his eyes. He walked past me, and I went back to what I was doing, but as I shut my locker, he startled me. He was leaning against the locker beside mine.

"I'm ruined for homecoming." He had a sadness to his voice. I almost felt sorry for him. Almost. He went on, "I was a dick. I was mad, and I don't know why I targeted your boyfriend and brother." I wondered if this was his form of an apology! *Wait for it,* I thought and didn't say anything. He continued, "I've got to find a way to make it up to the guys. I wanted to tell you personally that I didn't mean the things I said. I don't think you're inexperienced, nerdy, an artsy freak, or that there's something wrong with you. I think you're amazing actually. I'd like to make it up to you and take you to a nice dinner. Travis doesn't even have to know. We can just keep it between us." He winked at me, now apparently excited about the idea of a secret we could share.

"Thank you for the apology. It means a lot to me that you said it. I'm going to have to pass on the dinner invite though because I don't keep secrets from Travis." I paused while I let him soak that up. "I'm sorry that my brother hit you. That's not something he's ever done before, but now I can see why he became so angry. They wouldn't even tell me what you said, and whew, am I relieved to know that was all that was said. You could have called me so many worse things, like selfish, delusional, egotistical, and under the impression that I am God's gift to women, when clearly I'm not." I turned to walk away and found that a few people had paused to listen to our conversation.

"Why would I call you God's gift to women? You're a chick, and you date dudes," he called after me.

"Exactly," I sang, as I did a full spin, only slowing down when I caught his eye and continued on my way.

Lunch was solemn. By that time everyone had heard what happened after the game, what was said, and had seen Chiz's face. Some people congratulated Alex, but he told them that it wasn't something he was proud of. Others glared at him. I told Travis about my conversation with Chiz, but I didn't tell Alex because I feared that he might add to Chiz's already blue face. Abby had taken a hit, too. I could tell that she knew where her place was, but she had always been proud of it. The fact that Mason was put down because of her made her sad. Kiarah, on the other hand, was so animated by anger she insisted that Alex quit the team and boycott the games.

Very quietly, he said, "If art offended me, I wouldn't ask you to stop making it. I would just allow you to share it with people who appreciated it. Football is important to me, and if you care about me like you say you do, then you won't ask me to quit the team." We'd all frozen mid-sentences to watch their conversation. Kiarah stormed out of the lunch room, not even dumping her tray.

"I might be going stag to the dance if I even go." He threw his napkin on his plate and slouched, in his chair, obviously annoyed.

"Dude, you're going. You guys will make up," Mason said. The other guys agreed. Alex just shrugged.

After school, I began my homework, knowing that Travis and Alex would be later than usual. Out of my speech book fell a note that I hadn't realized was there. I smiled, thinking about how sneaky Travis was, as I opened it.

Gianna,

I really like saying your name. Sometimes I lay in bed at night and just say, "Gia, Gia, bo bia, banana fanana, fo fia." Just kidding, but I'd like to give you my idea of what your name means to me.

Before that day at the beach, I'd never heard your name before. I'd heard Anna, but not Gianna. Now, when I think of the name Gianna, instantly I think of a beautiful girl. She makes me feel warm inside, like I could light the world with the sun of warmth and light that she brings me. I could be the sun and she could be the moon, and together we could watch days turn into months, and the months turn into years. Secondly, I think of her soul, because when I look in her eyes, I see her soul. I hear the wonderful things that she says, and I see the way she thinks. Innocence is a quality that I would give her. Innocence that believed there was something in me. It made me think, not only this is an amazing person that I want to know more, but I have to be near her. I am amazed that she wants to spend time with me and get to know me. Everything can be going wrong in my day, and I just think the name Gia, and I smile. You make me smile, and I'm honored (I know it sounds cheesy) to be a part of your world.

Travis

As I finished reading, there were footsteps in the kitchen. I turned to see Travis standing there.

"I didn't think I'd have to knock since I'm here all the time, and I figured Oliver wasn't." I must have looked really confused. "Practice let out early. I'm going to go back in an hour to pick up Alex." I nodded, still affected by his letter. He tossed his bag on the floor by the table and leaned against the door frame, crossing his arms, and smiling at me funny. I felt my face turning red.

"Why do you do that?" he asked.

"Do what?" I was self-conscious now.

"Sometimes when I look at you, your face gets darker." He paused as if realizing. "Are you blushing?" I looked down at my hands and gave him a nervous laugh.

"Everybody does it." I didn't look back up.

"I didn't think you did. Usually people turn red, but you just look darker tan." He walked over to where I sat and knelt down beside my chair. "I think it's beautiful." He smiled, and I couldn't help smiling back at him. He looked over at what I was doing and his smile broadened. He stood and went to the kitchen humming the "Name Game" song. I leaned back in my seat laughing, as I rolled my eyes at him. He returned with two sodas and began his homework.

"You know, since we've been doing homework together, my grades are improving. I haven't even needed Abby's services; I must be breaking her bank."

"Well, maybe between you and Mason; I don't know," I teased him. He laughed, and we went back to work. Alex called when practice was over and Travis went to get him while I started dinner.

It was a simple dinner, large salad with romaine lettuce, cucumbers, cherry tomatoes, spices, chicken, croutons, and berries. It was one of my mom's favorite things for dinner—I think because it was so simple to make, and it always looked so pretty. As I tossed it, I thought about the first time she assembled it for us.

We were living in Louisville, and she had been working at the diner for a few weeks. She made really good tips there. Looking back, Louisville was really where we found hope. We lived in a small double. It was the kind of house where if you stood at the front door you could see all the way to the back door. None of the rooms had doors but we didn't care. It had a simple living room, two bedrooms, and a kitchen with the bathroom off it. That night Mom came home from work with a bag of groceries and a gleeful smile on her face. When she laid out all the packaging and I saw the prices on the black berries and the fancy tomatoes that would fit in your mouth in one bite, my eyes were the sizes of saucers. She simply patted my head and said, "Gia, my darling, things are finally turning around for us." She chopped and sliced, making sure it was perfect. She sprinkled the berries into each salad individually, giving Alex a few more because she knew he loved all berries. She diced the cooked chicken into perfect cubes and made vinaigrette from things already in our cabinets.

When we sat down, Alex and I didn't even know what to do. I didn't want to destroy the beautiful display she had made.

She began to eat and then paused, looking at us. Shaking her head, she said, "This is a beautiful salad, but if we don't enjoy it, it will go to waste. And it won't taste yummy after it has begun to wither. Little boys need their vegetables to grow into big strong men who will always protect their little sisters, Alexander the Great. Little girls need their vegetables so they will grow into strong, smart women because beauty will never be a problem, *la mia bella* Gianna. Eat up, little ones, because tomorrow this won't taste as sweet as it does right now in this moment." We did. And it was the best tasting salad I had ever eaten. After that, my mom made a point to make at least one night a month big salad night. So tonight I made a big salad. I cleared off our books and set the table using the nicest plates and glasses. Over the years, big salad night had also became the night we used the fancy dishes. Mom began to call it the dinner party night. Sometimes we invited friends over to show them how fancy we were, but most of the time, it was just for us. "Three plates, just like old times," I said to no one at all.

"If Travis is staying for dinner, then you should add another place." I stiffened as Oliver stood behind me hovering in the doorway. "What's for dinner? I swear sometimes I come home and the house still smells so good from what you've cooked, Anna. I go to sleep hungry." I went to the cupboard and took down another plate, glass, and silverware from the drawer.

"If you don't mind, please call me Gia, or Gianna. Anna was my mother's name," I said as if I had to remind him.

"I know, but you are so much like her. I am proud. She did an excellent job with both you and Alex. I know Alex only hit that boy because he wanted to hit me," he said it very matter-of-factly. I just stood there and stared at him. "But he has to learn that there are consequences to every action, and if he continues down this road. . ." He shook his head. "Well, God help his soul." He went upstairs without another word until Travis and

Alex came back. Dinner was a quiet event, and though I'm sure he enjoyed his big salad, Travis didn't say. We finished our homework afterward at the dining room table as Alex and Oliver cleaned up the dishes. Alex went to his room to do homework, and Oliver turned on the TV. We didn't rush even though Travis' leg bounced nervously. I put my hand on his to calm him. It helped only for a minute, but we finished around the same time we usually did. I walked him to the porch steps to say goodbye.

"Don't be offended, but that was the worst night I've spent at your house." He shook his head as he whispered, "The salad was delicious, but your dad, man, wow."

"I know, he totally creeped me out, too." I rested my arms against him as he casually put his hands on my waist. He kissed my forehead, then my nose, and finally he gently kissed my lips. Then the porch light came on.

"I don't know why he's acting like he's my dad. This is starting to scare me," I mumbled sarcastically.

"The world is a crazy place," he chuckled. "Tomorrow?"

"Yes, tomorrow." He squeezed me in a hug and turned to leave. I stood there until I saw his taillights turn off my street. Then I went inside and went to bed. I would see him again very soon. Tomorrow.

Chapter 13

A Splash of Color on Your

Wall, As Well As Your Heart

Travis

"My dress is olive green." Jillian leaned across the table; I could hear her smiling at me.

"Congratulations." I continued working on my formula, not bothering to look at her.

"You have to match me." She sounded annoyed.

"Why would I have to match?" Now I was annoyed.

"Because you are my escort." She rested her face in her hand.

"I'm taking Gia to the dance." I stared at her. She looked at her fingernail polish, still annoyed.

"Whatever. But on the float, and when we are announced at the dance, you are my escort." She spoke as though she was explaining it to a four-year-old.

"I thought Mason could escort you. I could escort Courtney." It's not like it mattered who was whose escort; it would only be one dance. She scowled at me.

"No, Mrs. Hendricks assigned us, mostly by height, but she said we couldn't change. Mason is escorting Courtney, you are escorting me, and my dress is olive green." She finally turned to her work.

It looked as though Alex and Kiarah hadn't made up yet when we all assembled at lunch. She sat across the room with some of her friends. She kept looking toward Alex who sat beside me. He looked down at his tray as though it was the most important, confusing thing he'd ever seen. Mason and the guys were engrossed in a conversation about the latest Monday night football game. I would have been right there in the middle of it, had I not been thinking about Gia, who kept glancing at her brother. I knew she was worried about him. He stood and took his tray full of food to dump at the return. There was still fifteen minutes of lunch left. Gia followed him, and I, of course, followed her. I was steps behind her, when she found him in the hallway.

"She's going to make up with you." She put her hand on the back of his shoulder as she caught up to him.

"I just don't need this right now." He pulled away as he turned to face her and leaned against the lockers. "I screwed up. I should have never gone after him." I leaned against the lockers across the hall from them. I might as well not have even been there; they didn't even acknowledge my presence.

"You did what you felt was right at that time. I'm not mad at you. I'm sure she will understand." She stroked his arm trying to comfort him.

"I don't care about *her*; I'm angry with *myself*. I gave into that anger. I'm just like HIM." He rested his head against the locker and looked at the ceiling.

"You are NOTHING like him." She stared at him, not believing what he said.

"Because I hit a boy instead of a woman?" He turned to look at her.

"Because you are NOTHING like him," she repeated. He hugged her.

"I needed that," he said. Then he looked over to me. "You sure you want to be a part of this messed up family?" Gia smirked, as she pulled away from him, suddenly looking shyly at me.

"Without a doubt," I chuckled. "You're still going to the dance though, right?"

"Yeah, Gloria said she'd be my date. I'm escorting her anyway." He shrugged. And just like that Kiarah was out of his mind. We went back inside and rejoined the conversation at our table, now a discussion about whether or not pink would look good on Patrick. His date's dress was Pepto-Bismol pink. I was so grateful that Gia had picked a color that wasn't too girly, even though her dress was, and I couldn't wait to see her in it.

Luckily, Gia was able to join me for dinner. Oliver was home when I dropped Alex off and agreed to allow her to come with me to my house. My mom had gushed about her after their shopping afternoon. She was pleased in everything about her. That only reinforced my feelings for her. I'd begun trying to come up with ways to tell her, and imagining the look on her face, when I told her I loved her. Then I'd imagine her saying it back to me. That brought a whole wave of emotions, along with dread and fear of what if she didn't love me? I tried to talk myself out of that. It was still in the back of my mind. What if it was too soon to feel this or too soon to tell her? I didn't really know what the appropriate time frame was to tell someone how you felt about them. I wasn't sure if there was one. I thought that if you felt a certain way about someone you should tell them. I wanted it to be special, and a surprise, even though I knew how she felt about surprises. I was almost sure she'd like this surprise.

All these things were still going through my mind during dinner, so I didn't hear the question Hailey asked me. I just looked at my plate until I felt eyes on me. I looked up and the three of them looked at me expectantly.

"Sorry, I was, well, what did I miss?" I looked from face to face.

"I asked if you were going to help me bring down my painting for Gia," Hailey said.

"Is it done? I thought you said yesterday you wanted to add some more things to it?"

"I finished it today. Gia said she would put it up in her room." Hailey caught me up to speed on the conversation. I stood and went upstairs and got the painting that looked like an abstract version of a vase of purple roses. My sister had many talents. It could have been sold in an art gallery. It was a large canvas with bright colors surrounding the roses. When she saw it, Gia gasped.

"It's so beautiful." She was sincere in her praise.

"I thought of you as I painted it. You were my inspiration, Gia." Hailey beamed. Mom beamed, too.

"You're so talented," Gia said, as she stood and came around the table and hugged her.

Hailey continued in a hushed tone, meant only for Gia and her to share. "I know you're sad a lot about your mommy, but I'll share mine with you when you need her." She patted Gia's cheek. Gia leaned her forehead against Hailey's.

"Thank you." I barely heard her whisper. "You are amazing." They hugged again. I put the painting by the door and sat back down at the table. We finished dinner, and Gia and I cleaned up the dishes with Hailey helping by putting them away. Then Gia and I went upstairs to do homework.

She sat down on my bed and began to drag books out of her bag. I closed the door. She looked up at me, surprised because we usually left the door cracked whether we were at her house or mine. Before she said anything, I lunged for her, knocking her on her back with me on top of her. She giggled, and I smoothed her curls away from her face. Then we were kissing. I didn't kiss her first; she didn't kiss me first; we just kissed. Our fingers entwined. At first, we traced each other's bodies over our clothes. Her fingers trembled as her hands went under my shirt, touching my bare stomach. I kissed her harder. My hands found her bare skin as I traced her side. It instantly goose-bumped up under my touch, and I smiled in our kiss.

"Your hands are cold." She giggled against my lips.

"Warm them up," I mumbled, as I moved my lips to her jaw and her neck. She took a jagged breath. Our legs tangled. Her toes traced up my leg, raising my jeans. It was driving me crazy, the way she was touching me, unsure of her moves, but somehow knowing exactly what to do. My hand moved to her stomach, and I felt her muscles tighten as she pulled my face to hers.

"I love being with you," I whispered, as my lips moved over her cheek to her ear. She crushed me to her, holding me tight.

"I like being with you, too," she breathed. I tried again.

"I love holding you like this." I lifted myself up to look in her eyes.

"I do, too." Her eyes hid something, but she smiled at me still. She wasn't ready. *Why was I trying to plan this out? I just wing things; I don't try so hard. That is how things come together the best. I'd just wing it and when it felt right, I would tell her.* I kissed her again. Then reluctantly, I let her sit up.

We did our homework and stole glances at each other. It was the least productive study session we had ever shared. I couldn't stop thinking about her in my arms, and I had a feeling she was envisioning the same scenario.

"Debate. What makes a good debate? It's not the topic you choose; it is more the research put into the subject. You can believe something, but if you can't prove it, well then, good luck convincing someone else to. But personal convictions alone do not make a good debate. We need facts and proof as to why your view is the one we should choose. I want you to pair up and pick a topic relevant in today's media, pick your side, and research your view on the subject. You will then debate your subject on Monday. We will decide who won the debate by vote. That is just for fun; I will give you your final grade based on your subject, research, and eloquence." Mr. Franklin waved his arms dramatically. "So pick your partners and discuss your subject." He left his podium and sat down at his desk. Gia turned sideways in her seat and faced me, and I smiled knowing we'd be working together.

"Any favorite, relevant subject?" she asked.

"I'd like to do something light-hearted, not too serious."

"I'd like that, too."

"We'll research it this evening." I winked at her. Then I paused, knowing I should tell her before she found out another way. So I leaned in close to her. "There's something I have to tell you though, not about the assignment." I motioned toward the front of the class.

"Should I be nervous? You're so serious." She leaned in closer so we were inches apart. I played with the corner of my notebook, bending it back and forth.

"I hope not. It's really no big deal. But I think you should know." I paused again until she nodded for me to continue. "I'm apparently going to be Jillian's escort for homecoming court."

She leaned away from me and barely whispered, "What does that mean?"

"It means I stand beside her on the float, on stage, and we dance together during the court dance." She almost looked hurt. I reached to hold her hand, but she pulled it away from me.

"I don't want you to escort her. It's wrong for me to say, but I don't." Her eyes didn't meet mine.

"I don't want to either, but it was the assignment Mrs. Henrick gave us. It sucks, but I don't want you to read anything into it or to be nervous about it. I'll do it, and then it will be over." She finally looked up at me and nodded OK. I knew she trusted me, but it still scared her.

At practice, we all ran extra laps because it seemed everyone was one step behind, dropping balls and missing blocks. I guess all our minds were on the coming weekend. Coach's face kept turning that dangerous red color. We all knew he'd had a heart attack two years ago, so this wasn't a good sign. Afterwards, when we were heading to the locker room, Chiz walked up to Mason and me.

"Guys, sorry about last week. I was out of line." He didn't look at us; he looked at his feet. "I hope we can put it all behind us. Coach is right; I guess we're a team and a family." He looked up hopefully at us.

"Sure," Mason and I said at the same with the same reluctance.

"Cool. Then after the game Friday, we're going to have another bonfire. We only have a few more weeks that we can surf before the gulf turns cold." He turned to begin the laps that Alex had already started. Then he called back over his shoulder, as an afterthought, "Bring your girls, too." He went back to running. Mason and I shrugged at each other. Like that, our fight was over, and we would be hanging together this weekend.

Chiz and Jillian didn't know, but shortly after I broke up with her, I found out that they were sleeping together. She also slept with Brandon and Ethan while we dated. I don't really care who else she slept with. It happened. There was nothing I could do about it. I regretted more now, since Gianna, that she was my first; but the fact that I didn't care about Jillian cheating said something about how I really felt about her. Sometimes I wondered if I just avoided conflict, or if I really did believe what I always told Mason—that some things just aren't worth getting angry about. My philosophy was that it all comes out in the end, and people get what they deserve eventually. Sometimes I think that I'd like to be there when Jillian gets hers, but whether or not I am, she will get hers one day.

As I waited for Alex, I sat in the bleachers. I leaned back on my elbows on the seat behind me and my feet stretched out in front of me. I heard footsteps approaching me. I turned to see Kiarah stepping up on the bleachers gingerly, her eyes focused on Alex. I turned to see him running, his back was toward us. She came and sat beside me. I looked back at her. She was chewing on her bright red lower lip. She took a deep breath.

"I screwed up with him." She looked at me with a pained expression.

"Maybe a little. He and Gia have been through a lot in the past year. I think he just wanted you to listen to him and support him," I sighed.

"Yeah, I realize that now. I just get so caught up in my own convictions." She continued watching him. He was running toward us now, and he saw her, too. He averted his eyes and focused on his running.

"This wasn't about you though. It was about them, Gia and him. Well, that's not true either. This was about Mason, him, and me. It wasn't fair to bring you guys into it, but after it was all over, and after you knew he already felt like junk, you should have just supported him. That's what being a good boyfriend or girlfriend is about; it's not how you feel sometimes." I shrugged. I felt bad having to tell her this, but she needed to know. Her actions caused my friend pain. I hated the fact that my friends were suffering.

"You're only a junior right?" she asked. I nodded.

"And you've only dated Jillian before Gia?" She knew the answer to that, but I nodded again.

"How are you the perfect boyfriend? Jillian is evil, and you are so good. Gia's lucky; I hope she appreciates you." I shrugged again.

"I heard today that he's going with Gloria." Kiarah watched him again.

"Yeah, he's her escort for the homecoming court anyway, so I guess it makes sense."

"He was out of my league anyway; I don't know what he saw in me. We didn't have anything in common. I guess I can be relieved that we figured it out earlier rather than later when I was in love with him." She looked at me again, her eyes sad. "Or more than I am now I guess." She stood. "I'll see you around, Travis." I held up my hand to say bye, and she left. Once she was gone out of sight, Alex came over to the fence in front of where I was sitting. I tossed him the water bottle I'd brought from the locker room for him.

"What did she want?" He looked in the direction she left.

"To admit that she screwed up; I guess she knew you'd get the message if she told me," I sighed.

"We both screwed up. Maybe I'll talk to her tomorrow." He paused. "I've got to shower and then we can go." He didn't wait for a response; he turned and went toward the lockers, finishing his water on the way.

Gia hung Hailey's painting on the wall that faced her bed. She centered it, and it really looked nice. We sat there on her bed listening to her '90s pop play list, songs from N'Sync, Backstreet Boys, and Britney Spears to Puff Daddy and Biggie Smalls. I couldn't believe that she was forcing me to listen to this. Then a song from En Vogue came on.

"You weren't even alive when this song came out!" I teased, as I threw one of her pillows at her. She deflected it and giggled.

"I was too! I was like three." She leaned toward me, shoving me with her shoulder.

"Friday after the game, the group is getting together for late night surfing and a bonfire," I said as casually as possible. She still stiffened.

"Who all is going to be there?"

"Probably everyone. Chiz apologized, so we're as cool as we can be; I mean he's not my friend, but I don't want to give him a black eye or anything." She cringed at my joke. "Too soon?" I asked. She nodded.

"I don't want to be his best friend; I just hate having this wedge in the team, you know?" I sighed and leaned into her.

"That's because you hate conflict." She rested her head against mine.

"I think that's a good quality, but you're making it sound like it's a bad thing." I hoped we weren't getting ready to have our first fight.

"Why can't you talk to Mrs. Henrick and see if you can escort the other girl—what's her name?" She thought about it for a moment.

"Courtney," I finally supplied.

She continued, "I don't have an issue with anyone else. You have a history with Jillian, and she still wants to be with you. I trust you, but I don't trust her."

"Believe me, I don't want to escort her either. It's too late to get out of it now. It's two days away. I told you I would quit, but you said you didn't mind." I didn't want to argue with her.

"So we're stuck?" She finally turned to me conceding.

"I think we're stuck." I pulled her to me as she scooted our books away.

"Promise me that I have nothing to worry about." She was looking at our fingers laced together.

"I promise," I whispered.

Chapter 14

Rolling Clouds and

Plastic Crowns

Gianna

I didn't know if the boys were still affected by the fight in the locker room a week ago, but they weren't playing that well. They were all missing plays, dropping balls, and missing interception opportunities. I wore my white Travis jersey t-shirt with my ripped-up flare jeans. I had a kelly green and black scarf tied in my hair like a head band with the tied corners hanging on each side of my neck. I sat with Abby, who looked equally worried. She kept chewing on her nails, and I kept pulling her hand down.

There were now two minutes on the board. Mason threw the ball to Alex. He took it almost all the way up the field, and then he was taken down. They huddled up. We needed one touchdown, and we would win the game. The score was seventeen to twenty-one. Mason threw the ball to Travis. He ran. We all stood.

I held my breath, and as I exhaled, I whispered, "Go, baby, go baby, go." Abby squeezed my arm. Two big guys came barreling toward him; he dove for the end zone. They piled on top of him. When the guys jumped off him, their entire team was waving their hands sideways saying it was no good while all of our team had their hands up like a referee signaling touchdown. The referee ran to him. It was as if everyone in the bleachers was leaning toward the field goal. His arms went up in the air for a touchdown. We all cheered. Travis stood up, took off his helmet, and kissed his two fingers and pointed to me. I kissed mine and pointed back at him. Abby and I hugged each other, jumping up and down and giggling.

We waited in the usual spot for the guys to get cleaned up. I was nervous about the bonfire, but not as nervous as I might have been had Abby not been going with us. At least I'd have her to sit with while the guys surfed. The three of them came up, and we all loaded into Mason's SUV. We made our way to the beach, but went through a drive-through first because the boys said they were famished. When we arrived, they got blankets out of the back of the truck. I suddenly realized there weren't any surfboards.

"Aren't you guys surfing?" Abby asked, realizing the same thing.

"Nah, we just want to hang," Mason said, draping his arm around her shoulders and kissing the side of her head. Travis took my hand as Alex went ahead of us to meet his date for the dance, Gloria, standing with the other cheerleaders near the sidewalk to the pier. We made our way and found a spot near the fire that was just getting started and laid out our blankets. I sat between Travis' legs and leaned against him. He smelled clean like the cologne he always wore. I shivered a little, and he handed me my sweatshirt. We sat there quietly while more people arrived, comfortable and enjoying the silence. Abby and Mason sat beside each other immersed in quiet conversation, and even though we were beside them, we couldn't hear them talking. Alex sat across the fire from us surrounded by cheerleaders, including Jillian, who was obviously flirting with him. He mostly ignored her, focusing his attention on Gloria, but I felt sorry for Brandon, who was Jillian's date to the homecoming dance. He sat off to the side completely ignored. In the distance I saw what looked like shadow figures in the surf. I knew there were about six guys out there surfing, including Chiz. They looked like ghosts from where we sat. I was relieved that Travis had decided to spend time with me rather than surf.

"What are you thinking about?" Travis whispered in my ear.

"Not much, just how nice it is to just be with you." I looked up at him. His arms squeezed around me.

"I like how you think," he whispered in my ear, brushing his lips against it.

Finally, after the boys who were surfing joined us, kids coupled up to go other places to make out, and after the fire died down, we folded our blankets, and Mason took us back to school to get Travis' car. Travis drove us home. Alex said goodnight and went in, leaving us standing on the porch. The evening was a lot crisper away from the bonfire. I watched Travis as he watched the door close behind Alex. He looked back at me. He held my hand, searching my eyes. He didn't say anything for a long moment.

"Will you be able to see me in the crowd tomorrow?" I asked, my voice a little shaky from his intense gaze.

"I'll find you."

"How will I know if you see me?" I looked down at the ribbed neck of his t-shirt, which suddenly seemed so interesting to me, only because I couldn't take his eyes searching my soul. I couldn't look into the eyes that penetrated me and knew me better than I'd let anyone else ever know me.

"I'll nod to you. I can't wave. Only the girls wave, but I will nod to you, so make sure you wave to me." He touched my cheek, guiding my face to look at him. "I don't think I could make it through all of this if I didn't find your beautiful face in that crowd. So promise me you will be there for me to nod to you." He was leaning into me now, about to kiss me.

"I promise," I whispered, as his lips pressed to mine.

At eight-thirty the next morning, I got a text with a picture Travis had taken of himself in his bathroom mirror, wearing his tux. He wore a white shirt and a white tie. He looked so hot, and I was very jealous of Jillian getting to stand beside him in front of our whole school district. There was a knock on my door. Alex came in without waiting for a response and did a twirl so I that could see his tux.

"Lookin' good, Daddy," I smiled.

"Mrs. Nichols just called and said that she can give you a ride, and you can sit with them at the parade. Then she said she got you a mani-pedi and hair appointment for after you guys do lunch. I don't know, but I think she really likes you," he chuckled, as he checked his hair in my mirror.

"I didn't know she was going to do that." I sat up in bed.

"Where are you getting ready for the dance, here or at Abby's?" He looked at me in the mirror.

"I guess here. I hadn't made plans with Abby to go over there." I shrugged.

"Good, because I think they are all coming over here first. We're going to take pictures, and this is where the limo is picking us up."

"What limo?" No one had said anything about a limo.

"Mason got a Hummer limo. Can you believe that dude? Just for the six of us, but it's a limo. He wouldn't even let Travis or me chip in." He shook his head in disbelief. "Don't say anything to Abby; he doesn't want her to freak out." I nodded OK.

"Better get ready if you want to get a good seat. You have to get there early." We heard the doorbell. "Gotta go." He turned to leave, but Oliver stood in the door and blocked his path to the hallway.

"Would it be OK if I took pictures of you and your friends this evening?" he asked Alex. Alex looked at me and shrugged. I just looked from one of them to the other, not saying anything. What could I say?

"I think that would be OK," Alex said, moving past Oliver and stomping down the stairs before I could object.

"Well, Gianna, it sounds like you have a busy day ahead of you." He gave me a weak smile and turned toward his bedroom, sipping his coffee.

I shook my head in confusion. Finally, I rose and found some black Bermuda shorts and a soft blue top. I got cleaned up, and just as I was finishing my orange juice, the doorbell rang again. I answered the door, and it was Hailey. Melanie sat in her car on the curb.

"You look pretty Gianna." Hailey smiled and took my hand, leading me to the car as I closed the door behind me.

"Thank you. So do you, Hailey." She wore jean shorts and t-shirt that had Travis' name and number on them. Her dark hair was in French braids that trailed to the middle of her back. She had green glitter all through her hair and the number 31 painted on the side of her face.

"Should I be wearing one of Travis' shirts?" I wondered out loud.

"I don't think so. You are his girlfriend, and you should look pretty for him." She climbed into the back seat, and I climbed into the front.

"Good morning," Melanie smiled.

"Good morning." She was wearing jean capri pants and a tank top. I felt a little better about not wearing his number. We arrived downtown and found a spot on the sidewalk. We sat at the curb while others who had brought lawn chairs were finding places of their own.

I leaned over toward Melanie and told her, "Thank you for making the appointments for this afternoon. I didn't even think to do that."

"I figured as much. Alex told me the other day when I called your house that this was the first dance you'd gone to in a while. So I thought you might not realize all the preparation that is involved. Pictures are at your house, too, right?" she smiled.

"I feel so out of the loop; I just found out about the limo, too. I hate surprises." I half-smiled and half-sighed.

"I know," she giggled, "but these are good surprises, don't you think?"

"Mom, ICE CREAM!" Hailey squealed beside me, pointing to a cart at the corner of the street.

"Do you want some ice cream, Hailey?" her mom asked sarcastically.

"Yes!" It was lost on her. Melanie handed her some money, and she was off to get her ice cream. We both giggled. I could hear the high school marching band in the distance.

"The parade must be starting," she said, as a man walked around passing out flags. He offered us two as Hailey came back with her packaged ice cream. He handed her one, too. She rejoined us on the curb and waved her flag as she ate her ice cream.

"Here they come." Melanie gleamed. The marching band came. We clapped along with the beat of the music. The band was followed by a float that the local boy scout troop had made. The fire department drove a couple fire trucks. The local Masonic lodge members drove small red Indian motorcycles. Then the cheerleaders who weren't in the homecoming court did some cheer routines as they walked along. Finally, the homecoming floats came. The freshmen and sophomores were on one, the juniors and seniors on a second. Travis, Mason, Alex, and Chiz stood behind four girls in beautiful gowns in an assortment of colors. Travis stood there, his hands on Jillian's hips. His face looked stoic from a distance. As he got closer, I could see that his eyes were scanning the crowd of faces. Finally, they found mine. He relaxed and smiled. I waved, and he nodded to me, almost bowing toward me. My smile broadened.

"He's found you," Melanie said to me. I nodded to her. Their float passed too quickly, and he was gone. There were a few more floats after that, and finally we were making our way to the car.

"Travis and Alex are going home to change and then meeting us at the sandwich shop." Melanie unlocked her car, and we climbed in. "Are you excited about tonight?" She was now checking her mirrors as she backed out.

"I'm more nervous than excited," I answered honestly.

"Just relax; you'll have a blast." She was right. We laughed and enjoyed our lunch. The three of us got mani-pedis. Hailey got little jewels on her big toes and her fingernails. Melanie and I got French manicures on our toes and fingers. Then she took me to her beautician, who styled my hair in an up-do with tiny braids leading to a cascading bun, hair curling and twisting around the nape of my neck. I couldn't believe how beautiful it looked. Melanie took me home and offered to come in and help me get ready. I smiled my thanks but thought I could get it from there.

When I came in, both Alex and Oliver gave me a low whistle. We all smiled a tense smile; there were some things that were in the DNA. I went upstairs and stripped down to put on my strapless bra and matching undies. Then I did my makeup, taking extra care with my eyes. I sprayed myself with my perfume. I took out my dress and stepped into it. I zipped up the side and surveyed myself. The sheer fabric layered over itself and clung around my hips to the floor. It was gathered in a way that showed all my curves—maybe even embellishing them a little. My chest looked larger, pushed together with cleavage, my waist looked smaller, and as I turned, my butt looked rounder. I sprayed my hair again, knowing that it was concrete and not going anywhere.

The doorbell rang. I began switching purses, putting my lip gloss, cell phone, and ID into my matching clutch. I went to my closet, got my heels, and sat them on the bed. Abby came in, in her coral dress. Her hair was beautiful, and she looked radiant. We hugged, and she gushed about how pretty I looked. I returned the favor, making her do a full turn. She messed with my makeup case and tried on another lip gloss that was in it.

"I'm borrowing this." She smiled to me through my mirror as I put on my shoes. I nodded OK. I stood, steadying myself. Travis stood in the doorway surveying me. It was like he didn't even hear Abby say, "Hey,

Travis." But he did. He just didn't take his eyes off me as he said, "Hey, Abbs." He was wearing the same tux but now with a yellow shirt that matched my dress against his white tie and vest. He held something behind his back. He brought it around and revealed a wrist corsage. I stepped to stand in front of him as he took it out of the clear plastic box. It had yellow and white roses, which looked like the tops of them had been dyed black. Then white filler, small white flowers with yellow centers and greenery. It was the most beautiful, unique thing I'd ever seen. I couldn't take my eyes off the roses. I looked up at him. He nodded and whispered, "You're still mourning." I held my wrist out as he placed it on me.

"Pictures," Alex said, as he rounded the corner from the stairs. We all nodded and went downstairs.

Parents took pictures as we stood staggered on the stairs. The guys sat around on the stairs looking very GQ, and we girls acted as if we were the best of friends by the fence in the front. After group pictures, each couple took a few pictures individually. A pearly white Hummer pulled up, and we all took pictures in front of it. Abby teasingly slapped Mason for keeping a secret from her. He laughed and grabbed her around her waist, hugging her to him. Oliver was pleasant enough to the other parents, even making small talk with Melanie. Hailey and I took a few pictures together, too. She loved it, telling me I looked just like a princess. Finally, we were on our way. We listened to the top forty radio station, talked loudly, laughing and enjoying the beginning of our evening. Gloria was very polite, jumping into the conversation easily. When we arrived, the first thing we did was get our pictures taken together. Then we got a drink and found a table. We sat with a few of the other boys from the team and their dates. After a few songs played, I convinced Travis to dance with me. We made it up to the dance floor as they switched the song to a slow song. He put his hands on my waist, and I put my hands on his shoulders. We rocked back and forth, turning in a full circle occasionally.

"This is fun," he said, nervously sarcastic.

"This is amazing." I ignored his tone, and rested my head against his chest.

"Yeah," he sighed. "This is amazing." After a few songs, a cheerleader came and tapped his shoulder. It was time for him to go backstage to be announced for the homecoming court. He kissed my cheek and followed the girl.

I wandered back to our table. I sat down and was talking to Abby when suddenly I felt something cold and wet slide down my back. I gasped and turned to see Lila, a cheerleader, standing behind me holding a cup with one hand and covering her mouth with the other.

"I'm sorry!" she gasped. I almost believed her. Almost. Abby was right by my side, taking my hand and leading me to the bathroom. We didn't say anything until we were in there. I turned and saw my reflection in the mirror; a bright red line traced down the middle of my back where my dress line began and ending just above my butt. I gasped and could feel a tear stinging my eye.

"Let me try to fix this." Abby went to get paper towels. There weren't any there. "I'll go get in the janitor's closet. They must have extras in there. Be right back." She left, and I turned, trying to see my back in the mirror. Suddenly the last stall opened, and Jillian came out smiling at me. I held her eye contact in the mirror for long moment before I gazed back at my back.

"Ah, that's too bad," she said sarcastically. "Who was the klutz who did that? Such a pretty dress." She washed her hands, even though I hadn't heard the toilet flush. "Sometimes bad things happen to good people." She pulled a paper towel from the dispenser out of her purse. I just looked at her in the mirror. She took out a lipstick and began slowly to apply it to her upper lip. "You know, Travis and I have been together for a long time. And sometimes we're on again off again, but we always end up together. I just get him like no one else." She was only half way done with one lip when she continued, "I know he's really mad at me right now, but he loves me. He told me all the time, every day actually, from the time we started dating. Has he told you he loves you yet?" She looked at me innocently as she began applying the lipstick to her lower lip.

"Not yet, but we haven't been dating that long." I looked down at the sink.

"Well, did you ever think that there might be a reason for that?" She rolled her lips blending the color. "I just don't want you to get hurt. I've heard rumors about your mom dying. I'm just looking out for you; I think you are clinging to something that's really not there." She was sugary sweet. It was stomach turning how sweet she was being now.

"I appreciate your opinion, but this is between Travis and me, so if it doesn't work out, I'm sure he has your number." I held her gaze and kept my voice as level as I could.

She smirked and closed her purse with a snap. She turned and left. I stood there for a few moments before Abby made it back in a huff.

"Someone locked me in the janitor closet. Can you believe that bull?" She sat the stack of paper towels on the counter. "Lila and Stacia let me out." She took a few towels and wet them. She began to tap at the wet spot. She rubbed gently, and the color began to fade. It didn't completely go away, but it was a soft pink by the time she was done.

"We can pull your hair down. It might cover it," she suggested.

"Yeah, but it would look crazy around my face." I contemplated her idea as I turned and surveyed my back again. I finally decided, "It's done. I

168

don't want it to ruin the rest of the night." She tilted her head into mine as she hugged my shoulders.

"You're so brave. I would be in tears right now." I didn't have the courage to tell her about the conversation I'd just had with Jillian. I drew from her strength even though she didn't know she gave it to me.

"Are we ready?" I asked, and she smiled grandly. We rejoined the crowd as they were announcing the students of the homecoming court. Each couple filed in, did a twirl as if they were going to dance, and then went to the stage. Travis found my face again and smiled at me; it was a little off though. Then they announced the homecoming queen, "Macey Graham." She stepped forward and took her crown. Homecoming king was "Darnell Abernathy." Chiz stepped forward beaming to take his crown with his two black eyes and crooked nose. I turned to Abby and mouthed "Darnell Abernathy?" She smiled widely and nodded yes. No wonder he went by Chiz. They stepped to the middle of the dance floor, and all began their ritual dance. They all actually looked like they were enjoying it. Alex and Gloria smiled and giggled. Mason looked pleasant, but kept looking at Abby longingly. Travis was engulfed in conversation with Jillian, his eyes soft, and a smile creeping into the corners of his mouth. He nodded yes and leaned down to her. She then brushed her lips to his, draping her arms around his neck. I gasped and began backing up, pressing against the bodies that surrounded me. They stood there for what felt like an eternity. I turned, pushing my way through the crowd. Abby reached for me, but I pulled out of her grasp. I heard a female say, "She should have known they would get back together. They belong together."

I got out of the crowd and ran. I slammed into the doors, plowing them open until I was out. I paused on the school's front stoop long enough to catch my breath, and then I ran. I've never run in heels before, but it didn't matter and I didn't fall. I ran until the school was out of sight. Then I walked. I walked several blocks blindly until I found myself at a park in the center of a neighborhood I didn't know. I walked to a swing and sat. I didn't know how long sat there alone, but I turned when I heard footsteps behind me.

Chapter 15

Shoulda, Woulda, Coulda

Travis

Mr. Dailey announced the homecoming court. As we came in to make the grand entrance that had been rehearsed for two periods on Friday, Jillian whispered to me, "This can be painless or difficult; it's up to you." I suddenly felt very anxious, but smiled to Gia as I stood on the stage. I didn't want her to be nervous. Mr. Dailey announced Chiz and Macey as the homecoming king and queen. Then came the part I was dreading, dancing with Jillian. We descended the stairs. We took our position.

"Your date is really pretty this evening." She looked sincere.

"Thanks, I think she is most days," I said.

"You two really do make a cute couple. I didn't see it before last night, but she needs you to take care of her. I get it."

"Are you on some kind of special medicine?" A smile crept into the corners of my mouth, and I leaned toward her adding, "It would mean a lot to me if you realized how serious I am about her." She smiled and breathed, "I do." And that was when she kissed me, wrapping her arms around my neck and holding me there. After what felt like an eternity but was probably more like seconds of struggling against her, I pulled her off me. I turned to where Gia had stood, but she was gone. I was still clutching Jillian's hands at the wrists hard.

"You're hurting me," she whined. I threw her arms to her side.

"Not nearly enough," I said, as I caught sight of Gia running for the back door, a red streak on the back of her beautiful dress that flowed behind her almost in slow motion. I tried to catch her but was pressed in the crowd. By the time I made it through to the front door of school, she was gone. Alex was behind me.

"Smooth, Nichols," he said.

"She just kissed me; I had no idea." I hit my fist against the brick.

"If you've broken her heart...," he began but stopped himself.

"I'll make this right," I said, as I took off running; I had an idea of where she might have gone.

I ran until I reached the pier. I walked to the edge that faced the shore line. She was nowhere in sight, but it was dark so I took off my shoes and socks and began to walk the beach. I walked until I was past most of the hotels. I turned and went back toward the pier. She was nowhere in sight. I found a bench and sat there. I needed to collect my thoughts. I wondered how last night we'd had so much fun and tonight it was ruined. Her dress was ruined; our relationship ruined. I walked until I found myself sitting on her stoop, waiting for her. I sat there for what felt like hours. The porch light came on. Minutes later Oliver opened the door and came out. I turned to look at him. He came and sat on the other side of the stairs. He looked up at the sky for a long moment.

"Tonight didn't go as you planned?" he asked matter-of-factly.

"What was your first clue?" I asked, not looking up from my feet.

"Well, you're here, and my daughter is not." *He misses nothing,* I thought sarcastically.

"Something happened at the dance that upset her. I couldn't get to her, and she took off. Now I'm just waiting for her to cool down so we can talk." I didn't know why I was explaining myself to him.

"Did you check the beach? She used to go there a lot as a little girl. I guess she always felt safe there. I used to go there sometimes and just watch her stare off into the gulf. She was so young to have such a serious face, full of serious thoughts. I didn't make their childhood easy. Sometimes the drink can turn you into someone you don't know. Or," he paused and looked at me, commanding my attention. I looked up at him. "It brings out the darkest person you have inside you." Then, shrugging, he said, "Not that there's any excuse for the mistakes we make in our lives. If we spend our time blaming other people, we are just as delusional as we were when we justified our decisions to do those things." His expression went soft. "Why don't you go home? I'll tell her you were here, and she can call you when she returns. That one, she spends a lot of her time thinking and makes her decisions on her own. You can't change her mind. In some ways, she's just like her mother when she was younger, before." He trailed off and looked up to the sky again. He stood and went back to the door before turning again to say. "Really, Travis, just go home." I stood and slowly began my walk home. I didn't even know what I would say when I did see her.

Chapter 16

What Becomes of the

Broken-hearted?

Gianna

"You look like you've lost your best friend." I turned to see Chiz approaching.

"It feels worse than that." I continued slowly to swing.

"Is there anything I can do to help?" He leaned against the pole, his hands in his pocket, his crown cocked at an angle on his head.

"How long are you going to wear that thing?" I tilted my head, appraising how goofy he looked.

"I'm the king, so as long as I want." He moved behind me and began to swing me, pushing me on my still damp back. "A few of us were worried about you. We split up to look for you. I'm glad I found you."

"Worse. Dance. Ever." I sighed.

"Yeah, I saw Travis and Jill kiss. That's harsh." It was one thing to have seen it; it was another to have Chiz confirm it. He continued, "I mean they probably just got caught up in the moment. You know, nostalgia." He held me at my waist longer than he should have to push me, but he pushed me again gently.

"Too bad about your dress, too. You were smokin' tonight, well, still are." I was glad I didn't have to look in his eyes. "Are you going to let him dump you like this?"

"Huh?" It was like he was speaking another language. I didn't understand the question.

"I mean, obviously they are getting back together. He wouldn't have kissed her if he wasn't. Travis' most annoying quality is that he's a stand-up guy. I just can't believe he dumped you like this. He's a jerk if you ask me." He held onto me again. I turned to look at him. The hurt had to be clear in my eyes.

"Sorry, were you thinking he'd still want to date you after that?" He looked apologetic. I turned back around.

"I was thinking it was a mistake, and we'd work things out." I leaned my head against the cool chain.

"I don't know if you want to stay in that drama. Him with you, wishing he was with her. You deserve so much better." Chiz came around and stood in front of me, taking my hands and pulling me to stand.

"I could protect you from him. All you have to do is ask." He didn't let go of my hands.

"What are you gonna do, rough him up? Give him an offer he can't refuse?" I used my best New York accent. He chuckled.

"Funny girl. No, I'll just tell him to leave you alone. But only if you want me to; I just think you shouldn't talk to him for a while." Then he pulled me into a bear hug. I had trouble breathing; he held me too tight. I pulled away as far as he'd let me to look up at him. He had this weird look in his eyes. Then his eyes closed as he leaned toward me. My eyes grew large as I realized he was going to try to kiss me. He held me too tightly for me to just step away. My only option came to me at the last second. As his lips were about to brush mine, I turned; giving him my cheek, my signature move. He planted it and then smiled at me, releasing me.

"I'll give you a ride home, if that's OK." I nodded, and he led me to his monster SUV.

Travis called me every half hour from eight o'clock in the morning all day Sunday.

I didn't take his calls, so he texted me.

I really need to talk to you.

Please let me explain.

I didn't know that she would do something like that; I would have never let her if I did.

178

And finally,

I'm sorry if I've hurt you.

I kept hearing Chiz's voice saying, "Him with you, wishing he was with her." I kept waiting for the tears to come, but they didn't. I stayed in my room all day listening to loud rock music. It was so loud that Oliver came to my door twice telling me to turn it down.

Alex came to my room mid-afternoon as I sat in the middle of my bed leaning against the wall staring at my beautiful painting. He sat down beside me and looked at it, too, for a while not saying anything. Finally, he turned the music down and said, "You can't hold him responsible for something that happened to him, something that he had no control over. He really likes you. He doesn't play games; you know that. He would never hurt you." When I didn't respond, he simply said, "Oliver's grilling steaks. If you're hungry they should be ready soon." I sat there staring at the painting. I didn't know how to gauge my emotions. I was hurt. I was humiliated. I felt betrayed even though it made sense that it wasn't his fault, but I kept thinking that there might have been a part of him, however large or small it was, that wanted to be with her. He promised me that I had nothing to worry about, but kissing Jillian or being kissed by Jillian still hurt me. My dress was ruined. My evening was ruined. My relationship, the one thing that had made this move seem as if it had a purpose, was ruined. I looked over to the pictures Oliver had already had printed up from the evening before. They had been waiting for me there on my dresser after Chiz dropped me off, being annoyingly charming by walking me to the door and introducing himself to Oliver.

We looked so happy in those pictures. There were actually a few pictures in which we looked in love with each other. I had stared at them into the early hours of the morning, willing myself to cry, but the tears didn't come. I had climbed out of bed with the first light and taken a shower, washing away the reminisces of the evening only to sit here in the middle of my bed the entire day staring at the painting his sister had given me only days ago. I was dealing with it the way I usually dealt with uncomfortable things, loud music and silence.

My phone rang again. This time it was Abby. I answered it.

"Are you trying to worry me to death? You didn't call last night; you didn't call today. What happened? Did Travis find you? Did he explain what happened? You know he didn't kiss her; she kissed him." I instantly regretted answering the phone.

"No, I'm not trying to kill you; I haven't called anyone. I don't know what happened. I haven't talked to Travis. I haven't taken any of his calls. I'm not ready to talk about it with him. I hope he didn't kiss her, but it looked to me like he did. And it still doesn't change the fact that I was humiliated when the drink was spilled on me, and then I had to watch another girl kiss my boyfriend. I might skip school tomorrow," I sighed and leaned my head against the wall.

"You guys aren't breaking up, are you?" Her voice was shaky.

"I don't know. I just am having trouble dealing with this." We spoke for a while longer and then hung up.

Oliver brought me steak, mashed potatoes, and a soda, and sat them on my dresser. I didn't even look at him as he shut my door behind him. I stared at the painting, suddenly lost in another memory, one that I had forced myself not to think about since it happened.

We were there in the hospital room, the room with stark white sheets and blankets on the bed which made it feel as if the gray walls were closing in on us. My mom looked like a shadow of herself, her bald beautiful smooth head, her beautiful brown eyes staring blankly straight ahead past me. Mitchell sat holding her hand. Alex stood in the corner, staring out the window. I stood at the foot of her bed. I could not say a word. I could not help. I just held her gaze, hoping for the recognition of me. She didn't. The doctors said it would be soon but gave no exact time frame.

We'd been in this exact position as we stood there for over an hour, but it felt like longer. Her breathing was labored, her eyes glassy and hollow, staring through me. A few times her breaths slowed and the monitor would blip slower, and we all looked at her, but the monitor would catch up. Holding our breaths, we would all three slowly let them out. Finally, after what felt like hours, she whispered through a raspy breath, "Gia, Lexie, my angels, I'm with you, always." Alex moved to my side with a speed I actually felt a breeze from. Her gaze rested on me as she looked at me, not past me. She smiled as her focus shifted to Alex. And then she was gone. A dullness entered in her eyes, and she exhaled slowly. The monitor made a final blip and then a long tone. That tone became so loud, deafeningly loud. I couldn't hear any other noise.

Mitchell buried his head in the bed. I had never seen or heard a grown man weep before. I heard him weep that day. Alex put his arm around me and squeezed me sideways. I buried my head into the crook of his armpit. He began to sniffle. I held him around the waist, and he leaned his head on mine and began to cry. I had tears in my eyes. I willed them to go down to my feet and away from my eyes. I couldn't lose it, too.

The doctor and nurse who had been hovering in the hallway came in. It was only a moment, but it could have been hours. Time stood still. I held my brother up as our mother slipped away. I had heard a psychic on a morning radio show say once that it took thirty minutes to reach heaven after someone died. It comforted me that maybe she was still hovering, probably watching me be brave for her family.

After Mitchell made phone calls and they took my mother away, we went home. It felt empty without her there. I stood in our foyer full of pictures of my childhood, of our struggle, of our courage, of our loss.

The funeral was surreal. I had family that I had never met come from across the country and even a great uncle from Italy. Everyone wept over the loss of "such a young life" they'd said. I just stood in the corner and watched. It was as if I were watching a movie, even watching myself— accepting hugs and getting Kleenexes for those crying when I had no tears. I stared emptily at all these strangers.

Mitchell had begged me to play a song for my mother on my guitar, but I refused. I couldn't force myself if she had come back from the dead and asked me herself. It was the only time he had become angry with me. He never apologized for calling me selfish. I didn't care. There were worse things he could have done, but he didn't. I forgave him. I understood he was mourning.

I woke up in my sweats and tank top on top of my comforter. My lights were off; my music was off; the only noise was a soft breeze against my window screen. I crawled under my covers and waited for morning.

When morning came, I put on a black jersey dress. It had a high neck line that fell off one shoulder. The sleeves came to my elbows, and the hem hit above the middle of my thigh. I paired it with a wide black leather belt around my hips. I put on my black leather knee boots and surveyed myself after I straightened my hair, flipping up the ends. I was fairly pleased with my appearance. I went downstairs, and Alex did a double take.

"Trying to make him suffer?" He threw his bag over his shoulder.

"I don't dress for anyone but myself, and I felt like I need to look my best today." I tried to keep my composure. I was afraid that I might lose it at any moment. I went to the cupboard and got two Pop Tarts and followed him out the kitchen door.

"Damage control, huh?" he chuckled. We made it to school, and Gloria was hovering near the front door waiting for him. I felt a lot of eyes and heads turn toward me as I walked down the hallway. Abby was waiting by my locker.

"Did you talk to him?" she asked, bypassing pleasantries. I just shook my head as I opened my locker. She looked at me with her head cocked to the side, then the stepped back and surveyed me. "Why do you look like you just stepped out of *Cosmo*?" Her expression was accusing. Then she looked up and smiled, "Incoming." She turned and was gone. I began putting my books in my locker as Travis leaned his shoulder on the locker next to me. I didn't say anything to him. I let him stand there. I was in my locker; this time he wouldn't make me late by blocking it. Finally, when I couldn't put it off anymore, I looked up at him. His pained look broke my heart, but I heard Chiz again in my head. *Him with you, wishing he was with her.*

"Can we talk?" he almost whispered.

"I'm going to be late." I shut my locker, turned, and walked away. I didn't look back; it would have hurt too much.

My classes were distractions. I took detailed notes. I didn't look at anyone except my teachers—not at the boys around me when they made comments about my obvious break up or asked if they could take me out, not at the cheerleaders when they made their snide remarks. I held my head high and ignored everyone. Lunch rolled around, and I was surprised to see Travis sitting at another table. I sat beside Alex, and he looked at me and shrugged. Travis sat beside Chiz in the center of the lunch room. My eyes found his almost every five minutes on the dot. I wasn't sure if his ever left me, but I'd look away as long as I could and when I looked at him, he just sat there slouched down, watching me, his tray untouched. He wasn't taking part in the conversation at his table. He just watched me. I didn't eat either or participate in my lunch table conversation. Abby kept squeezing my hand under the table encouragingly. Finally, I'd had enough. I stood, dumped my tray, and found my way to my speech class ten minutes before the bell rang. I lay my head down on my desk and waited for the inevitable. I waited, knowing I could no longer escape him, and I would be alertly aware of his presence sitting behind me.

I was not let down. He was the first person in the room after me. He sat in his seat. He didn't say anything to me though. He let me be in my silence, which almost felt worse. If he was going to dump me, I wanted to get it over with. I wasn't going to be a victim. I wasn't going to let him hurt me anymore.

Mr. Franklin, of course, decided this day he would be late, but his prop was a stack of newspapers. He surveyed the room from his podium before addressing the class, his eyes falling on me; then with raised eyebrows, he smiled at Travis.

"We're going to debate today." He pulled another podium that I'd not noticed before from the corner of the room. "Today we will be doing improv speaking, so bring a pen and a piece of paper up for your turn. I will give you a topic. You'll have two minutes to write down your points and then you can debate. Everyone else, I want you to pick a side and make your own notes. We will discuss points made and points that should have been made, so take notes. We'll be open for discussion. I'd like Gianna and Travis to go first, so please come to the front of the room." I stood and Travis followed me to the front of the classroom. We took our podiums as Mr. Franklin flipped through one of the newspapers. "Your debate is over 'the automobile industry's responsibility to the American public regarding defects and recalls.' Should they inform us of every defect no matter how small? Travis you will defend the automobile industry; Gianna you will defend the public." We looked warily at each other and made our points as he began his stopwatch. Everyone in the class wrote. When he said to stop, we all looked up. "You will now have two minutes to debate your point and then a rebuttal after your opponent takes their turn. Gianna, please go first." I looked at my classmates and began.

"The American people have a right to know when they are driving a lemon. As in, they are paying good hard earned money for a vehicle that should take them from point A to point B. The automobile companies have a responsibility to offer a quality product to their customers. Promising one thing and delivering another should not be acceptable on any level." I paused a moment and looked at Travis. Then I continued, "Where is the honesty that this nation was founded on? Now, it's about what they can get away with, and it doesn't matter who gets hurt in the end as long as they make a profit." I became passionate in my final statements. "It is time that the American people stand up and tell the fat cats that we deserve better. We deserve the best they can offer and if they don't want to give us their best, then they don't deserve ours," I concluded, and the class erupted in cheers and applause. I smiled triumphantly at Travis. He looked down at his podium, defeated. Mr. Franklin shushed the students and motioned for Travis to take his turn. He looked at me as he began.

"It was never the intention of the automobile industry to take advantage of the American people. We are the American people. Extensive testing is performed to provide for most scenarios. Sometime things happen that we don't anticipate. Sometimes the only thing that we can do is apologize and try to make it right for the future. We provide many jobs for the American people, and when our company suffers, so do our workers, the middle class of America. Like any tier of power, there can be corruption, but only when it is discovered, can it be weeded out. That is why I'm asking the American people to believe in us. Believe that we are trying to look out for what is best for them. Believe that we would never hurt them maliciously or intentionally." He finally took his eyes from me and looked down at his paper like he was reading something and then looked over to Mr. Franklin signaling that he was done.

"Miss Moretti, your rebuttal." He motioned for me to resume speaking, so I took a deep breath.

"Justifying mistakes by simply saying 'I'm sorry' isn't acceptable to the American people. There must be consequences for their actions. Mistakes, intentional or otherwise, should be explained. Also, the automobile industry should be required to give a plan to the American people as to how they intend to remedy the problems." I folded my hands together on the podium. Mr. Franklin motioned to Travis once more.

"Maybe the AMERICAN PEOPLE should not hold such high expectations of the automobile industry. We are only human. We cannot be held responsible for everyone else's actions. We are only responsible for ours and how we respond. If we reject the defective products, and they slip in anyway by mistake somewhere, all we can do is make it right. Holding us to higher expectations is not the answer." He was fuming, his face reddened, and he glared at me now. Someone in the back of the room let out a low whistle, and Mr. Franklin stood straightening himself.

"OK. Travis, Gianna take your seats. Did anyone have a point that was not mentioned during their discussion on either side?" We sat down, and I looked at my hands resting on my desk. I didn't listen to the rest of the discussion; I felt defeated. Even though they scored me as the winner, I didn't feel as if I'd won.

When class was over, I bolted for the door as fast as I could. I wasn't fast enough because he grabbed my hand and led me toward an empty classroom. I tried to pull away from him, but he was stronger than me. He pulled me into the room, blocking the door and turning the lock. I slammed my books on the floor and lunged for him. He grabbed my hands and pulled me to him and held me in a tight embrace around my waist, my hands crushed to his chest. I pounded on him, swearing at him, my fury unleashed. He took the abuse, and when I was done, he still held me.

After I calmed down, he took my face in his hands and lifted my chin so that I couldn't escape his eyes. They were pleading as he spoke softly, "How are you so mad at me?" He traced the side of my face.

"You kissed her," I groaned, as I pulled away from his hands and looked down.

"I didn't kiss her; she tricked me, and you have to believe me. The whole point was to break us up. Make us feel like we do right now." He loosened his grip on me, allowing me to leave his arms if I wanted to, but I didn't; I stayed there. I wasn't strong enough to pull away from him. Not yet.

"I don't want you to regret being with me if you want to be with her." I focused my eyes on the bulletin board beside us. I knew the next part would be harder for me. "So I think maybe we should take a break; maybe we need some time apart." My mind was clearer now than I thought it would be when I practiced saying it in my head.

"I don't need time. I know who I want to be with. I want to be with you." I was sure he was just confused. Chiz was still in my head saying, *Him with you, wishing he was with her.* I couldn't blame him; Jillian was unbelievably gorgeous. I couldn't compete with that, and I wouldn't anymore.

"*I* need time though, so I want to take a break." I refused to look at him as I broke his hold on me, turned away, and walked to the window, looking out on the bright sunny day. He came and stood behind me.

"Don't do this," he begged softly, but I didn't turn to him. I didn't say anything to him.

And after a few minutes, I heard him walking toward the door; then I heard it open and close. I buried my face in my hands, again willing the tears to come, but they didn't. I was empty of tears and just plain empty.

Chapter 17

Where There Is Hope

Travis

It was surreal. I couldn't believe she ended it so easily. There were no tears, no emotions at all. I didn't know the girl who was standing in front of me. I began to wonder if I'd meant anything to her. At first, I was relieved that I hadn't told her I loved her. Then I thought if I had said something maybe we wouldn't have broken up. I felt a void. I'm sure people talked to me after I left that room, but I didn't hear anything.

At practice, I told the coach I wasn't feeling well, and he let me sit out for most of it. I still had to run laps, but that was fine. I didn't have to interact with anyone else. I ran extra laps and was the last one in the locker room. I heard, "He's a mess. He didn't even look this bad when he and Jillian broke up." Mason was talking to Alex, and I stood on the other side of the row of lockers.

"She was, too, yesterday, sat in her room all day staring at a painting, listening to her music. The last time she did that was for three days after our mother died. I'm worried about her. She's taking this really hard." I heard him sit on the bench. "I don't know what to say to her either. I feel so helpless."

"Maybe they need to be locked in a room to work this out. You can tell how strongly they care about each other." *Didn't work,* I thought as I rounded the corner, saying loudly, "I'm here now; you can stop talking about me," in as light-hearted a tone as I could manage. They both looked at me, not believing my expression.

"I'm going to give Gia a call so she can come get me." Alex stood and turned to his locker to retrieve his cell phone.

"Dude, don't. I'll give you a ride." I pulled my shirt over my head so he couldn't see how badly I needed to take him home; I needed to be near her.

"Are you sure?" He turned and faced me.

"Of course." I turned to my locker, gathered my things, and headed for the shower.

The ride home was an awkward silence. We didn't talk much for the first half of the ride. "She wants to take a break," I finally forced myself to tell him, as if there were any question.

"*She* wants to take a break?" He looked at me like he didn't believe me.

"Yes, SHE wants to take a break. And there's nothing I can do but give her space. And it's killing me, man." I checked my mirrors and kept my eyes on the road to avoid his.

"Why would she want to take a break?" Alex's arm dangled out of the window.

"She thinks I still want to be with Jillian. That is so the opposite of what I want. Maybe she thinks it's too hard to be with me while Jillian is there trying to break us up. I guess now I know how far Jillian will go to do that. She's turning into quite a psycho. I wish Gia could see how much I care about her." I pulled in front of his house.

"I'll try to talk to her again; yesterday didn't help much. She wouldn't even tell me why she let Chiz bring her home Saturday. She really can't stand him, but Oliver said he brought her home, walked her to the door, and everything." Alex reached for his bag. I slammed my fist against the steering wheel. He looked up at me.

"You didn't tell me Chiz took her home! God only knows what that prick said to her. Now I know why at lunch today he wouldn't shut up about a mystery girl he met in the park. He said she was smart and pretty, but he didn't know her name, only where she lived. Said he kissed her. Do you think he kissed Gia, that she kissed him? And that's why she wants to take a break, because of him, because she wants to be with him and not me?" My mind was reeling.

"No, no way! She would have told me if she kissed him, and if she liked him. She knows how I feel about him, and she knows what he said in the locker room." He shook his head, but I could see that he wasn't convinced himself. "I'll try to find out. Either way I'll text you what happens." He opened the door to leave and turned to me to give me a hopeful look. "Have a little faith in her. She's been through a lot, and I don't know how much more she can take. I'm really worried about her." He got out and shut the door behind him, leaning in the open window. "I'll text you." I only nodded, the knot in my stomach growing ever tighter.

After dinner and after homework, I lay on my bed tossing a football in the air and staring at the ceiling. Her play list played on my computer, and I was lost in the handful of memories we had. The moments I swore I'd not take for granted, but that seemed so far away. The way she felt in my arms, the way her long curls sprang as she walked down the stairs. The way she cooked. I missed her food.

My cell phone dinged. It was a message from Alex.

Not with Chiz, doesn't want to be.

Good, is she mad at me?

No, really hurt, just needs time. She'll come around.

And that was it. I had hope. She wasn't angry with me. She didn't want to be with someone else. I wanted to prove to her somehow that I was still going to be there for her.

Gia,

I'm not going anywhere. Sometimes things look one way when they are completely different. That's what happened Saturday night. Maybe I should have done this first. You would have read this and seen that I don't want to be with anyone but you. I will be here, right where you left me when you are ready to come back to me. There is a reason for everything, and sometimes out of tragedy, you can find something really good. I think I was brought into your life to show you that you deserve the good. I know you were brought in my life to show me what true love felt like. I wrote it. Love. I can't believe I just *wrote that, but I did, and I do. I love you. I've never loved anyone like I love you. I don't know if I can ever love anyone else like I love you right now. And my heart feels broken. But I'm not going anywhere.*

Love,

Travis

I felt better after I wrote the letter, but also nervous because what if it was too late? What if it didn't matter anymore and it was over? I refused to think about that. All I knew was that tomorrow I would give her my letter, and I would leave it up to her.

I went to sleep finally, well into the morning hours. I didn't sleep well, and my alarm sounded too soon. I got up, showered, and was dressed and out the door. My mom gave me an encouraging hug before I left, whispering in my ear, "Hang in there champ." I had gushed uncharacteristically over dinner the night before. I told Hailey and her everything. I told them how awful Jillian had been last year. I told them how I'd first seen Gia and knew I had to know her. I told them why she was so special to me, that I told her things I'd never told anyone. And I told them I was in love with her. Hailey's eyes were wide the whole time. I probably told too much, saying things I shouldn't have in front of her, but I'd held it in long enough. It was time my mom knew who Jillian was.

When I made it to school and saw Gia hadn't arrived yet, I put the note in her locker and went to my class early. I was studying my notes when Jillian came in slamming her books down. I had completely ignored her the day before, making her do our experiment all by herself.

"You are such an ass." She plopped onto the stool.

"Fine with me." I didn't look up. She huffed and leaned into me, so close I could smell her perfume. It was nauseating.

"I get it; you're mad at me. And you want me to pay. I'm sorry I kissed you, but I didn't break you two up. You did that." I looked at her, her eyes steady on me. "If your relationship wasn't strong enough to withstand a little kiss, then maybe you aren't meant to be. You should be thanking me for getting you out of that mess. Did you know her dad was in prison?" she spat the words as she shook her head, appalled. I leaned back and surveyed her, her tight halter top and short skirt against her tan skin. She looked fake. Everything about her was fake. She realized I was surveying her and a smile crept into the corners of her mouth. She didn't say anything else to me as she turned, probably to give me a better look at her back side. She completely misinterpreted my expression. At this point I didn't care. I went back to work and ignored her the rest of the class.

I stood at my locker before lunch. Gia came around the corner, stiffening when she saw me at my locker. I smiled hopefully, but she looked away. I swallowed hard and turned to make my way to the cafeteria. I passed Abby and Mason on my way; they looked sadly at me. I didn't want anyone's pity. I wanted Gianna. Mason turned and put his arm around my shoulders.

"Hey, don't eat with the clique today; eat with us." He squeezed and let go.

"I can't sit that close to her." I looked down at the ground. "Besides she wants space from me so I'm going to give it to her," I added, as I sped up my pace leaving him behind. To make things worse she sat with her back to me. I couldn't see her face. I could tell by the expressions on Abby, Mason, and Alex's faces that she probably wasn't doing any better than I was. I thought that after she read my note and realized how I felt about her, that things would change. I hoped that she would confess to me that she loved me, too. I had hoped, but it looked as if once again I didn't know this girl as I thought I did. Maybe I was in love with the idea of her. Maybe I so desperately hoped that there was someone good out there after all those years with Jillian. Maybe I wasn't ready for a relationship, and Jillian had scarred me worse than I had thought. I stared at my plate, analyzing my emotions, trying to make sense of everything.

"What do you think, Travis?" Chiz asked.

"Um, yeah, whatever," I responded, not even caring what he was rambling about.

"I'm going to do it tonight then. She's amazing." He had a cheesy smile on his face.

"Do what?" I asked, scrutinizing his expression.

"Ask the girl out. She just broke up with her boyfriend, so it couldn't be better timing." He gleamed, high-fiving Brandon. I glared at him. He didn't notice.

I devised a plan. If she was going to move on from me so fast, I was going to at least make it difficult for her. Alex kept telling me that she didn't like Chiz, but I wasn't going to let him ask her out without making it a little uncomfortable. Alex agreed that if I were there, it would be harder for her to just agree and let him have his way. When dinner was over, I went back to their house with the premise that Alex and I were going to play video games. That was a logical explanation. Just because she wasn't my girlfriend anymore didn't mean that he wasn't my friend.

At seven-thirty I stepped up to the front door, hoping I wasn't already too late. I rang the bell. Mr. Morretti answered the door, and his eyebrows raised. He didn't address me; he just called to Alex, "Alex, your friend is here." He turned and climbed the stairs. I came in and shut the door. Alex appeared in the doorway between their dining room and living room, smiling and holding a big bowl of popcorn.

"Perfect timing, dude. He hasn't shown up yet," he spoke in a hushed tone, as he sat down and reset his game to two players. I sat down beside him.

"Where's Gia?" I asked, as I picked up the receiver.

"In her room, where else? She barely ate dinner and went right to her room." He didn't look at me, but I knew he was still worried.

We played for a good half hour before the doorbell rang again. I looked at Alex nervously. He smiled, "Show time." He answered the door speaking so low I couldn't hear him. Then I heard louder, "Sure, come on in. I have to go get her." He didn't turn toward me. He just climbed the stairs and disappeared. I kept playing the game with my back to Chiz, whom I knew was standing there between the front door and the back of the couch.

"Travis, man, hey. I didn't see your car out front." I turned to see him rubbing the back of his neck.

"Yeah, I parked a couple houses down. The neighbor was parked out front when I got here." Even though it was the truth, we had planned for me to park down the street.

"Ah, I see. I was just checking on Gia to see how she's doing. I know it's been a tough couple days for her, and I'm not just your friend, you know." He laughed, but he was a bad liar and a bad friend.

"You don't have to explain yourself to me." I continued playing my game. I heard the footsteps on the stairs. I turned to see Gia following Alex, and I saw her stiffen when she realized I was sitting there on the couch. She looked from Chiz to Alex, then to me accusingly.

"Do you mind stepping outside with me for a minute?" Chiz asked, as he moved toward the door, glancing at me anxiously.

"OK," she said. She had looked so beautiful today in her black dress, and though she wore sweat shorts and a tank top, she looked equally beautiful with no makeup and her hair pulled up in a ponytail. It was hard to look away from her, but I had no choice because she led him to the front porch. Alex shut the door and turned on the porch light. Then he motioned for me to come with him. I paused the game, and he waved his hand for me to leave it going, so I unpaused it. It was background noise. Maybe on the porch it sounded as if we were still playing the game. He squatted down by the front window. I sat beside him. The window was barely cracked. I hadn't even noticed before that it was open. I was grateful for his attention to detail. We listened. There was silence for a few seconds.

"How are you doing? You haven't looked so good. Well, you always look good, but sad," Chiz said.

"I'm as well as can be expected for the condition I'm in." I smiled, thinking it was such a Gia answer.

"I was hoping you'd be in a better mood by today."

"Well, I did break up with my boyfriend, so I'm not sure what the mourning period for that is." I heard the front step creak. I imagined her sitting there leaving him standing under the light.

"I think the rule is a day for every month you were together." His footsteps were heavy as he walked to where she was.

"I may be an exception to that rule then." That gave me hope again. Alex smiled at me.

"Well, I was thinking." He paused nervously. "Maybe I could help you with that." There was a long pause, and he continued awkwardly, something that was so out of character for Chiz. He was brazen and calloused when he spoke of girls and to girls. The girls he usually went after were needy and starved for attention and usually just as shallow as he was. I suddenly realized that maybe he really did like her as more than just a conquest. "I'd like to take you out for a nice dinner, maybe a movie, if that would be OK with you." She didn't answer. I was dying to peek my head over the ledge and see what her expression was.

"I don't think that's a good idea. When we moved here, I didn't have any intention of getting involved with anyone, and I think that was a good idea. I'm sorry." I heard the porch boards squeak again, and Alex grabbed me, pulling me to the couch again. My heart began to race as we picked up our controllers and began playing the game like we'd been sitting there the whole time. We heard voices again near the door and then it opened and closed. Gia stood by the door for a moment and then turned off the light and went back upstairs. I leaned back against the back of the couch with a sigh. Alex threw some popcorn at me and chuckled.

"I told you to have a little faith in her." We played for another hour and a half. I felt at ease for the first time since I'd held her in my arms at the dance.

I made it through the next week. I gave her the space she needed. It was the hardest thing I did—sitting behind her every day, staring at the back of her head, unable to talk to her or do anything with her. I missed the long talks we had; I missed just being with her.

When the weekend came around, I hung out at home Friday after the game and all day Saturday. Hailey was happy at first to keep me company but was complaining about my sour mood by the time lunch came around. I took her to get ice cream, and we walked the boardwalk. I saw a lot of people from school out and about but not the face I wanted to see. Finally, we went home. Mom was in the kitchen making dinner. I left again and went walking. I walked all around my neighborhood. I tried to clear my head; I tried to plan my next move. I needed to decide if I would let this be the end or if I would fight for her. I found myself at the beach at the exact spot where I first met her, sitting on the ground watching those waves. It felt like years ago, not just the few short weeks it had actually been. I stared at the waves, watching them come in and go out. I could only imagine how she felt that day. She probably felt as if her world were caving in on her, and here I was feeling the same way. She hadn't talked to me in days. How could my world revolve around one person I'd known for such a short time? But that was it; I did know her. I knew her better than I'd known anyone. The waves did have a calming effect. In the distance, a man played Frisbee with his dog, but other than that the beach was empty.

"You're in my spot." At first I thought I was imagining her voice. Then I turned and saw her standing there.

"Sorry, I thought it was public domain," I smiled and turned back to the waves.

"Do you care if I join you?" I did care; I wanted her to, but I just shrugged. She sat beside me, an arm's length away from me.

"Why do you want to join me?" When I turned and looked at her, she looked away from me to the tide and was silent for a moment before she answered.

"I miss you. It's not fair, but I do. I came to get some air; my walls were closing in on me, and I saw you sitting here. I hoped that it couldn't hurt to say hi, and I could stay out of the house a little longer. I'm sorry I've been so awful this past week, it's been--" she trailed off pulling her legs up to her chest and wrapping her arms around her thighs. I played with the sand in my hands and didn't have a response for her. I was just so relieved that she was finally talking to me. I didn't approach her; she came to me.

"I miss you too," I finally said in a low tone.

"Do you think we could be friends again? Eventually?" She looked over at me, laying her head on her knees.

"I would like that. I got a C on my math quiz this week. I miss our study sessions," I chuckled. She smiled.

"I miss them, too; it's nice to be able to talk to someone in between subjects." She continued to stare at me. I looked back down at the sand.

"Is it too soon? Can we be friends?" I looked back at her.

"I would like that." She looked back at the waves again. She didn't say anything else. Neither did I.

We sat there until the sun set over the horizon. I sat there as long as she would let me. Finally she stood, and I did, too. It was beginning to get chilly. I offered her my sweatshirt. She accepted it gratefully. I walked her back to her house, waiting for her to speak first, but she didn't. When we stood at the first step to her house, she looked up to the sky, and then smiled at me; it wasn't the smile I remembered, but it was a start.

"Thank you for walking me. You didn't have to." She unzipped the hoodie and handed it to me. I took it and smiled at her, too.

"I would do almost anything for you," I said under my breath. She cocked her head to the side, not completely hearing me.

"Good night, Travis." She took a step up backward.

"Good night, Gianna." I took a step backward, too. She held my eyes and stood there a moment. It was as if she wasn't ready to say goodbye, the same as I wasn't. I wanted to rush to her and kiss her. I almost envisioned myself doing that, and she would kiss me back. But I didn't. Instead I took another step away from her and said one more time, "good night, Gia."

"Good night." She didn't move this time. Her eyes fixed on me.

"Good night," I said one last time. She nodded and turned finally to go inside.

I put on my hoodie. It smelled like her, her perfume, a sweet smell. I walked home. It was quiet when I got there, and for the first time all week, I went upstairs to my room and fell into my bed. Not being able to sleep all week had exhausted me. Now that we were calling ourselves friends again, I felt better. So I slept deeper and sounder than I had all week.

Chapter 18

I Had One Wish; It

Was to See You Again.

Gianna

I closed the front door and leaned against it. I closed my eyes and let out a deep breath. Oliver came stomping down the stairs, his head tilted to the side and looking at me as I opened my eyes.

"Don't," I said, as I began to climb the stairs.

"Don't what?" A smile hovered in his voice.

"Don't say something that resembles fatherly advice. My life is a mess, and nothing will fix it. I can't fix it right now." He stood in front of me, blocking my way up the stairs.

"I wasn't going to say anything." He paused. I moved to pass him, but he remained in front of me. "Unless 'the heart wants what the heart wants,' or in my opinion, you and that boy are good together counts as saying something. I see more than you realize." He twinkled my nose, which annoyed me immensely. He stepped over to the side. I passed him, and he added, "Maybe you're just good for that boy." I paused and turned and looked down at him. "You are everything that is good that I could have done in my messed up life. I don't deserve you and your brother." He nodded and continued his descent of the stairs, leaving me standing there mouth open, just watching him.

On Monday, I entered the halls of school feeling renewed. Travis stood at his locker wearing dark denim jeans, his Cons, and a thin graphic tee that showed his shoulders and form. I was sure he hadn't seen me yet; he was relaxed and talking to one of the guys from the team. He threw his head back, laughing. I walked in beside Alex. He turned to see me. His smile widened. I smiled back and made a small wave as I walked past him, stepping up to my locker. Alex talked to him for a few minutes and disappeared into the crowd. He closed his locker and turned to me. I looked up, nervously.

"Enjoy your day." He smiled as he turned and walked away. This was definitely different from the last week. He had his confidence back. If our friendship did that to him and did that to me, then I could take it. This time I wanted to be sure he wanted to be with me. I could take whatever Jillian dished out as long as I knew he wanted to be with me. That kiss had done more damage than I thought was possible.

I turned to go to my first class. This was tricky. I had been avoiding Chiz since he had asked me out the week before, but he always found me between my morning classes. Like clockwork, I rounded the corner and he was there. He draped his arm around my shoulders. Well, it looked as if he draped his arm around my shoulder, but really he held me there and I couldn't move.

"Hey, honey," he said, too close to my face and pulling me in tight to him.

"Chiz, really?" I finally pulled out of his grasp. "We've talked about this. You're making me uncomfortable."

"I just want you to know how I feel." He looked down but kept pace with me.

"I know how you feel, and I thought I made myself clear. I don't want to be with anyone." *Except Travis.* I finished the statement in my head. No one could know that until I was sure it was really what he wanted. "Please respect me." I was at the door to my class.

"After the game, will you go with me to Brandon's party?" He leaned against the door jam. My classmates had to squeeze past him. They looked at me in annoyance; he didn't notice. I looked at each of them apologetically.

"I don't think so." I turned to leave, and he grabbed my arm.

"Just, just tell me you'll think about it. Give me that." I looked at my arm, and he released me.

"I'll think about it," I sighed.

"That's all I'm askin'." He bounced away, leaving me to turn and face a room full of annoyed juniors. I took my seat.

"Every day! Just go out with him, so he'll stop being a human door," the boy across from me growled.

"Or get back with Travis. Either way, make up your mind," another chimed in.

"OR," from the corner, "dump them both and give some of us others a chance." I turned to see who said it, but all the guys in that area were smiling.

"How about D none of the above and everyone just leave me alone." I leaned back in my chair. A few of the girls glared at me while the boys continued to smirk.

Travis joined us for lunch, finally. I was relieved. He didn't sit by me for obvious reasons, and I was glad for that to an extent. He sat beside Mason across from me. I really had missed him in the past week. It was shocking to me how attached I had become to him. This only reinforced my decision that I needed proof he was over Jillian. Unresolved feelings could still linger and would break my heart. At this point I felt as though anything could send me over the edge. I didn't think I was ready to deal with it.

I left the truck for Alex, letting Abby take me home. Travis had a dentist appointment and didn't go to practice anyway. I was the only one home when the doorbell rang. I knew we weren't expecting anyone, so I went to answer it. I pulled the door open and was shocked to find Mitchell standing there. I practically jumped into his arms.

"Hey, Gianna," he smiled. I looked over his shoulder to see a small U-Haul with a car hitched to the back of it. I pulled away from him, still smiling, and said, "Hey, Mitchell. What are you doing here?"

"I sold the house. I brought you and Alex some of your mother's things and a few presents. I also have to talk to Oliver about your trust funds." I looked at him quizzically.

"You sold the house?" I looked around him again at the U-Haul.

"Yes, I've bought a new one closer to my practice. I'm actually in Geist. Can you believe it? Right on the water." He smiled widely now.

"What stuff did you bring us?" I was on the verge of hyperventilating—my mother's house, my house, was someone else's now.

"Furniture, pictures, jewelry, papers. Stuff like that. I donated most of her clothes but brought a few of the pieces that she knew you loved." My knees went weak, and I lost my balance. He caught me just as I was about to hit the ground.

"Are you OK? Maybe we should go inside and call Oliver." He led me inside. He surveyed the old furniture with a raised eyebrow, and suddenly I felt defensive of where I lived now.

"I brought the great room furniture and the dining room set. I knew your mother was proud of that. She would want you guys to have it. It was the first major purchase she made, wasn't it?" I nodded and walked around to sit on the couch. "I also brought things from your and Alex's bedroom. Things you left behind." We'd left those things thinking we'd be returning to that house for visits and to live after we turned eighteen. The kitchen door opened and slammed. Oliver came in, his hair disheveled, huffing as if he'd run the whole way from the Pub, as he glared at Mitchell.

"YOU!" He pointed and crossed the dining room. Mitchell stood.

"Oliver, take it easy. I have some business to discuss with you and just wanted to bring the kids some things. I won't be staying long." I reached and clung to his arm.

"NO, say you'll stay for a while! Please Mitchell." He looked down at me, pushing his glasses up on his nose at the same time.

"I can't stay long, sweetie, maybe overnight. I have to get back. I have a big case that goes to court on Friday." He looked back at Oliver, who responded with a grunt. "I've got a hotel room for tonight. Where's Alex? We need to unload these things." He rubbed his hands together like he was about to do some work. As I stood, I could feel all the color drain from my face. Mitchell noticed and motioned for me to come to him. I did.

"Go get a soda; you look like your blood sugar dropped." He pointed toward the kitchen. I obeyed silently, and he followed Oliver out the front door. I heard their voices but didn't hear what they were saying. I texted Alex, telling him that he needed to get here as soon as possible. I didn't get a response. I went out and found Oliver was standing with one foot hitched up on the trailer that held the car while Mitchell stood on the bumper of the U-Haul with the door raised.

"What are we supposed to do with that furniture?" Oliver sneered.

"This was Anna's; it was important to her, so it's important to the children," Mitchell stated matter-of-factly. Oliver looked at me, and something on my face must have changed his mind. He simply shrugged and reached for the box already in Mitchell's hands. I was next. We took the boxes and stacked them inside the living room. Alex arrived and helped us finish unloading. Oliver made the decision to get rid of his furniture immediately, so they loaded it into the truck and took it to donate as Mitchell and I finished unloading the rest of the boxes. While they were gone, Mitchell lowered the red sports car from the back of the U-Haul.

"Follow me to the truck rental place, so I don't get charged for an extra day." He tossed me the keys. After we returned it, we arrived back just as Oliver and Alex did, too. Alex and I went into the living room and began cleaning and sweeping and mopping the wooden floor so that we could arrange the furniture. Oliver went to work in the dining room doing the same thing and sharing the tools. Mitchell went to the phone book and ordered pizza. Then we looked at the boxes sitting in the corner. There were about twenty of them, and they began to look overwhelming. How could you measure someone's life in boxes? It seemed like that was what had happened. This was what was left of the memories of my mother, of our life together. This was it.

The pizza came, and we sat around the too-familiar table in the too-familiar room but in two very different ways. Mitchell tossed Alex the keys to his car. Alex looked up at him questioningly.

"Gia told me how much that big truck is unreliable and scares her to drive. I thought this might give you better gas mileage and be a little more fun." He looked at Oliver. Oliver looked down at his slice of pizza.

"Mitchell, it's too much," I said, embarrassed.

"No, it's not. You two deserve it. You have to share it, you know. I couldn't afford two cars." He smiled at me as he reached and squeezed my hand.

"Thanks Mitchell," Alex said, shaking the keys at me.

"Yeah, thanks," I added. Finally, I excused myself and went to my room to finish my homework.

I stood at the side of my bed and dumped my bag on the bed. I knew there were some papers in the bottom that I needed to toss. My bag had become a magnet for loose papers. I separated the algebra notes from the history ones. I put the papers that were trash into a pile. I set my books over to the side, and then I saw it, a folded piece of paper. I had completely forgotten about it. The day after I broke up with Travis, he'd put a note in my locker. I'd stuffed it into my bag because I was running late, planning to read it later, but I hadn't. I had forgotten all about it. Here it was in my hand again. I sat down on the edge of my bed and opened it.

I couldn't believe what I read. He loved me? Was it true? Was this the sign that I had waited for? And could it have been so easy? I wanted to cry, this time tears of joy, but they didn't come either. I grabbed my phone, and I texted Travis.

U home?

Yeah what's up?

Can I come over?

There was a long pause.

Sure.

I had to tell him. I had to tell him I read his note and that I thought I might love him, too. I surveyed myself in the mirror and decided to change my shirt, refresh my makeup, and pull my hair into a ponytail. Then I put on the green hoodie with his number on it. I took the note and put it in my back pocket. As I descended the stairs, I heard voices in the dining room. I stood there a moment and listened. They were speaking in a hushed tone.

"I did my time, turning myself in when she filed charges. I continued my therapy even after the court dissolved it. I think I've proven how much I love them by allowing them to walk away from me. It killed me and made me see how much they really did mean to me. I even did what you asked. When she called me to ask my permission to allow you to adopt them, I told her no. You didn't even tell me my wife was sick. You only called me after she died. Those two are better off without me in their lives. But I guess they would do better without you in their lives more. You are no longer welcome in this house."

"I'm offering you help. I can't stand to look at them. Gia looks like her, and Alex reminds me of you. They aren't mine; they never were. Anna was mine. That was it. The day she died, she didn't even tell me goodbye. She only spoke to them. Maybe she didn't love me anyway, but I can't be near them anymore. I don't want to have any contact with them either. I've changed my numbers and my personal email account. You either take my money or you don't. It's your decision." Mitchell had an edge in his voice I'd never heard before. I sank to the step. What did he mean we weren't his? He had been the father Oliver never had been, hadn't he?

"I don't need your kind of help. Alex has made me proud, and I will pay for his and Gia's schooling even if I have to remortgage the house. They will be better than Anna and me." Oliver was firm.

"Your loss. I've set up the money from the sale of her house in a trust fund for them. It's theirs anyway; she willed it to them. She left me with nothing. Here." I heard a stack of papers hit the table.

"Why are you doing this?" I heard the keys hit the table, too. "You don't care about the children; so why are you giving so much? Do you feel guilty?"

"This was hers; it's theirs. I owe them that much." He still had the bitter edge to his voice. He let out a deep sigh. I didn't pity him though. "My flight leaves in two hours."

"Do you want me to call the children down?" I heard the chairs scoot.

"No, we've already said our goodbyes." We hadn't. Oliver walked him to the door. They didn't see me for all the boxes beside the stairs. But I saw them. He left without another word, and Oliver shut the door. He turned to come up the stairs and saw me sitting there, an empty expression on my face.

"OH, my Gia, I'm sorry *mia bella*, that you had to hear that." He walked up the stairs, patting my head as he passed me. He hadn't called me that since I was a toddler.

"You would have let us go? And you would have let Mitchell adopt us?" I didn't turn; I just asked him accusingly.

"Yes." He sat down a few steps higher than me. "I was never good to you or your mother. Back then I felt the world owed me something. I was angry at your mother. There is no excuse for the awful things I did to her. I drank too much. I was a monster. The three of you deserved better than I could ever be. I'll never make up for it, but I can only try not to be that man again." I didn't turn around. I didn't want him to see my face.

"I need to go out for a bit, is that OK?" I looked down at my hands.

"Yes, Gia, but please keep your phone on you." Then he added, "Take the car. I would rather you didn't walk around."

At this, I did turn to look at him and shook my head. "No, I don't want anything from him." I stood and went down the stairs. I turned on the porch light and closed the front door. I walked down the quiet street and over two blocks. Travis was sitting on his front steps, watching for me. I was pretty sure he saw me before I saw him, but as I approached, he stood to meet me.

Chapter 19

If Your Eyes Are The Window

To Your Soul, Are Your Lips

The Window To My Heart?

Travis

I didn't know exactly what it meant that she was wearing my hoodie, but I liked seeing my number on her. I met her under a street lamp. She didn't say anything. She walked up, stopping intimately close to me and then put her arms around my waist holding me close to her. She buried her face in my sweatshirt. I put my arms around her and held tightly for the quiet moments. Finally, she looked up at me. I couldn't read her expression.

"Hey, what's going on?" I wasn't sure I wanted to know, especially if it were bad. I was reveling in this moment.

"I had an interesting night." She let go of me but took my hand, and I led her toward my front porch again. This time we went to the porch swing. We sat down with space between us. She sat at an angle so she could look at me. She told me about Mitchell. She told me about how her heart broke when she learned of his true feelings for Alex and her. Then when I thought she would begin to cry, she looked at me, uncertain. She sat there quietly for a long moment.

"Go on," I encouraged.

"I love you, too," she barely whispered. I sucked in my breath. I wasn't prepared for that. "That's what I wanted to tell you when I texted you. I found your note." She reached into her pocket and pulled it out. "I actually read it tonight for the first time, and I'm sorry Travis. I, I..." she trailed off and looked across the street at a darkened house. I scooted closer to her, pulling her into my embrace.

"I love you," I breathed into her ear. She looked up at me, and her fingers traced my lips. Without even thinking about it, I pulled her up to me and kissed her. I kissed her deeply. I kissed her desperately. I kissed her long. When I let her finally breathe, she looked at me dizzily.

"I missed you, too," she said softly, leaning her head against my chest.

"I'm sorry for the whole mess of things. If I'd have known, I would have never taken you to that dance. I would have taken you somewhere else. Anywhere else," I sighed.

"I'm sorry, too, that I listened to Jillian and Chiz. I should have come to you and trusted you." I smoothed her hair. "I doubted myself, and I doubted you."

"You don't have to say anything else. It's over." I pulled her tighter to me, unwilling to let her go.

"I do, though, because I moved here and didn't expect to find anyone like you. But I did, and I threw it away so fast. I'm sorry." She held onto me, too.

"What are you going to tell Chiz? He'll feel betrayed because you told him you didn't want to see anyone," I laughed. She pulled away from me and looked at me, scrutinizing. My face suddenly turned red. I stammered, "I, I mean..."

"Shut up." She mock-slapped me on the shoulder and laughed, "I knew you two were up to something when he came over." She smiled, and it was the smile I remembered, the one I had been lost without the past few weeks.

"I have boxes to go through; will you help me tomorrow?" She pulled her feet up on the swing and shifted so that she was leaning against me, more comfortable in my arms. I began to rock us back and forth in the swing.

"Mm-hmm," I nodded. I twined my fingers in hers, and she kissed each of my fingers. I wasn't sure how much longer we sat out there, but eventually my mom turned on the porch light, signaling that it was time to come in. I ran in long enough to tell her I was walking Gia home. And we did, hand in hand. I walked her up the stairs to her front door, and there under the light I kissed her goodnight. I wished her sweet dreams and turned to walk back home.

I made it to the corner of the street when a monster truck pulled up beside me. I knew the truck and the driver. Chiz rolled down his window.

"Were you kissing my girl just then?" He leaned over and looked at me accusingly.

"I don't think she ever went out with you to be your girl, but yes, I was kissing Gia. We made up tonight. Sorry. That means we're back together." I kept walking as he rolled beside me along the curb.

"What lies did you tell her to convince her to take your sorry ass back? That when you kissed Jill it didn't mean anything?" I shrugged but kept looking straight ahead. I didn't owe him any explanation. "She deserves better than you." I heard him put the truck in park. I kept walking past his truck.

"That's her decision to make," I said, as he rounded the corner of his truck and was standing in front of me, both hands in fists. "Whatever you and Jill had planned, it didn't work. I love her and she loves me, and there's nothing you two can do about that." I was ready for whatever he was about to unleash on me.

"You just can't escape your attraction to Jill. You're going to break Gianna's heart, and I will be there to pick it up, whether you like it or not. She and I have this chemistry. It's like I know when she's near; I feel it." He trailed off and looked a little crazy in his eyes.

"Whatever, dude. Just stay away from her. I think you're better matched with Jill if you ask me, but stay away from Gianna." I moved past him.

He stood there stoically for a moment. Then he turned to me and said, "You'll see. I'll be there to pick up her broken heart." He walked back to his truck and took off, peeling out away from the curb.

We picked up where we left off the next day. I walked her to as many classes as I could, and we sat by each other as much as we could. We carried on conversations in hushed tones that no one else took part in. We were more affectionate than we had left off because every chance I got I pulled her into corners and kissed her. I couldn't stop kissing her. I didn't want to stop kissing her. She would giggle and push me away, only to pull me back to her with the same motion, kissing me.

After practice, I drove Alex home, and we came in to find dinner ready for us. Oliver was there, too. It wasn't as tense as it had been in the past. He slapped me on the back, welcoming me back. Alex looked at him curiously, but I just smiled.

I helped Gianna carry four boxes up to her room. We began to go through them. They were things she'd left at her home in Indiana. One box was full of sheet music. I flipped through a folder that said "favorites" on the cover with drawings all over it—roses, daisies, and other flowers I didn't recognize. She took it from me and flipped through it. I leaned over her shoulder and peered at all the squiggly lines. I wondered how any of it could make sense. Gia paused over one song called "Hero/Heroine." Her fingers traced the notes as if they were Braille and she was reading them. I stood and got her dusty guitar case and brought it to her. She sat there and just watched me. I sat it on the floor, opened the case, and handed the guitar to her. She took it and sat the folder aside. She put the strap over her shoulder and tuned it, looking nervously at me. Then the introduction to the song strummed from the guitar. Gia made her guitar sing. It was a familiar tune, and she played it precisely; then she sang. Her voice was soft but in perfect key. It had a raspy tone to it that made the moment feel surprisingly intimate.

She stopped singing when she reached the chorus, and playing as she turned and looked at me. "'Boys Like Girls,' one of my favorites, but you already knew that." She looked down at her guitar. "Thanks."

"For what?" I smiled and leaned back against her wall.

"For being you." She took off her guitar and placed it back in its case. Then she pulled out a shoe box with a lid on it from another box. She opened it and dumped a bunch of old pictures out. We looked through them and laughed as she told me stories behind them. Then she held one up with a concentrated look on her face.

"This one," she began, showing me a picture of a much younger Oliver holding a young Alex in his arms and her mother holding her, "was taken by my grandfather. It was the last time we visited him in Atlanta." She traced the faces. "He took this picture right before we left. That was the last time I saw him, too. He died a few months later of a massive heart attack. We didn't have the money for all of us to go to the funeral, so only my mother went. I barely remember him." She looked up at me and asked, "Do you think in ten years I'll look at these again and barely remember my mother? I don't want to forget her, but already sometimes I find myself trying hard to remember her expressions and her voice, and I can't." She looked past me then out the now-darkened window.

"I think that if you let your mind wander in those moments and try not to be so desperate for her, the memories will find you and remind you of what you're looking for. It's hard to imagine something if you've put a lot of pressure on yourself to do so." I patted her hand and found another picture and asked her about it.

After we put up some of her pictures on the walls and she stacked boxes on top of the already cluttered shelf in her closet, we went to Alex's room and kept him company while he put things away in his room. I sat on his bed and Gianna leaned against his dresser as he moved things around.

"Gia wants to sell our car; can you believe that?" he asked me but looked at Gia.

"We could buy something just as reliable and less flashy. It makes sense, maybe something that can carry the whole clan at one time like Mason's SUV." She shrugged.

"Or a minivan." He rolled his eyes as he put some trophies up on his shelf in the corner. He surveyed the rest of his boxes still half full.

"I should just put all this stuff in the attic or the basement. My room at home," he paused and looked at her, "or in Indiana, was a lot bigger than this. She nodded, agreeing with him.

"We still have to go through Mom's stuff." She looked down at the ring on her hand.

"We should take what we want and donate everything else. There's too much stuff." He plopped down on his bed beside me.

"I don't know if I should be here while you guys go through your mom's stuff," I stated, suddenly feeling like I was watching a very private moment.

"Travis, I couldn't do this without you." She walked over to where I sat and stood in front of me. I pulled her onto my lap, and she draped her hand around my shoulder.

"I hate to admit it, dude, but I don't think I could either." Alex shrugged. "This is a lot to deal with on our own." He stood and began consolidating boxes. "If we're going to do this, then let's do this," he added, as he stacked and carried them out of the room. We followed him downstairs where Gia and I began carrying boxes upstairs.

We began with the ones that said "clothes." She went through and held up her mother's designer clothes to herself. It seemed that they were similar in size. Her mother must have been a very small woman. I wondered how strong she must have really been to have survived and how she overcame such obstacles. I wondered if I were in a similar situation if I would have been so strong.

In the end Gia took only a few of her cocktail dresses and some of her shoes. She marked out "clothes" and wrote "donate." The next box was full of jewelry. Alex picked a few pieces out. Then they came across one of Mitchell's watches. Gia tried to get Alex to take it, but he wouldn't. She held it out to me. I looked at it.

"It's broken," I said, handing it back to her.

"I'll get it fixed. Would you wear it?" I looked at it again. I thought I would; it was an expensive watch. The name *David Yurman* was in small type across the face. I knew it had to cost a few thousand dollars. I couldn't believe that Alex didn't want it. He looked at it again.

"Mom bought it for Mitchell as a birthday present last year. It should work." He took it and pushed the pin on the side and it started ticking. She took it back and put it on my wrist. It was a little loose. She frowned, "I'll still take it to the jewelry store and get it taken up." Scrutinizing it, she noted, "Two links." Then she smiled at me. "Don't say I never gave you anything," she said with a wink. I hugged her around the waist and pulled her down on his bed. She giggled, and Alex breathed loudly, annoyed. We sat up and continued going through boxes.

I thought it was therapeutic for them, and I really got to know them both more. They bantered back and forth and talked about their memories with their mother. Finally, the evening came to an end, and it was time to go. Gia walked me downstairs and onto the front porch where we said goodnight. When we kissed, it was the sweetest kiss I'd known.

Chapter 20

Remove the Rose-Colored Glasses,

See the World in Living Color

Gianna

I think that I was the happiest I had ever been over the course of the next few weeks. I had good friends, and I had Travis. I still missed my mom, but the pain of the loss wasn't quite as piercing as it had been. It almost felt as if the pain were dulling. Only three months had passed, and though I missed her daily, I felt better. I didn't feel as guilty for finding a little happiness during my mourning. I was also relieved because neither Jillian nor Chiz were bothering us. In fact, it seemed that they had become the new "it" couple and were seen all over school in various stages of a continuing make-out session.

After practice one Thursday evening, Alex came in with Travis, bouncing off the walls.

"We sold the car! Brandon's dad wants to buy it tonight. Where's Oliver?" Alex bounced past me into the dining room then the living room, looking around.

"He said he had a meeting and then was closing the pub tonight," I said. I was surprised that Oliver's and my relationship had softened a little since Mitchell's visit. I had refused to drive the new car, and finally Alex put a for sale sign in it. I didn't want anything from Mitchell. I liked the fact that my boyfriend was wearing a watch that cost almost five thousand dollars, and that Mitchell had probably absentmindedly put it into the box of jewelry. Oliver had refused to let us donate any of our mother's stuff, especially her jewelry. He told us we would regret it when we were older, and it was better to give it to someone important to us in the future than just to let anyone have it. I'd seen his point, eventually.

"Oliver has to sign over the title. You wanna go try to catch him before his meeting starts? I think it starts at six-thirty." He looked at the clock on the microwave.

"Yeah, I guess we can," I said, and looked at Travis. "Do you want to come with?" He hugged me close to him and kissed the top of my head.

"I think this is a family matter. Besides my mom has been missing me. She wanted me to insist that tomorrow dinner is at my house. She and Hailey keep asking when they get to see you again." I nodded, and he squeezed me again and was out the back door. Alex and I followed shortly after he grabbed a sports drink from the refrigerator.

We headed toward downtown where our father was at his Alcoholics Anonymous meeting. We arrived, and there were still some people standing outside on the stone stoop and stairs, smoking cigarettes and drinking coffee as they talked to each other. Alex smiled at me encouragingly. We entered the old church. We followed the signs to the basement. There along the back of the wall was a table that had stale-looking cookies and coffee machines. There was a woman standing at a microphone at the podium in the front of the group. She was talking about the turning point in her life: living in her car, having her children taken away from her and the despair she felt. I looked at Alex apprehensively. He led me over to the corner to two chairs in the back of the room. We sat down and scanned the room. Oliver sat in the middle of a row toward the front. There was no way to get his attention without disrupting the meeting. There had to have been over one hundred people here. The lady finished and took her seat. A man who wore a brown tweed suit jacket stepped up to the podium. He thanked her and surveyed the crowd for a moment. Then he simply said, "Oliver, why don't you share your story with us." I took a deep breath, and Alex squeezed my knee. Then we both looked down at our hands. Oliver stood and sidestepped out to the middle aisle. He walked down the center of the room to the podium where he stood in front of the gathering and surveyed the room. I didn't think his eyes reached us though. He didn't look past the first few rows of people in both aisles.

He began, "Hello, I'm Oliver, and I'm an alcoholic."

"Hi, Oliver," the crowd said in unison.

"I met my wife after I graduated from high school. I had gone to Atlanta to work for my uncle. My parents emigrated from Italy when I was a tot, four or five. I was taught to work hard and be very disciplined. I worked for my uncle's landscaping company. He did the landscaping for a few of the schools. She was in summer school. I remember her looking at me from the window when I worked there. I liked her, and after a few weeks I had the nerve to wait around after her class let out and talk to her. She was intoxicating. Her will was strong, her opinions dominant, and she loved as purely and deeply as one could ever hope to find. We corresponded while she finished high school, and I moved back here working odds-and-ends jobs. When she graduated, we were married a month later. I'd like to say it was a happy ending, but it wasn't.

After a few years of marriage and the struggle of the day to day, we had our first child, a little boy, and he was a fighter, too. Oh, the spirit on that one; he had her strong will. I bought a house and a business, a bar. A year and a half later, we had my beautiful daughter. She was so delicate and gentle. I felt like the world was right, and everything had a purpose. The bar was a success, and I began to celebrate with my employees a few nights a week. I didn't see the harm in that. My Anna, though, she was fit to be tied. She would wait up for me, and we would argue, yelling back and forth at each other into the afternoons some days. On those days, I began to drink more. I didn't see what the big deal was; we were making money and she and my babies were taken care of.

It got to the point that I was drinking every night, coming home drunk and drinking during the day. A lot of those days were a blur." He paused and looked down at the podium like it would tell him what to say. He spoke softly now, the microphone barely picking up his voice, but it did. I heard every part of the next thing he said. "I remember the first day I lost my temper. Anna was so strong-willed, and she refused to be empathetic to my desires. She kept telling me that I had a drinking problem, and I denied it.

I guess what set me off was when she said she was going to go to her father's with the children. For some reason I lost it. I slapped her across her face. She screamed, and I immediately felt horrible and tried to hold her. I cried probably harder than she did and swore I wouldn't do it again. And I didn't for a while, but then we began arguing again, and I did it again." He paused a moment and swallowed hard. "I didn't stop drinking, and I didn't stop hitting her. I don't even remember some of the things that would set me off. It got to the point that even on good days, I came home and hit her. I was spiraling out of control. I was always drunk. She was broken, and I was the monster who broke her.

After four years of that, she had enough. She filed charges against me and got a restraining order. She left and took the children with her. At first, I was furious with her and contemplated hunting her down and killing her because if she wasn't going to be with me, then she wasn't going to be. That was the lowest point in my life. I am ashamed that I even thought such a horrible thing. But I began to wonder how I became such a wretched person. I stopped drinking the night they left. I turned myself in. I pleaded guilty with no contest and was given three years in prison." I vaguely remembered my mom leaving for a few days after we arrived in Atlanta. I wondered if she had returned to deal with his charges. Neither one of them had ever told us about this. He continued, "I entered a rehab program in prison and continued it after I was released. It was the least that I could have done. Anna kept track of my progress and would send me pictures of my children. She even asked me to visit, but I didn't want to upset them; they had seen enough of me. I thought it was over; I was living my life one sober day at a time, but then Anna passed away, and now I have my children again. It has been really frustrating for me, and for the first time in a long time, it has been a struggle for me not to drink." He paused and looked at the faces in the crowd. "Not because of what you probably think. It has been hard because in those children's eyes, I am still the man I was then. They are waiting for me to become angry and hit them. I see it, and it makes me want to escape their horror and their bitterness. They are two of the most amazingly strong young people I have ever known. They are that way because Anna's escaping me taught them that they are worth more than that. It's a struggle every day to get up, knowing that I had nothing to do with them being so strong, and knowing that they still despise me. I deserve it, but it doesn't make it less painful."

"Anna was the only woman I ever loved, and she is really gone. I was able to accept her being gone because I knew she was taking care of herself and our children. But now she's gone, and I never got to tell her goodbye. I don't think I would have gone to her, but I would have at least called her and said something. I don't know what I would have said, but if

I'd have known the last time I heard her voice was the last time, I'd have made more of it." He looked at the man sitting behind him and walked back to his seat. He was also broken. I realized he did love us as much as he could, and maybe I could give him another chance. The alcohol had made him a monster, and our leaving had not only saved us, but had saved him. I didn't even know he went to prison. There were things that my mother kept from us, I suddenly realized. The man in the tweed jacket encouraged Oliver to continue his sobriety and told him he was very proud of him. He also said he knew how far he had come and how hard it was for him to admit that he had a problem and work to quit it. We all applauded. Alex applauded and actually stood, causing some around him to stand. Oliver looked around embarrassed, but then he turned to the back corner where some people stood, and his eyes rested on his son, who now was smiling at him. He looked at me, and I nodded toward him, acknowledging him. He stood and began to come our way. The man in the tweed jacket ignored him and continued speaking. We left our seats and met him by the back door. Alex looked at him, appraising him for a moment, and then he reached out and hugged him. He hugged him so tightly, and they patted each other on their backs. Then he said, barely above a whisper, "I'm sorry, Dad. I love you." Oliver actually coughed, or it might have been the start of crying because he said in return, "You have nothing to be sorry for. I'm sorry, and I do love you, both of you." I squeezed into the hug. I wasn't ready to say the words, but I was ready to begin to forgive him. I at least owed him that much. If I had so easily given Mitchell a second chance after he had yelled at me, I could begin to forgive Oliver, if he had really changed his ways. It seemed as if he had. This time I could do something if he did choose to give in to his addictions again. We wouldn't let it escalate to the point that he was putting his hands on us. Maybe giving our forgiveness would give him the strength he needed to resist.

We left and met up with Brandon's father, who paid a nice retail price for our car and made our way home. It was getting late, and we had school and a game the next day. We went through the drive-through and ate dinner on the couch, watching prime time television together as a family.

The football team had another pep rally, and we all welcomed the chance to escape class. Abby and I sat toward the middle of the bleachers, and once the team was announced, several players found spots in the stands, including Alex, Mason, and Travis with us. I could tell he was nervous, and I let him pull me closer to him than I would have normally allowed for such a public place. His tension eased a little when that happened.

Later, I joined Travis and his family for dinner. I helped Melanie by tossing the salad while Travis and Hailey set the table. We had a nice dinner conversation, and Travis and I found ourselves in his room after the dishes were cleaned up. This was becoming normal. We always ended up in a bedroom with a closed door, especially lately. We always ended up kissing as our hands touched each other, over clothes, under clothes. We knew almost every inch of each other's skin.

"I want you so bad," he breathed in my ear.

I simply nodded. "So bad," he said again, as he moved his lips over my neck, his breath the only thing that touched me. It sent a wave of chills through me, and instinctively I arched my back, pressing myself into him.

"I do too, but," I paused and looked at the ceiling past him as he lifted up and hovered over me. I bit my lower lip and looked back into his eyes. I couldn't finish the statement.

"I understand." He leaned his forehead against mine. He took a deep breath and rolled over beside me.

"I'm sorry," I whispered. I still looked at the ceiling.

"No, don't be sorry. It's OK; we'll wait till when you're ready. But just so you know, I love you." He climbed back on top of me and held my face in his hands. "And I want you, too." He kissed me again, and we tangled ourselves into each other again.

The game was a close one and a tough loss because we could tell that the boys put everything that they had into it. Afterward, we went to a diner for a late snack as did most of the school. We grabbed a table on the patio that overlooked the beach. The five of us were joined by Gloria. I could tell that she was way more into Alex than he was into her. She hung on his every word, but he barely acknowledged her. We talked about the game and weekend plans. We were laughing at something Mason had said when Chiz sauntered over, his arm draped around Jillian's neck. He looked only at Alex as he addressed the table.

"My parents are going out of town for a week. Sunday we are having a gathering. Everyone is invited. You guys should come." We all looked at each other.

"Chiz, Sunday is a school night. You think that's such a good idea?" Mason asked.

"Well, I'm going to be busy tomorrow night." He winked at Jillian. She smiled. "What does it matter? Next week is a short week because of fall break." He walked off, Jillian in tow. I shrugged at Travis. He smirked at me.

"I'll be washing my hair." Abby gave her usual response.

"I'll probably be helping you," Mason added, nudging her.

"It would be fun; Chiz throws amazing parties," Gloria interjected.

"We'll see," Alex said, as he put his arm around the back of her chair. She seemed to like that answer and tried to snuggle closer to him. I gave him a wary look, and he shrugged.

We went our own ways. Travis and I walked along the surf. The water was starting to get colder, especially in the evenings. Though I rolled up my jeans, they still got a little wet. When we were in the dark, away from the boardwalk lights, he stopped walking and turned to me, taking both of my hands in his. I smiled up at him. We stood there silently for a few minutes. Then he leaned down and kissed me. He was so gentle in his touch I wanted to hold him close to me. I crushed myself to him, and our feet sank in the sand as the waves rushed over them and took it out from underneath us, only to come rushing over us again. I giggled, and he hugged me to him.

"You drive me crazy," he said, still holding me close to him.

"We'll be crazy together." I smiled into his chest.

"I'll save you a seat then." He laughed and kissed me again. Since we had reunited, it seemed as though our pull to each other was stronger than anything I had ever felt before. I didn't know that I could feel this way about anyone. My heart actually ached to be near him. It almost didn't feel natural. I wanted him with me always. I dreamed of him and waited for his letters in the mornings. I was beginning to feel a little addicted to him. I thought I might even understand what Oliver meant when he said my mother was intoxicating. If he felt anything like what I was beginning to feel about Travis, I didn't know how he was able to be away from her for a whole year. Travis kissed me again before we made our way back to the car. I felt on top of the world, but also as if I were on display on top of the world. No one watched us. I looked around, but I suddenly felt like we weren't alone on the beach and we were still being watched. He didn't seem to notice. He took me home and we sat on the porch for a little while, not wanting the evening to end.

"When I was a kid…" He leaned back on his elbows. "I used to play this game with my dad, that I was no good at, *Othello*. He didn't go easy on me either; I'd lose nine games and then he'd let me win one to keep me interested in it. We would play for hours. Then one day just before he left, I beat him like, five games in a row. I used to think that he left because I finally beat him. Then I realized he let me win to make me feel good about myself." I leaned on my side and watched him staring at the few stars that we could see over us. "Silly, for me to get so upset when I realized that, but I did. For a long time I thought that was the reason I was so mad at him, but it wasn't. It was because he left my mom when she was pregnant and needed him the most. It was because I was the first one in my class who didn't have a dad around, even on the weekends." He shrugged. "I don't know why I just told you that, but I wanted to. He called us the other day. He wants to see Hailey and me this weekend. I don't want to go, but my mom is taking Hailey. They are going to be staying overnight. I'm gonna be a bachelor for the night, have the whole place to myself." He looked over at me with a mischievous look on his face. It made me nervous suddenly. I sat forward and leaned my elbows on my knees and looked at him warily.

"I was thinking maybe you could tell Oliver that you were having a sleepover at Abby's, and we could spend the night together." He matched my move and held my eyes.

"I'm not comfortable lying to him," I lied. "We've reached this sort of understanding." This time I told the truth.

"We don't have to *do* anything. I'd just like to spend the night with you." Now he lied.

"I don't know." The thought of spending the night with him both excited me and terrified me.

"Think about it." He scooted closer to me and slid his arm around my waist. I leaned into his shoulder. "I love you," he said in a low, sexy tone. My heart began to beat out of control, and I was sure he heard it, but he didn't respond to it. He just held me close to him as I told him as evenly as I could, "I love you."

Chapter 21

The Tension So Thick,

You Could Cut with a Knife

Travis

Gianna came through like I had hoped she would. She was going to spend the night with me. I didn't know what I had planned exactly, but I just wanted to be with her. I wanted to feel her beside me all night and wake up with her in my arms. I didn't want to have sex with her if she wasn't ready, but if she *was* ready, I wanted to make love to her. She stirred such emotions I hadn't even known existed. I was getting even more nervous as it approached the seven o'clock hour. That was when Alex was dropping her off. He had called me, I assume after she had told him our plans, and asked for his help.

"If you make Gia do something she doesn't want to tonight, you'll have me to deal with." His voice was fierce, and I saw what Gia meant by how annoying it was when he didn't even say "hey" or anything.

"Alex, I just want to be with her. We're not going to do anything. Just sleep," I smiled to myself anticipating, then added, "I just don't want to be alone right now." I felt lame pulling that card.

"I'm just warning you. She's a virgin, and you're her first boyfriend. I don't want her to regret her first time if she's not ready." I already knew all of this. "She's on two different emotional levels. It's like she's teetering between falling apart and being blissfully happy. I see it on her face. You may not because you're too close to the blissful side, but I see both. And I don't know what's going to set her off but something might, and when it does, I don't know what will happen. She might become angry, she might cry, she might just shut down altogether. So don't pressure her to do anything." I was silent as I thought about what he said. "Are you still there?"

"Yeah, I'm here, I'm just—" I trailed off.

"I don't want to be such an asshat, but dude, it's my sister. I have to look out for her." His usual tone was back in his voice.

"I know. I love her. I'm not going to do anything to mess this up," I reassured him and myself.

"OK. I'll bring her over later." He hung up the phone without a goodbye. Gia hadn't complained about that; maybe he was still on the defense.

In preparation, I cleaned my room really well. I changed my bed sheets even though my mom had done it a few days ago. I cleaned the rest of the house and rented some movies. I showered and cleaned up then went to the Italian restaurant that we loved and picked up our dinner. I was in the kitchen when she came in.

"Travis?" She was barely audible. I came down the hall from the kitchen in the back of the house. She stood there in a pair of sweat pants rolled up to just under her knee and a couple of tanks layered with my hoodie, the one that I had loaned her during that first bonfire. She had a tote bag on her arm with her purse. I smiled at how adorable she looked, her hair pulled up in a bun piled on the top of her head. She really looked as if she were going to a slumber party instead of sneaking out to be with her boyfriend.

"Are you hungry?" I took her bag and purse and began to climb the stairs.

"You didn't fix dinner." She followed me, not believing her ears. I chuckled.

"No, I got Gigi's." She folded her hands in my back pockets as I now towed her up the stairs. I tried not to let her touch cause a reaction in me, but was failing. When I reached the top and turned to go to my room, she took her hands out. She still followed me. I dropped her bags at the foot of my bed.

"Careful, my camera is in there."

"Are we taking pictures? You gonna model for me?" I swung around and swept her up in my arms. As I did, we lost our balance and fell into my bed.

"I just thought we could take a few of us. My friends in Indy are dying for more, and this is a big night for us." She moved my hair around my hairline.

"I told you I'm OK with waiting." Just the thought of her and me generated another reaction. She looked at me strangely for a split second and then briefly smiled. I was embarrassed; I knew I should have taken care of myself before she came over. This night might be a long one.

"I'm not talking about that; I'm talking about what this night signifies. It's a cornerstone in our relationship. Like a milestone. Whatever happens, I'm going to remember it forever probably." She cut her eyes to the side of my room, not looking at me. I kissed her forehead and went to stand. She pulled me close again. Looking into my eyes, she traced my face with the tips of her fingers and smiled as she watched her fingers move. I couldn't take my eyes away from hers though. She looked back into mine, and the smile faded. Her eyes held the longing I felt, too. I sucked in a jagged breath. No one had ever affected me the way she did.

"Dinner. Will. Cold." I couldn't even think straight when she looked at me like that. She nodded as I loosened my grip on her and stood again. She let me go, too, and stood with me. I led her again down the stairs. In the kitchen I took down plates, and she looked at me with her head cocked to the side.

"What are you doing?" She began to unwrap our food.

"Getting plates, I thought it was obvious," I teased.

"We don't need to dirty your dishes if you don't want to." She went to the refrigerator and took out two sodas.

"I thought it would be nice, like a date. I was going to light candles and everything," I grumbled.

"Hopeless romantic." She giggled, conceding, and taking the plate I offered her. I took down two glasses and got ice for our sodas.

"I'm your hopeless romantic." I stepped too close to her and breathed into the back of her neck. I knew it affected her when I came that close to her and did that. She almost dropped the container she was holding. She looked at me with mock annoyance, but she smiled, and I smiled too.

We playfully flirted throughout dinner. Then I went to the living room to put in a movie, but she went upstairs. She came back down after a few minutes with fingernail polish and a file. She sat down on the floor, paper towel in hand as she spread out her toes and began painting them. I looked at her for a long moment.

"I'm at a slumber party." She looked up at me as if to say, "Duh."

"Ah." I leaned back and threw my legs up on the couch and watched the movie. Finally, when she was done with her fingernails and thought they were dry enough, she joined me on the couch. We didn't talk during the movie. It wasn't that it was very interesting; it was that I was alertly aware of her every move. She'd brush her hair away from her face, and I was watching her. She'd scratch her nose, and I was watching her again. I gave up on trying to follow the plot line. She snuggled up to me. I groaned unconsciously. She looked up at me.

"I'm just not into this movie," I sighed, not taking my eyes off the TV.

"Why? It's really good. Who do you think did it?" She looked back to the TV.

"The reporter," I said.

238

"But he's the narrator." She shook her head.

"Yes, but I just have a feeling that it was him." She still didn't trust me, I could tell.

"You're just saying that to mess with me."

"No, seriously, he's *'conveniently',*" I threw up my finger quotes, "stumbled on all these clues and is always there when something happens but never sees it. I think he has multiple personalities or something." It was one of those gritty movies that was advertised as having a shocking twist. She shrugged.

"We'll see soon enough, huh?" And we did. Within fifteen minutes she subscribed to my spoiler theory, and sure enough, he was the murderer all along. It got pretty gruesome toward the end, and she hid her face in my chest. When it was over she sat up, yawned, and stretched, showing a little of her belly. That was where my eyes gravitated. She pulled her shirt down self-consciously.

"Are you ready to go upstairs? We can watch this one up there." I held up the romantic comedy I'd gotten.

"Yeah, 'cause there's no way I'm going to sleep after that ending." She stood.

"Yeah, me too." I followed her up to my room. I put the movie in, and she pulled down the covers to my bed. "Do you need to change into pajamas or anything?" I nodded toward the bathroom.

"Yeah, but I can do that later. We're going to be up for a while, right?" She sat down and pulled the covers up around her. I pushed PLAY and climbed over to her. I pulled her close to me as the previews started. I kissed the top of her head, and she put her arms around me. I settled down and kissed the side of her forehead as she began to play with the hem of my shirt under the cover. The second preview started. She sat up a bit, pulled her hair down, and shook it out. I moved it away from her neck as she turned and looked at me for a second. I pulled her to me, and we were kissing.

We did the same thing we'd been doing every day. But this time was obviously different; there wasn't the caution that someone could come in on us at any moment. No one would stop us if we went too far. She pulled my shirt over my head. I pulled her on top of me as we kissed. My hands went under her shirts, and I helped her take them off. We kissed deeper, and I flipped her over and was on top of her. The menu was up for the movie, but we didn't care. I untied her sweats and wiggled them off her. She tugged at my jeans at the same time. I kissed her throat, her shoulders, her chest, her stomach. She kissed me, too, anywhere she could reach. I unhooked her bra and pressed myself against her. She began to breathe heavily. At first, I thought she was as excited as I was. Then she began hyperventilating. I jerked off her, leaning on my knees. She pulled the sheet up to her chest and refused to look at me.

"I'm sorry." She was still breathing heavily. "I thought I could, but I don't know what's wrong with me." She pulled her legs up and crushed the sheet around her.

"It's OK." I touched her arm, but she pulled away from me and looked at me as if she were scared of me or hurt. "What did I do?" I was confused.

"It's not you," she accused. "It's me. I must be wired wrong. I mean look at you!" And she surveyed me in my boxers. "I should be all over you, but I'm freaking out." She didn't look at me again.

"You're nervous, and it's all right." I pulled her to me. I settled us down in the bed and held her. We didn't dress; we just held each other and after a short time of me smoothing her hair, comforting her as best I could, she fell asleep. I turned off the TV and watched her sleep. Finally, I drifted off to sleep myself.

I woke up dazed the next morning, not sure what I'd dreamed and what actually happened. I rolled over and saw her lying there on her belly. Her hair spilled over her bare back and over her face; the sheet rested just below the band of her hipster panties. She still slept. I put my hands behind my head and stared at the ceiling. I was trying not to think about her lying beside me, and I was failing miserably.

"What are you thinking about so seriously over there?" I turned on my side to see her leaned up now, carefully covering her breasts in the morning light with her arms. It was very sexy.

"You." I didn't even look away from her as I said it as seriously as I'm sure I looked.

"I'm sorry, again." She looked away, embarrassed.

"It's OK, really. I hoped, but I didn't expect it."

"Soon, OK. I don't know how soon, but soon." She finally looked at me.

"Breakfast?" I asked, changing the subject. I stood and went to the bathroom and brushed my teeth. I came back into my room and got a pair of basketball shorts out of my dresser and put them on. She lay her head back down, watching me but not saying anything. I crawled across the bed and kissed her cheek. "I make the best scrambled eggs." She nodded. I left, giving her privacy so that she could get up and dressed. I put bread in the toaster and made the scrambled eggs. When I was dishing them onto the plates, she appeared in the doorway. She poured us juice, and we were at the table eating. My phone rang, and I answered it.

"Hey, honey, how is everything?" My mom's voice seemed a little strained.

"Everything's OK, Mom. How's Charleston?" I smiled and reached for Gia's hand, squeezing it.

"Everything is fine, but I think we're going to stay a few more days. Your father and I have been doing a lot of talking, and Hailey deserves a little more time with him. I wish you'd have come, honey. I'd hate for you to regret this." There was solemnness in her tone. I didn't understand it.

"I don't regret staying behind, Mom. What about school for Hailey? She shouldn't miss."

"I've already called the school; it's OK. Honey, I didn't want to tell you on the phone, but he's sick." I wasn't sure I heard her right.

"What do you mean?"

"I mean, the doctors are doing everything they can, but it's not a guarantee, he's in chemo—"

"He has cancer?" I interrupted her. I could feel my voice getting louder, and I couldn't even look at Gia.

"No, he has a tumor that they are treating with a sort of chemotherapy. It's terminal unless they can remove it." I didn't hear anything else she said after "terminal." My father was dying as Gia's mom had.

"I need to go," I said in a hushed tone.

"Sweetie, we need to talk about this. Do you want me to purchase you a ticket so you can come up here too?"

"No, I just want to be alone right now. I love you, Mom," I said. She said goodbye, and I hung up the phone. My hands began to tremble, and before I could say anything, Gia was standing beside me, holding me against her. I turned to her and felt the warm tears begin to stream down my cheeks. It had been a long time since I'd cried. He wasn't much of a father, but he was my father. Although I didn't want anything to do with him, I was overtaken with emotions of anger, fear, and sadness. She just held me to her as close as she could until I was done. Then she called Oliver and told him Abby was dropping her at my house. She would be spending the day with me, since I'd gotten some bad family news. He didn't hesitate with his approval.

"What do you want to do?" she asked me, pulling me to my feet and leading me to the couch.

"I don't know, but if this is how I feel hearing news about my dad, how did you feel when you found out about your mom?" I asked, rubbing my eyes.

"Um, at first I just sat there and stared at her. I remember she sat us down, and Mitchell was holding her hand. She said they would fight it and do whatever they could. I felt numb on the inside; I didn't cry. I thought I would, but I didn't. I thought I had to be strong for my mom, and I was.

"I helped her as much as I could. Alex turned to his sports and became obsessed with them. I quit playing my guitar; I only talked to my two best friends, but I refused to talk about my mom. This boy liked me." She blushed slightly and looked away from me. "And I liked him, a lot, but I wouldn't even talk to him after that. I felt like if I was good enough, then maybe God would make her cancer go away.

"Then I went through a phase where I was angry. I was angry at everyone, but that didn't last long. I sucked it up and got back to helping out. It changed me, though, obviously. Our lives are precious and too short.

We have to make most of every day. We have to spend it with the ones we love." She looked out the window. We sat there for a while. We watched the other movie, and we took a nap.

It was late in the afternoon when there was a loud banging on the front door. I wiggled my way out from under her and tried to not wake her, but she stirred. I answered the door, and Oliver was standing there with his fists clenched. He barged in and poked his finger into my chest.

"You were supposed to respect her! Gianna! Get your things!" he boomed. She sat up from the couch and looked at him.

"What's wrong?" she asked.

"I called Abigail's house and spoke with her mother. You didn't spend the night there. I trusted you." Her face turned red.

"Mr. Moretti, nothing happened," I began.

"Travis, keep your mouth shut. I will be calling your mother as soon as I get back home." He didn't look at me, just glared at Gia. She didn't say anything. She simply stood and went upstairs to get her things.

"You thought you'd get away with this?" He looked at me now.

"I just wanted to spend time with her." I looked to the stairs.

"Is that everything?" he asked, as she descended the stairs.

"Yes," was all she said to him. "Travis, I will call you later."

"Not likely," he said, as she led the way out of the house.

I stood and watched them. Oliver closed the door. They were talking all the way to the car, but I couldn't hear what they said. I just watched them from my window. I did catch his lips shape the word "virginity" though. I felt awful for getting her into trouble. I decided to give her time to get home and get lectured. Then I'd text her to test the waters. I turned on the TV to pass the time, but I didn't have to wait the whole thirty minutes. After twenty minutes, she texted me.

I'm grounded for a week, u're banned from coming over for a week.

That wasn't so bad.

It helps that we didn't do it. I told him about ur dad's tumor, I hope that's ok.

If it helped.

It did. He trusts us, he's talking to your mom, expect a call.

I sighed.

It will be worth it, if u ask me.

I think so too. I'll see you at school tomorrow.

Yep I'll see u first thing. I love you.

My mom called as soon as I hit SEND. I got a lecture and was told that I'd be grounded when she got home. I expected that. We said our goodbyes, and I went upstairs and took a shower. I was lounging on the couch playing video games when there was another banging on the front door. When I answered it, Chiz stood there with Brandon, Mason, and Abby.

"Are you ready?" he asked, as he came in and plopped down on my couch.

"Ready?" I looked at him, confused.

"My house, we're having a gathering of my subjects." I remembered his party.

"I'm not feeling up for it tonight," I answered, shaking my head.

"No excuses. Alex and Gia can't come out, but that doesn't mean you have to be a party-pooper, too. You never used to turn down a good time." He shook his head and stood.

"Come on, man, just a little bit. I'll bring you home in a few hours," Mason pleaded, probably because he didn't want Abby and him to be the only ones forced to attend.

"Fine, let me go change," I said. I ran up the stairs before Chiz could object. I changed and then came downstairs. I grabbed a sports drink from the refrigerator and followed the clan to their cars. I got into the front passenger seat of Mason's car.

On the way I filled Abby and him in on the evening and drama with Oliver. Abby already knew part of it, but they laughed at us and our bad luck. We arrived at a party that seemed to have been going on strong for a while. There were kids coming and going. We went inside, and Chiz made some random kids move from the couch so that we could sit. That's what we did for a few hours, just sat there and talked among ourselves.

Chiz came over a few times and offered us drinks, but we refused to drink; Mason was driving, Abby's parents were probably still going to be up, and I just didn't like the taste of beer. But when my sports drink was gone, I finally accepted Chiz's offer. One beer couldn't hurt. I watched him go to the pass-through counter between his dining room and kitchen. I watched him tell Jillian that I wanted a drink. She was playing bartender most of the night. She enjoyed making people beg for things. She popped the top off two bottles and reached for something I couldn't see. Then she produced them each with a lime on the rim. She handed them one at a time to Chiz, and he said something because she smiled at him with her conspiratorial smile. He returned and handed me a drink. I rubbed the lime around the rim, dropped it in, and took a swig. I scrunched my face as I swallowed a big gulp. It was cold, but it wasn't good. Abby looked at her cell phone.

"Are you ready to go?" Mason asked her.

"I am. It's already ten thirty," she groaned.

"Are you ready, Travis?" He turned to me.

"He's gotta finish his beer," Chiz interjected.

"If you guys are ready," I said.

"No, you know what, Brandon's not drinking." He pointed to Brandon standing in the corner with a bottled water talking to Lila. Brandon never drank. "He'll bring Travis home when he's done. We don't waste beer around here." I rolled my eyes at Mason.

"You guys go ahead; I'll hitch a ride with Brandon." I took another big gulp of the beer; the sooner I finished it, the sooner I could go home.

"You sure?" Mason asked.

"Yeah, I'm good," I said. They stood and left. Chiz, however, didn't. He sat there and wouldn't shut up. I took a few more drinks of my beer. Then suddenly, I felt a little off. I had trouble focusing on his face as he was telling me about the latest gossip from the cheerleaders.

"You don't look so good, dude," he said.

"I don't *feel* so good, dude," I said, leaning back.

"Let's get away from this crowd." He helped me stand. I teetered. Some kids looked at me; I waved. "Come on, lightweight." We stumbled to the stairs and up to his room. He literally threw me on his bed. I was there sideways with my face in the comforter. I couldn't move though.

"What-s-wrong wit me," I mumbled.

"Just shut-up," he said. He stood at the door. It was cracked, and he was looking out. The door opened, and I looked over and saw Gianna come in.

"Hey, babe," I said smiling.

"Hey, yourself, baby." It wasn't her voice; it was Jillian's voice.

"What-s-wrong with your voice?" I tried to sit up and get a better look at her.

"Nothing. How are you feeling?" She sat down beside me and held my face up to hers, scrutinizing my eyes.

"Better now that you're here. Are you still grounded? I'm sorry I got you in trouble." She cut her eyes to Chiz; he shrugged.

"Don't worry about that. We're together now. Are you ready to go home?"

"Yeah, I wish you could spend the night again." I put my hand behind her neck. She moaned and smiled.

"I love you, Gia," I breathed, as I closed my eyes. "So much." I opened my now heavy eyelids, and she was frowning. "What-s-wrong babe?"

"Nothing. Where's your phone?" she snapped at me. I reached into my pocket and handed it to her. She smiled, then whispered, "I love you, too." She put her hand on the back of my neck and pulled me to her. We kissed, but it wasn't right; it wasn't sweet; it was forced. I tried to pull away, but she only relaxed her hold a little. She climbed onto my lap, straddling me. I tried to kiss her the way we usually kissed. She pulled away and held her arm away from us. I kissed her neck, but it didn't smell right; it smelled like Jillian, not the soft coconut-like scent of Gianna.

"Gawd! Hurry up." Chiz stood by the door refusing to look at us.

"Almost done," she hissed. She pulled off her shirt. She pressed herself against me, and I fell back. I couldn't hold my eyes open.

"Travis? Travis? He passed out." She was annoyed now.

"That's because you gave him too much. Let's get him home." Chiz came over to where we were.

"One more." She lay across me and pressed her lips to mine. "Fine, now we just need the letters." *What was she talking about?* I tried to ask, but all I did was moan. "It's OK, Travis. It will be over soon, and everything will be as it should be." Everything went black. I didn't hear anything; I didn't see anything—just darkness.

Chapter 22

The Waves, Rushing,

Rolling, Pulling You Under,

Drowning You

Gianna

I stood by my locker until I had only two minutes before first period started. I tried to call Travis' cell, but it went straight to voice mail. I sent him a text right before class started.

Where are you?

He didn't respond. I was a little worried about him. Chiz was waiting by the lockers when I came out of my first period.

"You missed a party last night. Travis got smashed." He high-fived a boy that was walking the opposite direction.

"That doesn't sound like him," I said.

"Well, last night it was; he was funny."

"Really," I said flatly, apprehensive of Chiz. I was at my locker when Alex came up to me.

"Where is he?" he asked. I looked at Chiz. He looked innocently back at us.

"Who?" he asked Alex.

"TRAVIS!" he boomed. I shoved my books into my locker and grabbed his shoulders.

"What's wrong?" I asked.

"That DICKHEAD sent me a picture. Look." He shoved his phone at me. I opened a text that said,

Can you keep a secret?

There was a picture of Travis kissing Jillian's neck and her smiling at the camera. I dropped the phone and fell against the locker. Chiz reached around me and held me up at my waist. Alex picked up his phone and dialed a number. He cursed and pushed more buttons.

"I gotta get to class. Sorry to drop this on you now." He put his hand on my arm but turned to leave. Chiz loosened his grip on me, and I steadied myself against the locker.

"Are you OK? Do you want to get out of here?" Chiz asked me.

"No, I want to go to class." I took out my books and left him standing there.

I sat in my second period. I couldn't focus on anything, just the picture of Jillian there with bangs, smiling at me. She didn't have bangs, I suddenly thought. Maybe it was an old picture and somehow got sent to Alex. That had to be it; it was the only thing that made sense.

Then my phone vibrated.

I thought I loved you but I don't think I do.

"What?" I said out loud. Everyone looked at me, and my teacher repeated what she had just said. My hands began to tremble. I sat on them to try to steady them. After class, before I made my way to my third period, I stood at my locker longer than I should have and was almost late to class.

Where are you? we need to talk.

I sent him a text back. I settled into my seat, sat my phone at the top of the desk, and stared at it.

No, it's not working out, I have too much stuff to deal with right now.

I grabbed my phone and began frantically to text a response, not caring about the stares I was receiving.

"Miss Moretti, do I have to take your phone until the end of the day? I'm not telling you again." I looked up; Mrs. Thomason's eyes were glued to me. I put my phone away. I slouched in my seat and stared at nothingness. I didn't take notes, and I didn't speak when she addressed me again. I didn't get any more texts from him. I went to my locker before lunch. There was no note in my locker; he wasn't standing beside his locker. I wondered if he had skipped school. I didn't understand why he felt this way and was doing this. Abby found me at my locker.

"You look like hell," she said half-smiling. "What's going on?"

"I don't know. I think Travis broke up with me," I said, closing my locker.

"No way. Why do you think that?" I filled her in and showed her the texts I'd gotten from him. "Let me go find Mason." She disappeared into the crowd. I went to go into the cafeteria and was blocked by Chiz. I tried to sidestep him, but he moved to block me again.

"I'm not sure you want to go in there," he said, looking at me sadly.

"Why?" I asked, as I tried to look around him.

"It's pretty ugly in there."

"Is he in there?" I pushed past him. He held his hands up in the air and let me pass.

"This is my favorite one." Jillian began to read in a softer delicate tone, "*'I'm not a shiny new toy; I'm dingy and some of my parts don't work. Because they've been broken and glued back together. So be gentle with me.'*" There was a rumble of laughter as she shuffled pages. "Another line. *'I don't know how fair it is to be happy in here. It holds a lot of bad memories for me and Alex. And when I think of you, I am scared too. I think it's the good kind; it's the scared that makes my heart race and my palms sweaty.'* Talk about embarrassing." No one laughed this time; they were all staring at me, and I was staring at her back. She looked at her audience and held her hand up palm up. She slowly turned to see me standing there. Her new bangs were cut in a perfect straight line. I would have thought she looked really pretty. I might have even complimented her if I hadn't already seen the picture of Travis kissing her neck.

I ran to the hall and slammed myself against the lockers. I had to catch my breath; I couldn't breathe, and I couldn't move. The tears found my eyes, but they hadn't escaped yet. Standing in the door was Jillian, holding all the letters I'd written him over the past few months.

"You thought Travis would keep these a secret from me?" she smiled innocently. "We've shared a lot of firsts: first kiss, first time, first loves. Don't you see how little you mean to him now? I warned you. It's really your own fault for being so *stupid*." A single tear escaped my eye. "Aw, did I hurt the baby's feelings? Do you see me?" She waved her hand down her side as she said that. "I'm *everything* he wants, even when he doesn't know what he wants. I'm what most boys want. And he gets me. He gets me more than he'll ever get you. I get him, more than you'll ever get him." The second tear escaped my eye. "This is so embarrassing; he should have talked to you first. He promised he would, but we both know he has trouble keeping promises."

I straightened up, wiped my cheek, and avoided her eyes. I turned and walked down the hall with my head held straight ahead. I wouldn't cry anymore for her. I would do that at home, and I was going there right now. I walked past the office; Travis was standing there at the counter talking with one of the secretaries. I paused and watched him. He smiled politely, and she handed him a pass. I slammed through the front door and ran. I made it to the truck before another tear escaped. I drove aimlessly, as the tears slowly streamed down my face, one by one. I counted fifteen. They ended, and I finally found our street and our driveway. I went inside. I expected no one to be there, but standing in the kitchen leaning against the counter reading the paper was my father. I tried to walk past him unnoticed.

"Did school let out early?" he asked inquisitively.

"I didn't feel well, so I left early." I went to the dining room and up the stairs, grabbed some sweat shorts and a tank top, went to the bathroom, and took a shower. I let the hot water run over my head and down my body. The tears came again. All the tears of my father's abuse, my mother's death, Mitchell's betrayal, and now Travis's betrayal came rushing out of me.

Travis. I loved him. I missed him. But he didn't love me. I heaved and cried, sliding down in the tub. The water ran over me as the ocean of tears flooded me. I sat there with my knees pulled up to me until the water turned cold. I came out of the shower, toweled off, and put on my clothes without any undergarments. I brushed my hair and went to my room.

"Do you want something to eat?" I heard Oliver yell.

"No, I'm sick to my stomach." I went to my room and shut the door. My phone sang a pop song. It was Abby. I hit the REJECT button. Three missed calls. Abby, Alex, Mason. I put my phone on silent. I put my ear buds in and climbed into my bed. I covered myself in darkness. I listened to loud rock music. That would help me escape. My phone lit up under the dark covers I looked over at the name it displayed. The picture was Travis and me that first night by the bonfire. I'd thought all my tears had come, but then they came once more in numbers that I couldn't count, one drowning the other, making lines across my nose, tracing my cheek to puddles in my pillow. At some point I fell asleep because when I opened my eyes, my room was darker. The sun was beginning to set. My phone was lost somewhere in my covers or on the floor. I wasn't sure. I was sure it was almost dead. A light came on from the floor. I reached down and grabbed it, scrapping it across my hardwood floor. Twenty-three missed calls, mostly from Travis. A tear escaped my eye. I lay there staring at my white ceiling, wishing I could disappear. There was a knock at my door. I didn't answer. It opened anyway.

"There's someone here to see you." Oliver poked his head in.

"I don't want to see anyone," I said with a catch in my throat.

"He's been pretty insistent, been here for a while. And said he won't leave until I let him see you." He opened the door further. "Just hear what he has to say and then you can make him leave. I'll make him leave for you." I sat up and pushed the covers off. I stood to go to the door.

"You might want to change and brush your hair." He surveyed me in my short shorts and tank top.

"This will be fast," was all I said as I slipped on my flip-flops. I did, however, run my fingers through my hair as I began to descend the stairs. Travis leaned uncomfortably against the wall by the front door. I stood in front of him with my arms folded.

"Can we step outside?" He looked awkwardly at Oliver, who still loomed behind me on the stairs.

"Fine, whatever." I pulled open the door and went to the porch and sat on the first step, my arms on my knees.

"Tell me what happened?" He sat beside me and searched me earnestly.

"What do you mean? You gave Jillian my letters, the ones that I poured my soul into, and you gave them to her. Has she had them since the beginning?" I couldn't even look at him. Tear two escaped my eye.

"I didn't give Jill the letters. I don't even know how she found them or when. You came to the party last night—," he trailed off. I didn't want to hear what he had to say.

"I didn't go to a party. I was at home, grounded. Remember? They were laughing at me! She said you gave her the letters, and she was reading them to everyone, and they were laughing at me! You dumped me VIA TEXT!" I stood and moved to the walk-way; I had to get away from him.

He reached for me, and I scrunched my shoulders and held up my hands for him to stay away from me. He stood and followed me, grabbing my wrist and turning me toward him. He stepped to me as he held it to my side. His other hand cupped my face as he looked into my eyes.

"I didn't dump you. Chiz has had my phone since last night. He didn't give it to me until I came to school. I guess I forgot it at his house. I never sent you a text. How can I make this better? Can't you see what they're doing? She's trying to tear us apart again." He spoke barely above the whisper.

"It's working. How can I show my face?" I pulled away.

"It only works if we let her win."

"If you didn't give her the letters, then how did she get them?" The look on his face was suddenly filled with horror. I felt all the strength drain from my body as if I were about to collapse.

"I thought it was you, but even then it still didn't feel right." He shook his head.

"What?" I pulled loose from his now weak grip, clutching myself, bracing for whatever had given him such a look of fear.

"I must have drunk too much at Chiz's. I don't remember drinking more than one, and I don't even know how I got home, but I did. Before I passed out, I was in his room, and you came in, and I kissed you, and you kissed me back, and we held each other. Maybe it was just a dream and I imagined it," his voice cracked, and he swallowed hard.

"What are you saying?" I asked, not believing my ears.

"I think I was really kissing someone." He looked into my eyes, the horror still on his face. "I think I was kissing Jill." I stepped back away from him. He stepped toward me. I turned and ran. I ran as fast as I could. I ran even though there were sharp pains digging into my sides. I ran up three streets and over two to the pier. I couldn't breathe, but I had to escape and get away. The sun was setting over the horizon, and I walked along the edge of the sand where the tall grass began to grow. I'd lost count of my tears. I walked until my legs gave out. I heaved onto my knees in the sand. My face in my hands, I cried. I didn't know how long I sat there on my knees crying, but suddenly I felt arms around my waist from behind pulling me to him as he sat me down in between his legs. I was crying, and he held me. He smoothed my hair.

"I'm sorry, Gianna. I'm so sorry I've hurt you," he whispered in my ears. "I love you. I love you so much."

"I wish I'd never come here. I wish I'd died of cancer instead of my mom. I wish I'd never been born. This is what Hell feels like," I still cried, my voice a hoarse whisper.

"Don't ever say something so awful. You are amazing and strong and independent and brave. An angel, my angel!" He held me tighter against him as he looked off into the distance.

"Who do you think Hell was created for?" I whispered sarcastically, but I clung to him.

"You're not in Hell alone. I'm not leaving you. Ever. Believe me. Don't believe anyone else. Please?" He kissed my head. I looked up at him. He smoothed my hair out of my face and traced my tear line softly with the tip of his thumb. His eyes penetrated mine.

"I'm not leaving you." He pulled me to him and softly pressed his lips to mine. My hands found his neck, and I clung to him. His kiss became deeper as he traced my lips with his tongue. His hand finding the small of my back, he laid me down on the sand and hovered above me. He kissed my jaw line and my neck, moving to my chest between my breasts. My legs tangled around his waist, and his hands were under my shirt. He moved back to my lips again, kissing me hotly, urgently this time. My hands were all over him, in his hair, under his shirt, my thumb between the waist of his jeans and his skin. His hand moved to under my thigh. It moved between my shorts and my skin, squeezing my bottom. He pulled away slightly when he realized I wasn't wearing panties. The urgency grew with the desire. He kissed me deeply, crushing himself against me. I didn't want him to stop. His fingers found me. I let out a soft whimper. He kissed my neck again. I looked up to the sky; the stars sprayed the canopy above me. He moved his lips to my chest. I couldn't breathe. I felt shivers rise all over my skin, and suddenly, involuntarily, my back arched. He looked down at me, but he continued touching me.

"I want to show you how much I love you," he spoke so softly. "Please give me the chance to make it all right. I promise." My heart felt as if it would explode in my chest. I'd never felt anything like this before. "You're the only one I've ever loved. Never like this." He leaned down and kissed me again. Finally, he took his hand out of me, put it at the small of my back, and moved his other hand to cup my face. "I love you." His eyes locked on mine.

"I love you, too," I said, as a tear escaped my eye. He traced it and kissed me once more.

"Do you believe me?" His eyes searched mine. I understood that he wanted to be sure.

"I do because you broke me." Suddenly his eyes were full of pain, but I brushed my fingers from his eyebrow to his cheek, leaving my hand cupping his face. His eyes softened as he held my gaze, seeing the love in my eyes. "I needed you to cut me. In Indiana, my mom loved to garden, and when we bought our house, she loved it so much for the landscaping. There was this bush in the side yard that was puny. Our second year in the house she took her shears to it in the fall until all that was left was a stump. But the next year it bloomed and had the prettiest rose of Sharon blossoms. My mom had to cut it down to help it grow. Indirectly, you did that for me. These past few months have been the worst, hardest, happiest, and most beautiful of my life. When I met you on the beach, it was chance. When we sat together at the bonfire, it was circumstance, but when you fell in love with me, it was fate. I won't throw that away so easily ever again. I promise." I looked past him again at the stars shining above his head. He didn't say anything else. He just held me close to him.

Chapter 23

Would You Like Your Justice

Served Medium, or Well-Done?

Travis

Gianna went inside. I stood on the bottom step of her porch as she closed the door. I had to make this right. She had been so beautiful in my arms not more than a half an hour ago. I could still hear her moans. I could feel her and taste her lips and her skin. She was all that is good with the world. I took out my phone and made a call. I would make this right.

The next morning I felt so alive. I wasn't really sure if I'd ever been alive before last night, before I kissed her, before I felt her. I was alive now. I was at school bright and early. Bryan approached me on the front stoop.

"You got it?" he asked.

"Yeah, I got it." I handed him the flash drive that held the article I had spent less than an hour writing the night before. I'd never written anything so important so fast.

"Are you sure you want to do this? There's no going back." He raised his eyebrow as he unlocked the front door.

"I've never been more sure of anything in my life," I smiled. "This will run today, right?"

"Yep, that's why we're here early. Journalism class is third period so it's out by lunch. Mrs. Henry has already proofed it, so we can put it in now and it will be good to go." I followed him into the dark halls.

"This way." He motioned for me to follow him. I did. He went to the computer and started it up. I looked out the window at the most beautiful day I'd ever seen.

"Here we go. We just take out Madison's exposé on Jillian, and insert yours." My heart raced as he cut and pasted my document. "Nice picture." He paused momentarily as he looked at a picture of Jillian that one of the cheerleaders had texted me right after we broke up last year. She was standing over another cheerleader, with a scowl on her face and her mouth opened so wide she was shouting at her. The text had said, "You really dodged a bullet with this one."

"Thanks, man."

"Done. Saved." He handed me my flash drive back. I put it back on my key chain. "Now we wait."

"Thanks again." I slapped his back. He nodded.

"I've been waiting for a moment like this. She is a wretched person." He stood as he shut down the computer. "See you in speech." He turned and left the room.

I went to the gym and put on some gym shorts and my running shoes and went to the track to run off some of my sudden burst of energy. I ran for thirty minutes. When I saw other students begin to arrive, I went back inside, showered, and cleaned up. I was leaning against her locker with one leg propped up behind me when she walked up. The smile on her face said she was happy to see me. Before she had a chance to say anything, I grabbed her around her waist with one hand and pulled her to me. I gave her the strongest, deepest kiss that I could. I put my other hand on her neck just under her ear, my fingers tangling in her hair at the back of her neck. Finally, when we were done, I looked around, and everyone had stopped what they were doing to watch us.

"You've just embarrassed the hell out of me," she smirked, her face turning that darker shade that I liked.

"Never like this," I said, reassuring her, as I kissed the top of her head. She giggled and hugged me around my waist.

"I'll see you at lunch?" I asked, as I pulled away and stepped toward my locker.

"Yes," she sighed nervously. Everyone was still watching us.

"Well, until then, here." I handed her a note I had also written last night.

"Um, OK. Thanks." She surveyed the gawkers and finally met my eyes.

"Don't worry about anything; you'll see. This will all blow over." I leaned in and kissed her forehead one more time and turned to go to my class.

I sat at my stool, and I reread the passage that we were going to be quizzed on, waiting for everyone to come in and to lay my ground work. Jillian came in and sat beside me. I dropped my folder, and it popped open, spreading papers across the floor between us. I knelt down to pick them up, and I kept my head low as Mr. Jackson began his review. I leaned closer to where she was reading, too.

"Don't look up or say anything, just nod," I whispered. She did.

"I've been doing some real soul searching these past few days. We need to talk, but I can't until after lunch. I've got to talk to Gia first, let her know how I really feel about her." I paused; she nodded. "But I think we should talk, too." Again she nodded. "You should keep your distance from me until I've had a chance to take care of her." She started to turn to look at me, but I held my hand out to keep her eyes off me. "Just know that everything will be right between us very soon." She nodded. I stood and returned to my seat; Mr. Jackson began to pass out the quizzes. When she passed me the papers, she smiled her brilliant smile and winked at me. I smiled back at her, very pleased with myself.

Second and third periods, I kept waiting to hear the office call me to the principal's office, telling me that I'd been busted. The call didn't come. I met Gia as usual before lunch. Abby and Mason were there waiting for me. I got the copy of the school paper and carried it under my arm like it was the *New York Times* and I was in my forties. I paused just inside the door, and they turned to look at me. I opened it to the article.

"A Deeper Look at Jillian Thomas," I read in my most professional voice. Mason and Abby groaned, and Gia looked at me nervously. I continued, "Mason, will you take over?" He took the paper, found where I left off and began to read.

"Everyone knows Jillian Thomas. She is our ever-fearless leader. Her résumé includes class president, homecoming court, head cheerleader, and organizer of the annual clothing drive for the local shelters. Jillian has been a leader since she realized there were followers. But being the most popular girl in school has its price. Jillian donates many hours to helping those less fortunate than she is.

That was how Madison Erikson's original profile article about Jillian Thomas began. I wonder how many people actually believe Jillian is our fearless leader? As long as Jillian reigns, we will live under a dictatorship. She runs the halls with an iron fist that most fear. I would like you, the student body, to realize she has no power over us. This may sound like a bad break up rant, but I'm writing this and hijacking this article because Jillian has crossed a line. I was wrong not to come forward with this information before. I didn't want to get involved, but I should have. I'm only hoping that now it's not too late. I will accept the consequences for my actions, both of not coming forward and inserting this article. I am sorry, Madison. I understand you worked really hard to shine a positive light on Jillian, but the truth must come out.

Everyone knows the rumor that surrounded Mr. Monroe and an inappropriate relationship with a student. We all know that student and her family moved away after the embarrassment of it all. Here is what you didn't know. Mr. Monroe was innocent. The pictures were planted on his school computer in a locked file that he didn't even have the password to.

Mr. Dailey probably thought he just refused to open the file because he didn't want to get into trouble, but he honestly didn't have access to it.

Everyone knows my break-up with Jillian last year was TMZ-worthy. You remember the soda in my face, and all the rumors that began shortly after we broke up as to my sexual orientation and all. At that point I didn't care about my reputation or any of the rumors. Not that I'd ever be ashamed of who I am, I'm just not gay. It was all worth it, though, because I was rid of her, and as you see, all the rumors blew over. If I had wanted revenge, I would have come forward with my information. I didn't come forward then because no charges were filed against Mr. Monroe, and he is working again. In case you were wondering, he's in Chicago. I reached out to him last night and explained what I've done and have asked for his forgiveness. He sends his love to the students and families that supported and believed in him.

Here is my bombshell. Jillian took those pictures of the girl at a slumber party. She sent them to me a month before they showed up on Mr. Monroe's computer. I also believe that the police can tell when a file has been added to a computer. I'm not a betting man, but I imagine that date is after I received my email. The grade Jillian was receiving in Monroe's class would have failed her; she would have been off the cheerleading team. After Addison's "accident" last year, ensuring Jill as head cheerleader, she was willing to do anything to hold onto her position. When he refused to change her grade, she threatened him. I actually heard her tell him he would be sorry. Only I found out too late why he would be sorry. So I am now forwarding the email to Mr. Dailey as proof of Mr. Monroe's innocence.

I want to make sure the people I care about are protected, and I WILL do whatever it takes to ensure that.

Travis Nichols"

Mason looked up at me, Gia eyes were huge, and Abby's jaw was on the floor. My thumb hovered on the SEND button. Gia looked at my hand holding my phone. I pressed the button.

"Principal Dailey has the email," I sighed, as I heard a roar of cheers coming from different tables in the cafeteria. I saw Jillian enter the lunch room out of the corner of my eye. She looked at Gia with the tear streaming down her face and smiled at us. I stepped forward to Gia and took her hands in mine. She looked up at me, the love in her eyes making me catch my breath.

"I would do just about anything for you. All of this will keep her busy and away from us for quite a while." I spoke softly now, not positive about how much trouble either Jillian or I was in. Abby and Mason still stood there staring at us, as was most of the cafeteria now, including Jillian. "This is just the beginning to make it up to you." I clutched her hand in both of mine, holding it to my chest. People were talking in a low roar about the article. Others looked accusingly at Jillian. She began to survey the cafeteria nervously. A girl who played in the marching band walked up behind her and dumped her tray over Jillian's head.

"Mr. Monroe was my favorite teacher." She turned and walked away, as a cheer rose from the tables near where Jillian stood now drenched in spaghetti and pudding. Food from across the room was flung toward her. A boy sitting beside her shook up his unopened can of soda and popped the lid toward her, spraying her in a sticky mess.

"WHAT IS GOING ON HERE?!" she screamed in a shrill voice as food continued to pelt her. Suddenly Mr. Dailey and several other teachers appeared in the doorway. One teacher snatched her by the elbow while others grabbed a few other kids in the middle of slinging food. Mr. Dailey walked over to where we stood, his eyes boring a hole through me. My heart began to pound; I had known this was coming. I dropped Gia's hand from my chest and held it at my side. Gia squeezed my hand encouragingly.

"Mr. Nichols, will you come with me please?" He was all business. I let go of Gia's hand and followed him.

"WHAT DID YOU DO?" Jillian screeched at me, stomping her feet.

"Miss Taylor, please, SHUT UP," Mr. Dailey addressed her and led us to the office. Six of us sat down in the waiting area. They told Jillian to stand in place. One by one each of the students who had been caught throwing food were brought in and then brought back out after about fifteen minutes. They had all been slapped on the wrists with detentions for a month.

"Travis, Jillian, would you please come in?" Mr. Dailey stood in the doorway to his office. We walked in silently, Jillian sending me daggers. She looked innocently at Mr. Dailey.

"Mr. Dailey, I was attacked for no reason," she began. He raised his hand to cut her off.

"Travis, you have had these pictures for so long and never came forward; you obstructed an investigation. We have to contact the police as there was an investigation into the matter. What do you have to say for yourself?" He frowned at me from behind his desk. I looked over at Jillian as she began to piece together why we sat in his office, me in the soft cushioned chair, her in a folding chair.

"I understand that I'm in trouble. I didn't come forward because I didn't piece everything together until well after the fact. Then I wasn't sure if it was my place. I broke up with her and thought removing myself from the situation would be the best. Apparently it wasn't." I glanced at her sideways; she gasped, and I continued. "I've told Mr. Monroe everything and have offered to help in any way I can to remedy my mistake. I think Jillian is the worst kind of bully because she feels invincible. She has been pretty indestructible since I've known her." I looked down at my hands. Mr. Dailey leaned back in his seat.

"Well, you are suspended for breaking into school and putting that article in the paper. Did you have help with that?" He leaned forward on his elbows.

"No, it was just me." He scrutinized me, not believing me.

"OK. Now go to the office and call your mother. If she gives permission, you can drive yourself home. I don't want to see you until after fall break."

"She has some of my personal property that she stole." I knew I was pushing my luck.

"She will return it. Now you need to go call your mother before I change my mind and suspend you for two more days next week." I stood and left the room as he began. "Jillian, these are criminal acts. The police are on their way now to question you." I shut the door. In the office I found out the other students had gone back to class. I used the office phone and called my mom. I told her the short version of what happened. She was disappointed in me yet again. She told me we had more talking to do when she got home from her trip after fall break but for now, just to go home. I hung up and left the office. Hovering in the hallway outside of the office was Gia. She stepped close to me so no one in the office could see her face.

"I told Mr. Franklin that I was sick. Mrs. McCurdy seems to think I'm sick enough to go home." She winked at me, keeping her voice solemn.

"Well, you haven't been feeling very well these past few days." I put my arm around her shoulders. We walked out of the school together. In the

270

bright sun of the most beautiful day I'd ever known was the most beautiful girl I'd ever seen. And she was mine.

Epilogue

What Doesn't Kill Us

Only Makes Us Stronger

Travis

Jillian was prosecuted as an adult. Because it was her first offense, she didn't have to go to jail; she did have five years of probation and had to register as a sex offender for the next twenty years. I thought it was a little harsh, but the judge said he wanted to send a message to teenagers who sent naked pictures of under-aged children over the web. She was expelled from school and had to attend the alternative school. What surprised me was the complete turnaround it made in her. She is spending her spring break at UC-Berkley speaking about bullying and the effects it has on young people. She has actually spoken across the country and had to do a public service announcement that aired in our state.

I got six months of community service for my obstruction of justice, but it wouldn't show up on my permanent record because I was a minor. I volunteered at a local shelter for women and children from abusive homes. Gianna volunteered, too, and though my sentenced ended last Saturday, we plan to return to our weekend volunteering after spring break.

Today we are on our way to spend spring break with my father. I'm actually flying hundreds of miles to visit him for the first time in eight years. Hailey sits by the window staring out at the blue sky. Gianna sits between us with me in the aisle seat. My father's tumor is in remission. He has a new take on life and wants to start over, beginning with us. I only agreed to come if he paid for Gianna to come. He agreed, overjoyed that I would even consider it. I know we have a long way to go, but if he is serious about making an effort, so am I. Gia squeezes my hand as I soften my hard stare at the seat in front of me, contemplating the immediate future.

My strength comes from her. She is also a new creature. Since she had her breakdown and finally cried, she was able really to mourn her mother. She truly is beginning to put her life back together. Oliver has taken to fatherhood well this time around. The three of them are becoming very close. She's my rock, and I have a feeling that I am hers, too. I've never loved her more than I do now. It seems that I can't love her more, and the next day I do. She has revived something in me that I never knew I'd lost. We still spend evenings in her once safe haven that is now our spot. And on those days that we watch the sun set and the tide roll in, I am grateful that she moved back, and that she gave me not one but two extra chances. No matter what happens, as long as we love each other, we will make it over any obstacle.

www.ingramcontent.com/pod-product-compliance
Lightning Source LLC
Chambersburg PA
CBHW071120170626
46809CB00002B/440